Robert G. Barrett was raised in Bondi where he worked mainly as a butcher. After thirty years he moved to Terrigal on the Central Coast of New South Wales. Robert appeared in a number of films and TV commercials but preferred to concentrate on a career as a writer. He is the author of 24 books which includes the bestselling Les Norton series.

ROBERT G BARRETT

LES NORTON IN

BETWEEN THE DEVLIN AND THE DEEP BLUE SEAS

PAN
Pan Macmillan Australia

First published 1991 by Pan Macmillan Publishers Australia
This edition published 2019 in Pan by Pan Macmillan Australia Pty Ltd
1 Market Street, Sydney, New South Wales, Australia, 2000

A catalogue record for this book is available from the National Library of Australia

Typeset by Post Pre-press Group
Printed by IVE

The author and the publisher have made every effort to contact copyright holders for material used in this book. Any person or organisation that may have been overlooked should contact the publisher.

This book is dedicated to Midnight Oil. Because the oils are oils. And always will be.

As usual the author is contributing a percentage of his royalties to the environmental organisation, Greenpeace.

ACKNOWLEDGEMENTS

The author would like to thank the following people
for their help with this book:

Jens Ward, senior journalist at *People* magazine,
Sydney.

David Winterflood, J.P. Sydney.

Dr. John Kearney, M.B.B., F.R.A.C.C.P., Sydney

And my barber, Karyn Booth, at Bateau Bay, NSW.

By rights it should have been all doom and gloom in Price Galese's office at the Kelly Club on that pleasant Saturday evening, the last day in October. A warm, balmy evening that was now fast approaching 4 am on Sunday morning the first of November. After all the Kelly Club was closing down and it was the end of an era so to speak. An era of illegal gambling, corruption, murders, associated crime and vast profits going into a certain grey haired gentleman's pockets. But still, the end of an era no less.

Not wanting to panic his faithful staff any more than necessary, Price had told them as they left a little earlier than usual that it would probably only be for two weeks; another political hiccup so to speak. They were all paid accordingly and told to ring George Brennan in a fortnight, he'd tell them what was going on. In the meantime have a nice holiday on the boss. But in the plush seclusion of his office amongst his inner core Price had told the boys it would be for at least a month, and this time more than likely for good. The Kelly Club had rolled its last dice, spun its last wheel, bribed its last cop and politician. It was enough to make you cry. Good, honest, hard working Australian men all about to lose their jobs through no real fault of their own, and employment prospects in Sydney at the present time were rather

1

skinny to say the least. Plus who would give you a decent job in Sydney when your last job reference said you worked in an illegal gambling casino for so many years. You couldn't exactly hope to start a new career at McDonald's or Coles or the ANZ Bank. It was truly a bloody sad picture all round. Yet why the levity?

George Brennan's double chins were working overtime as he laughed his way through vodka and tonic about number ten. Eddie Salita was happily devouring rusty nails. Billy was chortling away while he gave a bottle of Old Grandad an awful nudge and Les Norton was tipping stubbies of Fourex down his throat like he was expecting a brewery strike. Even Price, destitution and ruin staring him in the face in his twilight years was cracking all sorts of jokes as a bottle of Dimple Haig got lower and lower and going on as if he didn't give a stuff. It was a funny one all right.

Of course the boys had known something a little more serious than usual was in the air when Price had told them earlier in the week that they'd be closing down and had added to expect to have a bit of a late drink on Saturday night, which was why Billy and Les had left their cars at home. But then again, they'd heard it all before. The Kelly Club was always closing up for a few nights or a week here and there. And Price was always saying that this was definitely it. But no one was really expecting a month, and this time Price did seem a little more sincere than usual when he said that this time was definitely it. So there was absolutely no need for levity. No need at all.

'So this is definitely it, eh, Price?' said Billy Dunne, easing back in his seat after pouring himself another quadruple Old Grandad and Coke.

'Yep. 'Fraid so, Billy, old mate,' replied Price. He looked at Billy over the top of his glass and tried not to smile. 'We're goners, the lot of us. Gowings.'

'Yeah, but fair dinkum, Price,' said Les. 'How many times have we heard this now? Eight hundred?' Norton shook his head and took another slurp of beer and looked around the room. 'I've been booked on cruise ships, got ready to go on camping trips in the bush — even lined meself up to take a sheila out. And then ring ring. On the phone. "Les. Les, old mate. It's Price. It's all sweet. I need you here tomorrow night."' Norton took another drink and grinned at his boss. 'This'll be the same. You wait and see.'

Price smiled at the Queenslander's cheeky, if not blunt honesty and shook his head. 'No,' he said seriously. 'This time it's different. I got the drum from right up the top. And it's one hundred per cent we'll be closed for a month.' The grey-haired casino owner eased back in his seat and let his eyes run round the room. 'There's gonna be a change of government in this State soon. I know for sure. The mob that's in don't want to win the next election anyway. You only got to look at the mug they've shoved in as premier since shitbags bailed out. He's got as much charisma as a dead cat. I wouldn't give him my vote if he promised me a bigger dick.' Price took a sip on his Scotch and soda. 'They'll let the other mob carry the can for a while — who are no better anyway. And seeing as there's no way this new pack of dummies can fix up the mess this State is in they'll get behind their favourite old smokescreen...'

'Law and order,' butted in Eddie.

'That's right,' nodded Price. 'Just like they've been doing lately. Which comes straight back on...' He made a helpless gesture with his hands.

'Can't you get to them though?' asked Billy. 'And the coppers?'

'I already have, Billy,' replied Price. 'And they don't particularly want to close me down. But they're just gonna have to. I mean, they're only out to get whatever earn they can while they're in. But you can't get to everyone. I mean, I've done my best. I've corrupted more than my share. But there's just some cops out there too fuckin' dumb to take a sling. The dopey pricks.'

'What?' said Les, blinking over the top of his stubbie. 'You mean to tell me there's actually some honest cops in NSW?'

3

'Yeah,' nodded Price, trying not to laugh. 'Not very many. But they're out there. Like a fuckin' cancer, eating away at the decent ones I can get to. Bastards.'

'Christ?' joked Les. 'An honest cop in NSW.' He shook his head. 'I never thought I'd see the day.'

'You'd need to be Sherlock Holmes to find them,' chuckled George. 'But they are out there.'

Norton shook his head again. He finished his beer and rose to get another one. 'So what do you reckon you'll do, Price?' he asked from behind the bar. 'If — and it's a big if — if this does mean the end?'

'Probably take a well-earned rest,' smiled his boss. 'Just concentrate on my horses. To tell you the truth I'm sick of looking at coppers and politicians and sick of giving them half my hard-earned money just for not doing their job. The pricks. And I'm getting sick of gambling too. I've been at it over twenty years. One thing's for sure,' he added, nodding his drink for emphasis. 'I'm not gonna start playing Russian Poker. They can stick that in their arse.'

A collective shudder ran round the room. The boys had seen Russian Poker in some of the places that had changed over to it. It was a cross between Manilla, baccarat and poker and was played predominantly by Asians, most of whom were suffering Vietnamese refugees down to their last quarter of a million dollars worth of gold bars and diamonds they'd managed to escape with when they fled oppression. The places stayed open twenty-four hours a day; and the Asian punters, who all hated each other's particular nationality, chased one big bundle of money that changed hands every week. You won it and you were Jack the lad or Trang the lad, as the case might be, till you did it all back and the bundle went round again.

In the meantime they'd break into a house in their own community, rip the owners off to get a stake to get going again. The people whose houses got broken into were mostly shonks themselves, and rarely called the police. There was no glamour attached and guns,

4

knives and drug money were the order of the day. The Russian Poker joints stayed open only because of some flimsy loophole in the gaming act. Villain and all that he was, Price would have no part of it.

'Anyway,' smiled Price, 'I've managed to put a few miserable shillings aside over the years, so I'll survive somehow. If I go bad I can always get another milk run. I might even sell hot dogs outside Souths Juniors on fight nights.' He chuckled as he took another sip of his drink. 'Anyway, who gives a stuff about a poor old mug like me?' he said, glancing around the room. 'At least I don't think anybody here'll starve.' Price caught Norton's eye. 'What about you, old fella? What are you gonna do now that we've all fallen on tough times? You reckon you can survive without old Uncle Price to look after you?'

'Look after me?' snorted Les. 'Hah! I'm lucky I'm still fuckin' alive after working here.' He took a drink and looked directly at George Brennan. 'No, I'll go up to the CES, get on the jam-roll. Let them find me a job.'

'You would too, you miserable drop kick,' George Brennan almost shouted. 'You *would* have the hide to apply for the fuckin' dole. And blow up if they didn't give it to you.'

'And why not?' Norton looked defiant. 'I'm a worker being laid off. I pay my taxes. I'm entitled to it.'

'Entitled to it?' snorted George. 'What have you got your occupation down as. Head-crusher?'

'No. Public relations. My accountant over at Double Bay has got me a tax file number and I'm listed as working in public relations. Same as Billy. Ain't that right, old mate?' said Les, turning to his workmate.

'Yep,' nodded Billy Dunne sagely. 'That's us. Meeters and greeters — as in public relations.'

'Meeters and greeters,' sniggered Eddie Salita. 'Between the two of you, you've made more work for the nurses and interns in the casualty ward at St Vincents than twenty years of natural disasters. Johnson and Johnson should give you a medal each.'

5

'About the same amount of work as you've supplied for the local funeral trade, Edward,' replied Norton evenly.

Eddie grinned and pointed a finger at Les. He was going to say something but he didn't bother.

From then on it was non-stop bagging and everybody copped it, as more bottles of booze went steadily down and the level of laughter went steadily up. It was well after six and the sun was bright in the sky when they all fell roaring out of the Kelly Club, mule, stinking drunk. And it was closer to seven when Les got out of the taxi he and Billy had somehow managed to catch between them.

And it was close to two when Les got out of bed on Sunday, barely able to open his eyes, his tongue feeling like you could strike matches on it and a hangover that big you would have been flat out fitting it inside an aircraft hangar.

Jesus bloody Christ!, thought Norton, holding his head as he stumbled from his bedroom to the bathroom and out to the back verandah. How sick do you have to be to die?

The sun was beating down from a beautiful clear blue sky. It was a perfect summer's day — perfect for going to the beach, picnicking or just being outside. Four seconds of it was enough for Les. With the sunlight coming at his eyes like a First World War bayonet charge, he retreated back into the kitchen and put the kettle on. There was no sign of Warren, but an 'office memo' next to the fruit bowl on the kitchen table told of his feelings: *Do you have to make so much fuckin' noise when you come home in the morning. You fuckin' big goose. It's like sharing a house with Frankenstein.*

Norton laughed as he screwed up the note and tossed it into the bin. But even a few seconds of laughter made the pain in his head worse. He beat another retreat into the bathroom and rummaged round until he found Warren's packet of Panadol Fortes. Shit, how many of these do you take again? I reckon three ought to

6

do. He got them down with a glass of water, thought for a moment they were going to come straight back up, but when they didn't, went back to the kitchen to make a mug of coffee with plenty of honey in it.

Now what happened again last night, and why am I so bloody crook? he reflected into his coffee. It was an easy enough night out the front; there were no stinks. The staff all went home early, along with the punters. Then it started to come back. Ohh yeah, that's right. I ended up drinking every bottle of Fourex in the office then me and Billy finished off that first bottle of Old Grandad and another one. That Coca Cola's got a lot to do with it too.

Half an hour later, the Panadols had started to work, the coffee stayed down and although Les still felt tired and completely shithouse, at least the pain had gone. He decided to walk down to the beach and have a swim. The walk might do him good and it'd be useless trying to find a parking spot on Sunday afternoon. He climbed gingerly into a pair of shorts, T-shirt and thongs and set off, still squinting uncomfortably through a pair of dark sun-glasses.

Bondi Beach wasn't all that crowded but there were plenty of people sitting on the grass or walking around the shops. Norton found a spot on the sand just up from the south end next to the wall with a little shade. He had intended going down the north end where he knew a few people in the surf club but decided at the last minute that conversation might not quite be on the agenda this particular Sunday.

The water didn't look too polluted. The nor'easter seemed to be blowing most of the 'murk' into Bronte and Tamarama. Oh well, Les thought, walking down to the water's edge, legionnaire's disease, anthrax, even bubonic plague couldn't make me feel any worse than I did earlier. He made a mental sign of the cross and plunged in. Despite the germs, industrial waste and pollution, the water still felt good. He flopped around for a while and even caught a few small swells onto the beach. After a while he lay on the water's edge checking out the punters and perving on the girls sunbathing topless. But his heart wasn't really in it and he still felt tired and hungover. What he needed was a feed, a rest, then a good night's sleep; it was getting late anyway. He had a shower, got some takeaway Chinese and two litres of orange juice and headed for the cool, darkened sanctity of Maison Norton in Cox Avenue. It was a day completely wasted.

The soya sauce chicken and fried rice went down well, as did the orange juice. All I need now, thought Les, feeling a little better, is a nice early night. Shit, I'll be getting plenty of those from now on he mused, as he watched some travel documentary about the Himalayas on Channel Two. The gravity of what last night was all about and some of the things Price had said were starting to come back to him. He was thinking heavily on this when the sound of the front door opening told him Warren had come home.

'G'day, mate,' he said, as Warren walked into the lounge. 'I got your note. Thanks.'

Warren stood there staring at him. 'You know what time it was when you got home this morning?'

Norton nodded. 'Roughly.'

'It sounded like Jesse the elephant coming through the front door.'

'Wouldn't surprise me.'

'You fell over in the hall. You nearly slammed the front door off its hinges. You knocked over the bowl of fruit in the kitchen; plus all the dishes draining next to the sink. You left every light in the house on. And you pissed all over the floor in the bathroom. You've certainly got some style, haven't you? Even for a fuckin' bush Queenslander.' Norton's face coloured and he gave a self conscious smile. 'You were still snoring and farting your head off when I left here at one o'clock. The girl I was with said she'd never seen anything quite like it. And she used to work on a pig farm up on the Darling Downs.'

8

'Thanks, Woz. You're a real pal.'

Warren continued to stare at Norton, then wrinkled up his nose. 'You still smell of stale piss too.' He continued to stare at him as Les tried to concentrate on the TV to try and hide his embarrassment. 'So what was the big occasion? You win the lottery or something?'

Norton kept staring at the TV. 'I'm out of work.'

'Out of work?' Warren's eyebrows knitted for a second. 'What do you mean? Out of work?'

'The Kelly Club's closing down for a month. Probably for good. And I'm out of a job. We all are. That's why we all got so pissed.'

Les told Warren about the previous night and what Price had said. Warren stared at him in disbelief. He was still staring at him after Les had finished. But it wasn't a look of sympathy; it was more like trepidation, bordering on shock-horror.

'That doesn't mean you're gonna be home here all the time now, does it?'

Les grinned and nodded.

'In other words, I'm going to be constantly seeing your big boofhead around the place. Including Friday and Saturday nights when I like to play chasings with the girls.'

'They don't call you lucky Warren for nothing.'

'Ohh, shit!' Warren looked up at the ceiling then back at Les. 'Can't you get another job? You'll have to. Your money'll run out before long.'

'Don't worry. I've thought of that already,' enthused Les. 'I'm getting another three boarders in. I'm putting two in the spare room, and you're going to share yours. I've lined up three footballers. They've all come down from Queensland to play for Easts. You'll love 'em. Plus the rent's going up. Don't worry about old Uncle Les, mate. He'll survive, all right.'

Warren looked at Norton for a moment, then went into the kitchen to make a cup of coffee. He came back out into the lounge room, sat down and continued to stare at Les who continued to stare at the TV.

9

'No, fair dinkum, Les. What are you gonna do? You can't sit around here all day and night, mate. You'll start to veg out.'

'Warren,' replied Les, 'the only thing that would make me veg out is being near you — 'cause you're a half-baked little fruit. Mate, I'll have plenty to do. Cleaning up after four boarders is going to take up a heap of my time — beds to make, garbage to empty, rents to collect.' Norton looked directly at Warren. 'Which reminds me: yours is overdue — again. And me out of work too. You rotten little cunt.'

Warren sipped his coffee and started to laugh. He could see just where he was getting with Les on this particular topic of conversation. Nowhere.

'So what are you doing tonight?' he enquired. 'You going out?'

Norton shook his head. 'No, mate. I'm too fucked. Besides, I couldn't look a beer in the face at the moment.'

'I've got a good party to go to.'

'Yeah?' replied Les, disinterestedly.

'Yeah. It's only up at Bondi Junction too.'

'Sounds terrific. Who're you taking? Whatever scrubber it was you dragged back here last night?'

Warren nodded over his coffee. 'She's no scrubber, she's a good sort. Her name's Ximena. She works for a publisher.'

Les turned to Warren. 'That's one good thing about me being home more often now. I get to keep an eye on some of these dogs you keep dragging in here behind my back. Make sure they're not old crackers full of hookworm and various forms of STDs.'

'Ximena's got a girlfriend — an aerobics instructor. She's a good sort too.'

'I couldn't give a fuck if she was Victoria Principal and her old man owned a brewery. I'm staying home. I'm rooted.'

'Please yourself, you miserable big prick.'

'Mr Miserable Big Prick to you, soupbones.' Norton grinned at Warren. 'Jesus, am I ever looking forward

10

to the next few months. Plenty of exercise, plenty of early nights and plenty of keeping an eye on you. There's gonna be plenty of changes coming up at Maison Norton in the next few months. Guaranteed, old fellah.'

Warren nodded over his coffee. 'I can imagine. But I bet it still won't be your underwear.'

Wearing designer jeans, a blue striped shirt and reeking of expensive aftershave lotion Warren said goodbye and left about eight-thirty. The same time as the movie came on — Charles Bronson in *The Streetfighter*.

This'll do me thought Les, placing a cushion from the lounge under his head as he heard the front door close. For the next five years. Fuck the money.

The movie ended around ten-thirty and Les was in bed not long afterwards. This time he didn't piss all over the bathroom floor and he didn't leave any lights on. He also slept like a log; not hearing Warren stagger in alone some time after two.

When Les rose around seven on Monday morning, he still wasn't one hundred per cent but, compared to Sunday's effort, he felt like the bionic man. Sipping a mug of coffee on the back verandah it was a carbon copy of the previous day; sunny and warm with just a slight northerly wind; a good day to be out and about and do a bit of training. Norton did just that. He threw on an old pair of shorts and headed for North Bondi Surf Club.

He had no trouble parking his car and was in a fairly good mood as he strolled down to the club, nodding to the regulars and a few old-timers who still, almost religiously came down for their early morning swim. He left his gear in the club, wrapped a sweatband round his head and, after a bit of limbering up, set off for a lazy eight laps of the beach.

It was more than pleasant trotting along the water's edge. Sometimes the waves would surge up round his ankles as he weaved around the other joggers or people just out having a stroll; a surfer would leave the water and head back to his car on the promenade.

11

The surf crashed pleasantly against the shore and the city could have been a million miles away. It was the ideal situation for an early morning jog. It was also an ideal situation to do a bit of thinking, especially about Saturday night at the Kelly Club. This thing could go either way. Either he'd be back there in a month, or he'd be looking at a new life style. Sooner or later though, the Kelly Club was going to close: if not this year, the next — it was inevitable. The good old days — or bad old days — take your pick were coming to an end. It was like the man said in the song, 'And the times they are a'changing'. And Price had had a better run than anyone.

No matter what happened, Norton wouldn't starve. He had money snookered away in bank accounts and fixed term deposits all over the place; he even had some buried. The earns that had fallen in while he was working at the Kelly Club had mounted up and it was debatable if Les had ever spent his wages the whole time he worked there. He owned the house in Cox Avenue. He'd missed out on the giant earn with Peregrine and that painting but it was comforting to know that Peregrine, although not quite all right, wasn't dead. The army had eventually fished him out of the loch in Scotland. And not long after Les had received a letter from Peregrine's father saying that, although badly burnt and suffering brain damage, his son was alive and now in a clinic in the South of France where he would probably stay for quite some time. The Van Gogh was destroyed in the blast; thanks for your help anyway, Les. Or as Warren had so succinctly put it, the painting went west and Peregrine went south.

Norton jogged steadily on with another two things slowly turning over in his mind. One was what he had said to George on Saturday night about how his accountant, Desmond Whittle, had him down as a public relations consultant. That was something he was definitely going to have to do now that he had some time to himself: sort out his financial affairs with Whittle.

Norton didn't know too many accountants but Whittle had to be the best in Sydney — he could get Les claims on things that were almost unthinkable. He'd even advised Les to put an old typewriter in the spare room in his house and got him a rebate on it as office space. George had tipped Norton into Whittle and it was the best thing that could have happened to Les as far as making his money legal went, and on top of that Whittle was a pretty good bloke all round. Yet Norton absolutely loathed going over to his office in his unit at Double Bay and talking to him. It wasn't that he disliked Whittle, it was just that Les abhorred anything to do with figures, book-keeping, numbers, adding and subtracting and just plain arithmetic in general. It almost gave him a migraine. Norton was flat out writing down the date and handling money was simple. You just put it in the bank and left it there. Why spend it if you don't have to? Coming last in arithmetic in every class he was ever in at school didn't help much and he always felt embarrassed when he confronted Whittle, which was another reason he saw him as little as possible. Good little bloke that he was, Norton still regarded him as a dentist with a degree in economics.

But Whittle had been ringing him fairly often over the last few months, saying it was time again to get his affairs in order. There was also something important he had to discuss with Les that he didn't wish to talk about over the phone. Norton had a good idea what that was too. The second thing that had been turning over in his mind.

Norton's big investment. Blue Seas Apartments. About three years previous Les had been talked into buying an old block of flats in Randwick not far from the Prince of Wales Hospital. It was an old run-down block of five flats with a resident caretaker and the whole thing was managed by a real estate agency in Randwick Junction. Norton didn't particularly want to buy the block, but Price had lined it up for him, a deceased estate, the same as the house he lined up in Cox Avenue.

Price along with George Brennan had kept berating him he'd be a mug not to buy the old block of flats. All he had to do was put down a deposit, the rents would pay off the balance, and the land value alone would treble in three years. Price would have snaffled it up himself but he wanted to do a favour for Les, if Les would have a go. So rather than be a mug that wouldn't have a go, Les had forked out seventy-five thousand dollars, which nearly killed him, borrowed another seventy-five and the next thing between Price, Whittle and the estate agency in Randwick Junction Les Norton was the new landlord of Blue Seas Apartments.

But that was as far as it went for the big Queenslander. He was not the slightest bit interested in collecting rents, doing maintenance or meeting his tenants. Everything was in the hands of Whittle and the estate agency. Apart from driving past now and again or having the odd beer at the Royal Hotel in Randwick, Norton kept away from Blue Seas Apartments, much the same way he kept away from his accountant. He never told anybody he owned them — the only people who knew were the inner core at the Kelly Club, and even there it rarely if ever, came up in conversation. Which at times did seem a little curious to Les, seeing how Price had pestered him to buy them. He at times thought his boss might be interested to know how his big investment was coming along. Then on the other hand this suited Les. Talking about high finances and ways of making money bored him shitless and he was still in a way sorry he'd bought them.

Then on the other hand again, there should be a bit of a whippy in hand. It had been almost three years since he'd checked on the old block of flats with Whittle. By some devious means, the money involved with Blue Seas Apartments was kept separate from Norton's other finances. The place could be worth anything by now; maybe that's what Whittle was ringing him about. He'd had an offer from a Hong Kong syndicate or some Americans. The Japanese? The property boom was on and Les Norton, property tycoon, was right in the middle

14

of it. Donald Trump, eat your heart out. Grasshopper, it was time to sell.

So who really needs the bloody Kelly Club? thought Norton, as he jogged the final lap back to the surf club. I can do all right. Les had to laugh to himself — it was money for old rope though, and you couldn't ask for a better boss or a better bunch of blokes to work with.

He had a work-out on the heavy bag, did a bit of weights and sit-ups and after topping this off with a swim and shower went home where Warren was in the kitchen, looking almost as bad as Les had the day before.

'Well, if it isn't the party-time kid.' Norton stood in the doorway glowing with health from his run, his hair still wet from the shower. 'And how was the party?'

'Good,' croaked Warren. His eyes were closed and he didn't look up from his coffee.

'Yeah. It sounds it.' Les moved across to the sink and poured himself a glass of water. 'You look like the portrait of Dorian Gray,' he grinned. 'How come you got so pissed? And where's the fiancée?'

'The bitch gave me the arse at the party.'

'She what!?'

Warren winced. 'Please, Les, not so loud.' He took a deep breath and sighed. 'An old boyfriend turned up so I got dropped to reserves.'

'The filthy, low moll.'

'That's what I said.'

'So, crushed with remorse, you pitched for every other tart at the turn, they all gave you the arse as well, so you hit the piss.'

Warren nodded almost imperceptibly. 'Five bottles of champagne. Christ, I'm crook.'

Despite himself, Norton couldn't help but sympathise with his flatmate. 'I know just how you feel. You goin' to work?'

'Got to. There's a heap on today — of all fuckin' days.' He downed his coffee and rose unsteadily from the table. 'In fact, I'd better have a shower and get going.'

'Have a nice day,' smiled Les.

15

Warren had a shower then stumbled around a bit more while Les had breakfast and read the paper. He mumbled something about seeing Les tonight, the door closed and Warren was gone.

Norton shook his head and thought about his condition yesterday and Warren's this morning. This getting pissed out of your head was fast becoming a no-result. And now that he had a lot more time to himself, and knowing how much he loved a drink, he was going to have to watch it. He drummed his fingers on the table. What I should do is go on the wagon for a month. All I'd do is save money and brain cells. He drummed a bit more. Yeah, I might even give it a bit of serious thought. I wasted a whole fuckin' day yesterday. In the meantime; I've got to make a phone call.

Les expected to get Whittle's answering service. Instead he couldn't miss his accountant's well modulated and measured voice.

'Hello. Desmond Whittle.'

'Hello Des. It's Les Norton.'

'Oh hello Les. How are you?'

'Good mate. I've been meaning to ring you, but I've been busy at work. That and other things.'

'That's all right Les.'

'You said you wanted to see me about something.'

'Yes. Yes I do. When's a good time for you?'

Norton shrugged. 'Today. Tomorrow. Whenever.'

'Today I have to go into the city. How about tomorrow morning? Say ten-thirty.'

'Yeah righto. Ten-thirty tomorrow.'

'Don't forget to bring all your receipts.'

'No worries. See you tomorrow Des.'

Well that was short and sweet thought Les, looking absently at the phone. Now what am I going to do for the rest of the day? He grinned to himself. How about sweet fuck all? How about I go down the beach, sit on my arse and read a book in the sun? That's what I'll do. This could be the start of a whole new exciting life style for me. Why rush into it?

Norton did just that. He got a couple of magazines out of Warren's room, drove back down to North Bondi, propped on his banana chair and spent the rest of the day reading, swimming and ogling the girls sunbaking topless. He went for a couple of strolls along the beach, bumped into some people he knew for a bit of a chit-chat and it was an extremely pleasant day all around. He was almost tempted to have a couple of beers in the afternoon, but didn't bother. He got some pork schnitzels and came straight home instead. Les was in the kitchen getting tea together with the TV tuned to the news in the lounge room when Warren arrived home around six.

'So how are you feeling now?' he asked when Warren walked into the kitchen.

'Still pretty bloody seedy.'

'You hungry?'

'Starving. I've been flat out all day. Hardly had a chance even for a sandwich.' Warren poured himself a glass of milk from the fridge and looked at what Les was doing. 'What's for tea?'

'New fashioned pork. Just like the ad says on TV.'

'Sounds good,' Warren took some money from his pocket and handed it to Les. 'Here's your rent, Shylock.'

Norton counted the money several times, held one bill up to the light and pulled it around a bit then folded it up with the rest and put it in his pocket. 'Yes, that all seems satisfactory. Thank you, Mr Edwards.'

While Les was fiddling around with the schnitzels he told Warren about his proposal to go on the wagon for a month, did Warren want to join him. Warren said that didn't sound like a bad idea at all. He'd certainly give it some thought. He poured himself another glass of milk then had a shower while Les cooked tea.

The pork schnitzels and vegies turned out delicious. Les even had a go at making a garlic and mushroom sauce; which didn't turn out too bad either. One thing Warren mused to himself, Les hanging around all the time, might be a bit of a pain in the arse after being

17

used to having the place to myself most of the time, but at least I'll eat well. They finished with coffee, then after cleaning up watched the Monday night movie. *Ghostbusters*. Warren was yawning and in bed by ten-thirty; Les wasn't long behind him.

I wonder what it is Whittle wants to see me about besides my tax return he mused just before he dozed off. Hope it's good news. I reckon it will be. He let go a cavernous yawn and shoved his head further into the pillow. This coming month could prove to be very interesting. What is it the Chinese say? May you live in interesting times. That's me baby. The next thing he was asleep.

Tuesday was as good a day as any to see Whittle. It had come over cloudy, the nor' easter had turned southerly, it was cooler and looked like a chance of rain. This didn't prevent Norton from getting up around seven and ripping into some more training, opting this time for a run in Centennial Park and about two million sit-ups and push-ups. Although sweaty, sore and momentarily stuffed, the big Queenslander was still feeling like a million dollars when he returned home to find Warren standing on the back verandah, sipping coffee and listening to the radio. At first Les thought Warren was doing *tai chi* or some sort of mild exercise; but he was only jigging around to the music, a new song by Girl Overboard. He turned around when he heard Les, and compared to Monday morning, Warren looked like a two-year-old at the AJC Spring Carnival.

'Les. My man,' he beamed. 'My main, mother-fucking man. How goes it baby?'

'Not too bad,' smiled Norton. He studied his flatmate for a second or two. 'I must say, you look a bit different than yesterday. You look almost alive.'

'I feel it too, don't worry about that.' Warren looked evenly at Les for a moment. 'You know,' he intoned, nodding with his cup of coffee for emphasis. 'I've been mulling over what you said yesterday about giving up

18

the piss for a month. I'm willing to give it a go. Especially after yesterday.'

'Yeah, righto,' nodded Les. 'We'll see how we go. Sunday's effort was enough for me.'

Warren raised his coffee cup and grinned. 'Then here's to sobriety.'

'Fuckin' oath. On the wagon,' winked Les.

Warren followed Les into the kitchen and rinsed his cup while Les got a bottle of mineral water from the fridge.

'So what's on today, landlord?'

'Today? I got a million things to do. Starting with seeing my accountant over at Double Bay. Today marks a new turning point in my life, Woz, and I feel I must go for it.'

'Yeah?' I thought you might be taking it easy for a while. Sit back on your arse and do fuck all. It's what you do best.'

'Well, Warren, you know the old saying: dogs don't piss on moving cars. And that's just what I'm doing, baby. Movin' and groovin'. Walkin' and talkin'.'

'Good idea,' nodded Warren. 'And I'm off to the office. Where I'll be makin' and shakin', wheelin' and dealin'.'

'Yeah! Right on, brother.'

Les gave Warren a high five, nearly snapping the young advertising executive's hand off at the wrist then got into the shower. Shortly after he heard Warren call out something about seeing him when he got home and the front door closed. Then it was a nice, long relaxed breakfast reading the paper and before Les knew it, it was time to go and see his accountant at Double Bay.

Norton was whistling to himself and for the first time he could ever remember, actually looking forward to seeing his accountant when he pulled up in Fairlight Avenue Double Bay. With a large, brown paper bag full of receipts, phone bills, dry-cleaning dockets etc, he walked into Whittle's modern block of units and pressed the intercom.

19

'Hello?' a polite voice crackled over the tiny speaker.

'Hello, Des. It's Les.'

'Come straight in, Les.'

The security door buzzed open and Norton let himself in.

Whittle's unit was on the ground floor not far from the entrance; he had the door open before Les had a chance to knock. The accountant looked just the same as the last time Les had seen him: half his size in a sober, chalk-striped shirt, sober maroon tie and sober black trousers and shoes. The same twinkle was in his soft brown eyes, and his short hair still looked like it needed combing. The youthful, almost boyish face, still intrigued Les, because although Whittle was in his forties, he hardly looked a day over twenty. Having a slim, wiry build helped and even though Whittle didn't train all that much, Norton was surprised to find out that he had been a champion fencer at Sydney University and had once taken out a silver medal for Australia at the Commonwealth Games.

'Hello, Les,' he said, his voice slow and distinct. 'It's good to see you again.'

Norton took his handshake. 'Yeah. You too, Des.'

Whittle closed the door and Les followed him into the lounge room of his one-bedroom unit which he had turned into a fairly spacious office, complete with a computer, fax machine and photocopier. He hit a folding lamp above a table and motioned for Les to sit down, which he did dropping the paper bag full of documents in the middle.

'These are all your receipts, are they, Les?' asked Whittle.

'Yeah, that's them, Des. It's been pretty quiet in the public relations rort lately.' Norton gave a bit of a grin. 'In fact, the club's closed up for a month. Might even be for good.'

'Yes, I heard a bit of a rumour to that effect.' Whittle removed all the documents from the brown paper bag and went through them quickly but carefully. 'Mmm,' he nodded. 'These all seem to be in order. We should be able to get you some sort of return from this.'

'Good,' replied Les, now feeling at ease and just a little pleased with himself. He watched his accountant for a few moments then shuffled on his seat. 'So what else was it you wanted to see me about, Des? Is it that block of flats?'

'Yes, yes, I was about to come to that.' He looked up from the table. 'Would you like a cup of coffee, Les? Or how about a glass of beautiful, clear spring water? I've got a dispenser in the kitchen. It tastes ten times better than tap water.'

'Okay, Des. Sounds good.'

The accountant brought Les out a large glass of cold, clear water which tasted as good as he said. While Les was sipping it he got a white manilla envelope from a filing cabinet which he placed in front of Norton. Norton noticed the official seal of Randwick Municipal Council on the front.

'What's this?' he asked.

'I think you'd better read it first, Les. Then we can discuss it.'

Norton's eyebrows knitted slightly and his ears pricked up at the ominous way Whittle had said 'discuss it'. Some sixth sense told Norton this wasn't going to be quite the good news he had expected.

The letter was addressed to D. Whittle, Accountant of Blue Seas Apartments, Aquila Street, Randwick. Norton studied it as best he could and it all looked kosher until he came to the part that said, 'Mr Whittle, as you are aware under section 16a, Rule 46b of the Local Government Act of 1902, Council has the power . . .' That's when Norton's dark brown eyes nearly fell out of his big red head. He read it again and his jaw almost hit the table. He stared at the letter for a moment, then glared up at Whittle, his face a mixture of disbelief and accusation.

'What the fuck's this? You're fuckin' kidding, aren't you? It says here the fuckin' council's reclaiming the land my block of flats is on!'

'That's right, Les.'

'They can't fuckin' well do that.'

'Oh, yes they can, Les.' Whittle pointed to a part of the letter. 'See here, where it says "Secretary of The Department of Main Roads" and that other part that says "section 26b of the —"'

'Yeah, yeah,' interrupted Norton. 'The Local fuckin' Government Act of sixteen fuckin' twenty or some fuckin' thing. Fuckin' council workers. Where do they think they are? Fuckin' Romania?'

Whittle watched in silence as Les took a long drink of water and glared at the letter. Then he seemed to settle down a bit.

'Oh well,' he shrugged. 'If they take it, they take it. They're doing me a favour really. I was never all that interested in the joint. Just tell 'em to send me the cheque.' Les looked at Whittle. 'What's the place worth now? It's got to be around three and a half hundred grand. At least.'

Whittle made a small gesture with his hands. 'Les, I hate to tell you this. But when a council or the department of main roads reclaim your land, no matter what the circumstances, they only pay you the V.G.'

'The V.G. What's the fuckin' V.G.!'

'Whatever the Valuer General's Department says it's worth.'

'And what's the V.G. on this?'

Whittle paused for a second. 'A hundred and fifteen thousand dollars.'

'WHAT!!?' roared Norton. 'A hundred and fifteen grand? The fuckin' joint cost me a hundred and fifty!'

'Plus the interest, Les. Sixteen and a half per cent. Plus other expenses.'

'Jesus fuckin' Christ! What fuckin' next?'

'That's why I've been ringing you for the last three months. I think you'd better sit back and have another glass of cold water. There's a few things I have to explain to you.'

'Like what? "Les, I've got some good news and I've got some bad news".'

22

'Well, Les, if you wish to be jocular... Firstly, there is no good news. And secondly, the bad news only gets worse.'

When Whittle had finished with him, Les Norton the Donald Trump of the Eastern suburbs face looked more like a badly-iced sponge cake that had been left out in the rain and if there had been a length of rope in the flat, Les would have hung himself in the accountant's shithouse. Norton's one hundred and fifty thousand dollar investment had turned out to be a bigger lemon than the movie *Cleopatra*.

The old block of flats was practically falling down and in constant need of repair. The most the agents could let them for was $110 per week, and one, it appeared, had been vacant for over three weeks now. The income from the flats covered the bank payments and interest but constant maintenance, council rates and Whittle's expenses had taken up what was over. Plus there was a live-in caretaker, who got $100 a week. So after three years of all this, instead of having a bit of a whippy waiting for him, Norton was nearly $2,000 in the red. And climbing. If Randwick Council had not decided to reclaim, the land alone would have been worth at least $300 000 on today's value. But Randwick Council must have known Blue Seas was a dog and decided it was the ideal place to put in a roundabout and divert the traffic away from Belmore Road and the Prince of Wales Hospital and Randwick Junction. And while they were on the subject of public relations, there was also a large girls' college behind Aquila Street, Saint Bridgettes, who had a covenant on the land going back to the turn of the century. If it was ever reclaimed, the college got part of it for a small reserve: Saint Bridgettes Park.

To compound the whole shemozzle, council didn't intend to reclaim for around another five years. So for the next five years Les was stuck with an old block of flats that would never increase in value and, even after the rent money, would cost him about $400 a week.

23

And like they say in the army, there wasn't thing one Les could do about it.

From across the table Norton stared in silence at his accountant, his face a mixture of grief, anger, disbelief and a myriad of other emotions; not one of them even resembling joy or happiness. Whittle couldn't work out whether Les was going to burst into tears or start taking his home-unit apart. He thought this might be as good a time as any to get a nice cold glass of spring water himself. He returned with the glass plus a folder which he placed on the table between them.

'So that's about it, Les,' he said softly. 'As far as Blue Seas Apartments go, financially you're not in a very sound position. But you can't blame me,' he added quickly, pointing to the folder he had just placed on the table. 'Look through all the documents. You can see where I've negative geared it, offset it against your current income. There's a complete breakdown analysis of your capital expenditure. I even tried for an assets revaluation reserve. Have a look.' He shrugged, and pushed the folder in front of Les.

Norton flicked disconsolately through all the facts and figures. He may as well have been looking at a Chinese newspaper.

'What about that fuckin' lawyer in Paddington who handled all this? What's his name? Aubrey Spenser. I'll go and have a nice word with him. He should have known about all this.'

Whittle tried not to smile. 'Well, if you are, I suggest you pack a suitcase. He's in gaol in Ireland. For currency fraud.'

Norton closed his eyes. 'That figures,' he snorted. 'That fuckin' figures.'

'I'm truly sorry, Les,' said Whittle, taking another sip of water. 'But unfortunately that's the way it goes.'

'Yeah,' grunted Les. 'The way it goes. You win some, you lose some.'

'That's right. Caveat emptor. Or damnum sine injuria.'

Norton just glared at his accountant.

24

'Look, Les, why don't you go home and have a look through those papers yourself? You never know, you might just come up with something I've overlooked.' Whittle was telling a complete falsehood; Norton was stuffed six ways to Sunday. But it was a polite way of getting him out of the flat. 'In the meantime I'll attend to your tax returns. There may possibly be something there I can do.'

Les snorted a burst of air out through his nose. 'Yeah, righto.' He rose from the table picking up the folder as he did. 'I'll give you a ring early next week.'

'Do that.' Whittle moved across to the door and opened it. 'Good luck, Les. And don't let it get you down too much.'

'Yeah, terrific. Thanks anyway, Des.' Norton gave his accountant another brief handshake and walked out to his car.

He didn't start the engine straight away, he just sat there staring at the folder, not able to believe his rotten luck. Norton's gilt edged dream of riches had suddenly, unexpectedly crumbled to dust. Worse — dried-up dogshit. He moved his gaze from the folder, to the window and to the sky. You've always been crooked on me for some reason, haven't you? Why? Why fuckin' me? What have I ever done to you? He returned his glare to the folder. Fuckin' Price. And that fat fuckin' George Brennan too. 'You'd be a mug not to tumble into this, Les. Now's your chance to make some big bucks, Les.' Big bucks, huh! I'm about eighty grand down the gurgler so far and I've got five years to go. He closed his eyes and shook his head. He still couldn't believe it. Well there is one thing I can do to save some money. I can sack that fuckin' caretaker. And I'll do it right now. What's the name of that stinkin' estate agency? He flicked through the folder. Here it is. Steinberg and Ringblum Licensed Real Estate agents. That figures. Yeah, that fuckin' figures. Les's face was an unsmiling mask set in cement as he started the car and drove to Belmore Road, Randwick Junction.

25

The traffic wasn't too bad between Double Bay and Randwick and Les was there in about fifteen minutes; only abusing all the pedestrians and just about every other driver on the road. He found the estate agency after turning left off Alison Road and fluked a parking spot about twenty metres away.

Steinberg and Ringblum's was in between a boutique and a travel agency underneath a large motel. The front window was full of photos of houses and blocks of flats and stencilled on the door was Isaac Steinberg, Licensed Real Estate Agent and Marvin Ringblum, Licensed Strata Manager. Behind a counter inside, three girls sat typing beneath a large map of Randwick and Coogee. A sort of corridor along the grey carpet separated them from a row of filing cabinets and further down the room glass partitions formed three offices. Les stepped inside and waited at the counter.

A young blonde girl in a light blue dress got up from her typewriter and walked over. 'Yes?' she smiled. 'Can I help you?'

'I'd like to see either Mr Steinberg or Mr Ringblum, please,' answered Les.

'Mr Steinberg is out at the moment, but Mr Ringblum is in. Who shall I say wishes to see him?'

'Mr Norton. The owner of Blue Seas Apartments.'

'I won't be a moment.'

The blonde girl walked down to the furthest office, said something to a man in a shirt and tie, who looked up briefly, then came back.

'Mr Ringblum will see you. The second office on the left.' She opened up part of the counter and Les walked through.

Marvin Ringblum, a telephone receiver resting on his left shoulder, was about fifty, balding, with a paunch pushing out against a white shirt tucked into a pair of brown trousers. With a podgy hand he motioned Les into a seat, muttered a few more unsmiling words into the phone and hung up.

'Mr Norton,' he said through an oily, insincere smile,

26

'such a long time since we've seen you. How are you?' He offered Les a handshake which felt like a slice of veal steak. 'And what can I do for you?'

As if Marvin Ringblum didn't know. Sitting before him was one big, dumb goyen with red hair. A goyen straddled up with a block of flats worth about two and a half shekels. And now the goyen was probably going to start crying on his shoulder. Norton's troubles Marvin didn't need. Sympathy Les wasn't going to get.

'As you probably know, I'm the owner of Blue Seas Apartments in Aquila Street,' said Les, pointing to the folder in front of him.

'Of course, Mr Norton. A nice... a nice little block of units.'

'I'll get straight to the point, Mr Ringblum. I want to sack... dismiss the caretaker.'

Ringblum shrugged and made an open-handed gesture. 'Of course, Mr Norton. You're the owner. You do as you wish.'

'Yeah. But I want to do it straight away. Today.'

'Good,' nodded Ringblum. 'Do it.'

Les looked at the estate agent quizzically. 'Well, you're the agents. What do you do? Send him a letter? Go down and tell him? What?' Surely there had to be some kind of protocol involved here? You just don't sack someone without a reason or at least some sort of an explanation — do you?

But as far as Steinberg and Ringblum Real Estate agents were concerned, Les could do what he liked with Blue Seas Apartments and whoever lived in them. The block was a lemon and an eyesore and for the amount of commission they collected from the rents, not worth having on the books. And as far as any feelings for the caretaker... Marvin and Isaac were a couple of good Jewish boys who had come out from Russia fleeing persecution by the communists. Their mothers wanted them to be doctors but they couldn't afford uni fees at the time. Politics didn't interest them, or being heroin dealers and joining the parking police didn't pay enough.

So they became real estate agents instead. Norton could have taken the caretaker out into the street and had him publicly beheaded then fed his body to the hyenas at Taronga Park Zoo for all they cared.

'No problem at all, Mr Norton. You just go down to the apartments and tell Mr Olsen he's been dismissed.' Ringblum sat back and gave Les another oily smile.

'That's it?' blinked Les.

'You want I should give him a gold watch?' shrugged Ringblum. The phone rang and he picked it up. 'I'm sorry, Mr Norton, but I'm terribly busy,' he said, cupping his hand over the mouthpiece. 'If there is some sort of a problem, come back and see me. Thank you, Mr Norton.'

'Yeah righto, terrific. It's been really average talking to you.' Norton picked up his folder and left the office.

Sitting outside in his car Les didn't quite know what to do. He'd never sacked anyone in his life and no matter what, he couldn't have done it just like that, anyway, no matter what sort of a mood he was in. And the last thing he wanted to do was go down and have a look at his gilt-edged investment rotting away just down the road; it was too vexing and too depressing. He thought about it for a few moments, then started the car, took the next on the left and drove home.

It was close enough to lunchtime when Les walked in the front door and normally at this time he would have cooked himself something tasty to eat, but for some reason he seemed to have lost his appetite. Instead, he made a cup of coffee and contemplated his miserable fate while he flicked through the folder Whittle had given him. The pile of documents with all the facts and figures made no sense at all. The letter from Randwick council did, though, and he was able to grind through that. The only other thing he could understand was that the flats were insured for $150 000 with Erin. A. Insurance Company. Hah! That figures, snorted Les. Erin means Ireland where that stinkin' lawyer's in gaol and you can

28

bet your life he's set that up and pissed off with all the funds. So it's a lay-down misere that's not worth the paper it's printed on. On an impulse he picked up the phone book and then the yellow pages. There was no Erin. A. Insurance Company in Sydney. That figures. Yeah, that bloody well figures. He put the useless insurance policy back in the folder and tossed it on the dressing table in his bedroom.

Norton switched on the TV to watch the midday movie, but ten minutes of Joan Crawford in *Autumn Leaves* almost had him reaching for the hemlock. Ahh, bugger this, he cursed, switching off the TV. I know what I'll do. I'll get a bottle of Bundy and a case of beer and blot the whole stinkin' day out. He went to his room to get some money then he remembered that he and Warren were going on the wagon for a month. Christ! What a time to try and stay sober. No, bugger getting on the piss. I've only got to wake up again tomorrow and Warren will want to know what's going on.

He fiddled around the house for a while then drove up to Bondi Junction and hung around the shops and the Plaza for the rest of the cool, cloudy, November afternoon. When he left, he bought a kilo of cheap mince; being in a lousy, miserable mood he decided to cook a lousy miserable tea.

The mince was stewing on the stove and Les was stirring it disconsolately when Warren arrived home about six.

'Hello landlord,' he said cheerfully, as he breezed into the kitchen, holding two large bottles of mineral water. 'What's doing?'

'Not much,' grunted Les.

Warren took a deep breath, held out his arms and flexed what little muscles he had. 'You know, I've never felt so good in my life. This getting off the drink is the best idea we've ever had.'

'Yeah? That's good.'

Warren moved across to the stove. 'So what's for tea?'

29

'Mince.'

'Mince!' Warren peered distastefully into the pot. 'Fuckin' mince. They feed you that in Boys Homes.'

'You don't like mince Warren?'

'I'm fuckin' sure I don't.'

'Well, don't fuckin' eat it.'

Warren stepped back from the stove. 'Jesus! You're in a good mood.'

'I'm all right.'

'Yeah, terrific.'

Warren got cleaned up then joined Les in a very ordinary tea. So much for a month of gourmet cooking, he mused. This tastes like shit. And Les is in the same sort of mood. I think having him hanging around the house is going to be like I pictured it in the first place. Very bloody ordinary. They did the dishes and watched TV. The TV was quite good, but the conversation on Norton's behalf was very limited.

'You know what's wrong with you?' said Warren, half way through 'Beyond 2000'.

'What?'

'Withdrawals. Two days off the piss and you can't handle it.'

'If you say so, Warren.'

'You fuckin' big sheila.'

'If you say so, Warren.'

They watched TV till around eleven then hit the sack. Norton managed to get to sleep after a while but he definitely wasn't looking forward to the following day. Or the following five years for that matter.

Wednesday was pretty much like the day before; scattered clouds being pushed along by the southerly, cool but in no way cold. Les was up at his usual time for another run in Centennial Park, trying to enjoy it as best he could, despite what was sitting uneasily on his mind. Warren had left for work when he got home and Les remembered his saying something the night before about having to start a little earlier because of some new advertising campaign. He got cleaned up and had a leisurely breakfast and read the morning paper, making it last as long as he could. Finally he got into a pair of jeans and a T-shirt and headed for Randwick. It was getting on for eleven when Les turned into Perouse Road and found a parking spot almost out the front of Blue Seas Apartments.

The old block looked pretty much the same as the last time Les had seen it, which was so long ago he couldn't remember when. It was situated on the corner of Aquila Street and Perouse Road, about two hundred metres down from the Royal Hotel. Aquila Street was a dead-end street, about a hundred metres long, with a couple of blocks of flats on one side and Blue Seas on the other, the rear of which backed onto a lane with St Bridgettes College taking up the entire end of the street. Unlike the better blocks of flats opposite, Blue Seas only had two storeys: three flats on the top level and two on the bottom, along with the small caretaker's residence, a storeroom and laundry.

The front of the building was old, daggy brown brick smeared with pigeon shit; Blue Seas was written above some windows in what once might have been dark blue but which was now almost faded to a light grey. A waist-high brick fence stood under this stopping at a side passage where an old wooden, paling fence hung with letter boxes ran alongside the house next door. The brick fence cornered from Perouse into Aquila and past the main entrance till it became more wooden palings which went round the back of the flats where the alley separated them from St Bridgettes at the rear. The whole place looked old and neglected and again Les wondered how he'd let them talk him into buying it. Shaking his head he got out of the car and walked over stopping to look at the small front yard. The grass was overgrown and a few different types of cactus plants almost gave a hint of colour where some dog turds sat amidst a number of yellow dandelions pushing through the weeds. Some fuckin' caretaker I've got, thought Les. He shook his

31

head and walked around to the old wooden doors at the entrance in Aquila Street next to a number of dirty wooden boxes that held the gas meters.

The foyer consisted of more dirty brown bricks above a floor of chipped, slate tiles edged in a kind of red and white diamond pattern. A staircase with thick wooden handrails ran up beneath a splintery wooden panel with ancient electricity meters clinging to it. In the light from the old lead-lined windows in a kind of blue bow design Les could see wires and leads poking and hanging out everywhere. Again, he shook his head then thought seeing as there didn't seem to be anybody around, he might check the place out before he saw the caretaker.

The doors on the flats upstairs were the same as the ones below: white with brass knockers and milk serveries in between. He pushed a door open onto the fire escape. It had a wooden staircase and a handrail made of pipe and cyclone wire which had been painted a garish red; more wires and leads hung off the walls and more pigeon shit smeared the dirty brown bricks. Another flight of stairs led to a door that opened out onto the roof. The roof was flat — plain grey tar with a few old boxes, bricks and other junk strewn around. A TV aerial jutted out to one side and behind that, if you twisted your neck around enough, you got a distant glimpse of a few swells out on the horizon. So that's why it's called Blue Seas Apartments, thought Les. The panoramic ocean view. He shook his head and walked down to the back yard.

The concrete back yard held the empty clothesline and several long metal stakes jammed into the concrete held the back fence up. Someone had stacked a number of housebricks into two squares filled with soil to make a bit of a garden, and the few red flowers within, along with the cacti and dandelions out the front added the only colour to what was undoubtedly a very dismal scene. How could I have been such a mug thought Les again. No wonder I kept away from the prick of a joint. He stared absently at the flowers for a moment then went in to see the caretaker, checking out the laundry as he did.

The laundry was dark, dirty and stunk of mildew. Old papers, bottles and other junk littered the floor amongst the dirt and dust that seemed to be everywhere. There were five copper tubs with a gas meter above, each fitted with a lock. Cobwebs, dead flies and more dirt festooned the windows that overlooked the backyard. Water on the floor, a few pegs scattered round the tubs, and a couple of dried-up bars of Sunlight said at least someone had been in there recently. How could I have been such a mug? thought Les again. And again he shook his head.

The storeroom was locked and the caretaker's flat was next to the laundry. Les knocked, not too loudly, and waited. He heard a shuffling movement inside then the door opened.

If Warren was half Les's size, the caretaker was a quarter. He looked around sixty, with thinning brown hair edged with grey, little ears, a little flattened nose and a little mouth full of stained teeth, all set in a heavily-lined face. Wearing an old pair of shiny blue trousers and a matching flannelette shirt he looked up at Les through a pair of watery eyes.

Norton gave a double blink at the wizened shape in the doorway. 'Are you Harry Olsen?' he asked.

'Yeah,' was the tight reply.

The caretaker being so puny Norton felt worse than ever. 'Ahh... look, mate,' he said hesitantly. 'I've been sent down by the estate agents.'

'Yeah?' The caretaker's voice was tighter than ever. 'And what do those two arseholes want?'

Les was taken slightly aback. 'Well, mate. They're ahh... they're thinking of putting on another caretaker.'

'Oh, are they?' sneered the caretaker. He gave Les a pretty heavy once up and down. 'And I suppose you're it, are you?'

'Well, yeah — kind of, in a way,' replied Les sheepishly.

'And do you think I really give a stuff?' The little caretaker puffed out his chest and raised himself up defiantly.

'Well...'

'Well, I bloody don't. So there.'

Norton gave another double blink. 'Well, good for you.'

The caretaker half smiled at Les. 'Come in anyway, big fella. And I'll tell you what's goin' on. And what you can tell those two slimy reffos to do with their greasy caretaker's job.'

Norton followed the caretaker into a gloomy sort of a bedsitter. The carpet was a threadbare brown and there was a grey vinyl night-and-day shoved against one wall with a small laminex table and two chairs. The cold water kitchen had a gas heater, a small stove and a fridge and from the sickly yellow glow of a single light bulb, in a white shade hanging from the ceiling Les noticed a bit of a wardrobe against another wall and a door that probably led to a bathroom. A large bottle of opened beer sat on the table and, oddly enough, a suitcase half full of clothes sat on the night-and-day. The Ritz it wasn't and the stark poverty of the surroundings made Les feel quite uncomfortable. So this is how the other half live eh? Yet what the little caretaker had said about the two estate agents made him curious.

As the caretaker moved around the table and poured himself another beer, Les noticed he had a pronounced limp.

'So what's your name anyway, son?' he asked.

'Les.'

'I'm Harry,' replied the caretaker, offering his hand. 'But everybody calls me Hoppy.'

Norton took his callused handshake. 'Nice to meet you... Hoppy.'

The caretaker looked evenly at Les. 'So, how come you got the job?'

'I... just saw it in the local paper,' lied Norton. 'I didn't really know what was going on. I hope I'm not doing you out of a job.'

'Hah! You're not doing me out of job, mate. I was pissin' off anyway.' Acting like he'd just got one up on Les, the little caretaker continued to pack clothes into the suitcase.

'My sister's husband just died up in Newcastle. Left her a big house and plenty of money. She's on her own and I'm going up to join her.'

Norton's day suddenly brightened up. 'Ohh, that's real good then.'

'Reckon. I can get out of this flea-bitten dump.' Hoppy looked at Les a little suspiciously. 'So you're gonna be the new caretaker of Blue Seas, eh? You sure don't look like you're short of a quid.'

'I just got divorced, Hoppy. The bloody moll took the house, the kids and every zac I had. I'm doing it tough, mate, don't worry about that.'

'I know what you mean. I got divorced myself. I also used to be a pretty good jockey once, till a couple of horses went over me at Rosehill about thirty years ago.'

'Shit! That's no good, mate.'

The little caretaker patted his right leg. 'That's why the limp. And why they call me Hoppy.' He took a mouthful of beer. 'You want a glass?' Les shook his head. 'Coffee?'

'Yeah. I could go a coffee.'

Olsen nodded to the kitchen. 'Well, help yourself while I finish packing.'

'Okay.'

Norton fossicked around in the kitchen finding the jug, coffee and a clean mug. As he waited for the jug to boil, he thought it might be a good time to pump the caretaker for a bit of information.

'So, how long've you been here, Hoppy?'

'Close enough to three years.'

'You know who owns the joint?'

'Haven't a clue. I think it's one of the estate agent's reffo mates. But I'm glad it's not me,' he added with a chuckle. 'The place is a dump.'

'Yeah, I got to agree with you there,' said Les, trying

35

not to sound depressed. He made his coffee and pulled up a chair while the caretaker finished packing. 'When are you leaving?' he asked.

'Soon as I finish packing this suitcase,' replied Olsen. 'I'm off, quicker than Moshe Dayan's foreskin.'

'What about your furniture and that?'

Olsen laughed. 'Mate. It's all fuckin' yours.'

Norton had to laugh back. 'How are you getting to Newcastle?'

'Train.'

'I can give you a lift to Central, if you like.'

'Okay, Les. That'd be good.'

'On one condition.'

'What's that?'

'You've got to tell me a bit about the place. Who lives here and all that.'

The caretaker gave a wheezy laugh. 'Who lives here? I'll tell you who lives here. Some of the greatest weirdos I've ever come across. Wait till you meet them. You'll love 'em.'

Norton sipped slowly on his coffee. 'Like who, for instance?'

The caretaker rolled up several pairs of tatty socks and pushed them into the corners of his suitcase. 'Okay. We'll start with downstairs. Firstly, in flat two, you got old blind Burt and his guide dog, Rosie. He's on the pension and he sells papers. He's not all that blind, but he's blind enough.' The caretaker seemed to laugh at some private joke. 'You're gonna love old Burt.' He took another mouthful of beer. 'Then in flat three, you got Sandy. She's an artist.'

'An artist?'

'Yeah. Not a bad sort, either. Sandra Jean Garrett's her real name. She's got a boyfriend — or two. She's also got some old bloke comes round and porks her just about every weekend. I think he's got a fair bit of money. He buys nearly all her paintings.'

'Like a rich benefactor?'

'Something like that. Right, now upstairs in flat four

36

you got an all-girl rock 'n' roll band. The Heathen Harlots.'

'The fuckin' what?' exclaimed Les.

Olsen laughed out loud. 'Wait till you meet the Heathen Harlots, Les. You'll love them too. They look like fuckin' vampires and dress like aliens from another planet. They *could* be vampires too. I can't remember the last time I saw them in the daylight.'

'Christ!'

'Flat five's empty. Used to be a bikie lived there.' The caretaker shook his head. 'Bad lot too, him and his mates. There was a terrific stink up there about a month ago — screamin' and yellin'. These other bikies took him away and I ain't seen him since. Just between you and me, I think they killed him.'

'Shit!'

'Though, when I think about it, Jimmy wasn't all that bad a bloke. Only a little fella for a bikie; not all that much bigger than me. Just before it happened he got me to put some stuff in the storeroom for him. Bits of a motorbike and that.'

'Is it still there?'

'Yeah.' Olsen finished the bottle of beer. 'And in flat six you've got a team of hippies.'

'Hippies?'

'Yeah, just like out of one of those sixties movies.'

Hello, thought Les, here we go again. I'm back in Yurriki. 'How many living up there?'

Hoppy shrugged. 'About half a dozen — I think. They drive an old blue kombi, it's generally parked out the front. Wait till you meet them. They wouldn't have a brain between them and I don't think any of them have had a bath since the War of the Roses.'

'Un-fuckin'-real.'

'They're all on the dole and all they do is get out of it and sit up on the roof playing didgeridoos.'

'Didgeridoos? You're kidding.'

'Wait till you hear it when they go off. Albert Namatjira'd roll over in his grave.'

37

Norton shook his head and stared into his coffee. Christ! What have I got myself into here?

He looked up as Hoppy threw an old pair of tan shoes into the suitcase, shoved them down then closed the lid and turned the locks.

'Well, that's it,' he said, picking up a cardigan from the back of a chair. 'I'm packed and out of here.'

'That's it?' echoed Les.

'Yep.' The caretaker gave the suitcase a tap. 'That's it.'

Bloody hell, thought Norton. Poor little bastard. Three years in this dump, he's half a cripple nearing the end of his life and what's he got to show for it? A lousy suitcase full of old clothes. Well, at least he's going somewhere decent. Then a guilty thought struck Les. What if Hoppy didn't have that sister in Newcastle? He was going to toss him out on the street. Les swallowed hard and looked at the little caretaker standing there putting on his cardigan.

'What about the rest of your stuff?' he said, nodding to the kitchen.

'Like I said, Les. It's all yours.' Hoppy smiled at Norton. 'You're gonna need it, mate. You've got alimony payments and all that coming up. I remember my divorce. I know what the bastards are like.'

Les gave the little caretaker a soft smile. 'Ohh, that's what I meant to tell you. The estate agent said to give you this. I think it's a bit of a square-off from the owner.' He fished into his jeans and pulled out two hundred dollars which he handed to the caretaker. 'Better than a poke in the eye with a chopstick.'

'Well, bugger me!' said Hoppy, staring at the money. Then he laughed. 'This proves one thing for sure. Whoever the owner is, he couldn't possibly be a mate of the agents. 'Cause those two pricks wouldn't give you the steam off their shit.'

'You still want that lift into Central?'

'Yeah,' nodded Olsen. 'Let's go. And don't even drive past the agent's. If you hadn't come round I wouldn't even have closed the door behind me.'

Norton picked up the ex-caretaker's suitcase, switched off the light and led him out towards the car. As they got to the front, Olsen stopped in the doorway, unzipped his fly and pissed all over the front of the flats.

'You're the caretaker now,' he winked at Les. 'You can clean it up.' He zipped up his fly and followed Les over to the old Ford.

On the way into town, Hoppy gave Les the key to his flat and the storeroom. There was no master key to any of the other flats but he did have a key to flat five; the bikie had left it with him when he put his stuff in the storeroom. He told Les when the garbage went out and one or two other things. All in all nothing for Les to get too enthused about. Then they were at Central.

Olsen said there was no need for Les to help him with his bag, there'd be a train before long and he wanted to sit on his own and have a couple of beers and read the paper while he waited. They shook hands. Les wished Olsen all the best in Newcastle and Olsen wished Les all the best with his new job at Blue Seas and hoped his divorce worked out okay. Then as if by magic, the little caretaker was swallowed up in the crowds of other country travellers coming and going with their suitcases among the platforms at Central Railway.

Norton sat in his car for a moment and had a think. There wasn't all that much to think about, except that he was now another two hundred down the drain. He started the car and for some reason headed back to Blue Seas Apartments.

Well, me old mate Hoppy sure travelled light and didn't believe in too many luxuries, mused Les, as he had a bit of a browse round the ex-caretaker's flat. There was nothing in the wardrobe except a few coat hangers and an old copy of the *Herald*. The remains of some coffee sugar and detergent sat in the kitchen and the fridge contained a bit of milk, margarine and half a tomato. There was no TV, no radio and no blankets. Then again thought Les, he probably knew he was splitting and got rid of all that, if there was any, before

39

he left. He had a quick look out the kitchen window into the backyard: there was still no one around and he hadn't noticed anybody when he came in. Norton left the fairly dismal scene and decided to check out the storeroom.

The key fitted and there was a light switch near the door. The storeroom was windowless, gloomy and just as grimy and dusty as the laundry, with possibly more cobwebs and dead flies. Boxes of old newspapers and bottles littered the floor along with some paint tins and dried-up brushes. A battered empty suitcase and a couple of empty overnight bags sat in one corner near a yard broom, a rake, a mop and bucket and an old push mower. Up against a wall was Jimmy the bikie, or late bikie's motorbike. Les was expecting a Harley Davidson or a BMW; instead he was surprised to find a rusting old BSA Bantam resting on its forks, the wheels and flat tyres behind it. Christ, thought Les, when was the last time I saw one of those? Old Tom, the postman back in Dirranbandi, that's right, he used to get round on one. Wonder what a big, bad Sydney bikie was doing with an old BSA Bantam? Norton ran his hand over the handle bars and empty saddlebag. Probably restoring it. He shook his head. The remains of the gutted motorbike seem to fit in perfectly with the whole cheerless scene. Les switched off the light and left.

Well, thought Les, standing out in the light of the foyer, while I'm on the subject of bikes and bikies I may as well check out whatever's left in the alleged late Jimmy baby's flat. There was still no one around as Les trotted up the stairs, but he thought he could hear a radio playing in flat four.

The two bedroom flat was a corridor as you walked in with a bedroom on the left then the bathroom, the lounge room, another bedroom off it and the kitchen adjacent.

Norton didn't know what to expect when he stepped into flat five but he sure as hell wasn't expecting what he found. It was complete chaos. The flat had been tipped upside down and absolutely wrecked. It looked like one of those scenes in a movie where the drug squad hits a place and gives it a thorough going over, except flat five had been methodically almost destroyed. It didn't appear as if there'd been a great deal of furniture in the lounge in the first place, but what was there, was smashed and splintered. Posters had been ripped from the walls, the carpet was torn up and even the cheap curtains had been yanked down. Then Les noticed the dried blood spattered across the white walls of the lounge room. It was the same in the kitchen. Every cupboard and drawer had been tipped out, ransacked and smashed. Cutlery, plates and what few pots and pans there were were strewn all over the floor and even the fridge and stove had been ripped apart with rotting, mouldy food and water from the ice-cube trays spread amongst the debris strewn all over the kitchen floor.

'Jesus bloody Christ!' exclaimed Les. 'What the fuckin' hell?' He'd never seen anything like it.

Same in both bedrooms; there was more blood on the walls showing up as rusty, dark stains on the old brown carpet. The wardrobes were smashed and even the mirrors had been shattered and torn off their hinges. Someone had smashed up the beds then taken to the mattresses with a knife, spreading kapok and springs amongst whatever already littered the floor. A dressing table in the front room looked as if some maniac had attacked it with an axe.

'Bloody hell!' muttered Les.

The bathroom was the same only they'd torn apart the sink and ripped down the medicine chest above. They'd even kicked in the sides of the bath and torn out the shower fittings. Worst of all was the amount of congealed, browning blood all over the bath. An attempt had been made to wash some away but what was left showed the sheer ferocity of the attackers.

'Shit!' said Les.

Norton walked slowly through the carnage double blinking. He'd seen some sights in his time, but nothing

41

quite like this. And to think he owned it. It was fairly obvious what had happened though. Jimmy's bikie pals had come around looking for something — more than likely drugs. They'd started to bash some information out of the hapless Jimmy and, going by the amount of blood in the bathroom, they'd overdone it and killed him and then taken the body away, just like old Hoppy had said.

Norton toed his way through the shoes, shirts, jeans and other torn clothing that littered the floor; an old brown sports coat even had the shoulder pads cut out. Whatever it was they were looking for, thought Les, they were sure keen to find it. And now I gotta clean all this fuckin' shit up. Not today though. Then Norton's eyes darkened. One thing's for certain. If ever I find the cunts that did this, I know who else'll be getting cleaned up.

He was still shaking his head and staring at the havoc around him when he heard it. At first it sounded like a squadron of bombers flying low overhead, vibrating down one wall and coming in through the open window of the flat. Les had heard the sound before, though not so much in Sydney. But he knew where this was coming from and who was behind it. He had a last look around him, then closed the door and walked up to the roof.

It was the hippies from flat six all right. There were three of them, sitting cross-legged in a semicircle, out of it blowing for all they were worth into their didgeridoos. But unlike the hippies Les had seen up in Yurriki, who were clean and fairly tidy, these three made your average park wino look like Trent Nathan. Their hair was like greasy rope, the soles of their feet were absolutely pitch black and even from where he was standing Les could smell BO that bad you could have photographed it. They wore filthy sweatbands and equally filthy tie-dyed T-shirts and singlets hanging out over crushed velvet pants. The main reason they were crushed velvet was because they'd never seen an iron since the day these chats had more than likely flogged them off some clothesline.

Then Norton realised where he'd seen these three grubs before. It was up at the stalls in Oxford Street, Paddington one Saturday afternoon. Some sheila Les had been taking out had dragged him up there and this mob, plus more, were out on the footpath with a sign saying, *Didgeridoo Massage $5*. They had one of their team lying down on the footpath as a stooge and were running the didgeridoos over her as she writhed in absolute, bunged-on joy. It was one of the best cons Les had ever seen and only her black stinkin' feet gave her away. The best part though, thought Les, was that they were actually getting mugs in at five bucks a toss.

They noticed Les standing there but chose to ignore him as they howled away into the long, wooden pipes. After a few moments, Norton walked over and placed his foot over the end of the nearest hippy's didgeridoo. He stopped blowing, as did the others, and looked up at Les as though they half expected him to be a cop.

'Hey, what's the hassle man?' he said.

Norton looked distastefully at all three of them, then back at the one whose music he'd interrupted. 'No hassle, man,' said Les, sarcastically. 'I'm the new caretaker.' Although not actually taking Les to their breast, the hippies did seem relieved that he wasn't a cop. 'You got any idea what happened in flat five? And what happened to the bloke that was living there?'

There was a chorus of. 'No, man... We didn't see anything, man. We weren't here whenever what it is you're talking about happened, man... Sorry, man... We can't help you at all, man.'

What they really meant was they'd seen and heard everything but were too terrified to talk about it. You didn't have to be Sherlock Holmes to figure that out. But what was the use of grilling them. They probably wouldn't be able to tell him all that much. And what they could would come out like a load of shit, anyway.

'Yeah, righto,' nodded Les. 'Don't worry about it.' He left them to their music, or whatever it was, and went back downstairs.

43

There was still no one around out the front and as Les walked across to his car he noticed the old blue kombi Hoppy had told him about. It was just as rough and dirty as the people who owned it. There was a pair of rusty roof-racks on top and various environmental stickers on the windows: Save the Whales, Solar Not Nuclear, Stop Japanese Drift Netting. Oh well, mused Norton, the hippies might stink, but at least their hearts are in the right place. He got in the old Ford and headed for Bondi.

Seeing as he had almost insulted Warren with that horrible mince the night before, Les thought it might be an idea if he got his act together and cooked something a bit decent that night. So he bought a corner cut of topside. He also thought it might be an idea if he stopped being so moody and quit sulking or Warren might start to smell a rat. He'd never told Warren about Blue Seas and he sure as hell didn't want to bring it up now or what was on his mind.

While the roast was cooking and Norton was fart-arsing around the house he reflected on the day; thinking about it only made the situation worse. Blue Seas was a bigger dog than he had ever imagined — he should have checked it out more thoroughly when he bought it. His tenants or what he'd seen of them so far, were a soapy-looking lot to say the least. And now it looked like there'd been a murder on the premises. So what to do about that? Call the police? Yeah, they'd probably try and pin the thing on him, knowing his record. Flat five would just have to go on hold for the time being. The only bright spot of the day, if you could call it that, was getting the old caretaker out so smoothly. And even that had cost him two hundred bucks. Fuck. What a schemozzle.

But if anything was wrong that night Warren would never have known. The roast beef was the grouse and Les bubbled away, saying he'd spent the day with some mates playing cards and a bit of snooker and drinking mineral water. Yes, Warren was right, it had been withdrawals Les

44

had been going through the night before. There was no escaping the brilliant, young advertising executive's amazing powers of perception. Warren rubbed it in and said he'd never felt better in his life and added quite confidently that he didn't care if he never had another drink in his life. Les added that he only wished he had Warren's iron backbone and phenomenal resilience. They watched a video Warren had brought home and were both in bed around midnight.

Thursday was pretty much like the day before when Les rose at his usual time; the southerly was still keeping the temperature down but it didn't seem as cloudy. Again he had another run in Centennial Park and again when he got home Warren had left for the office early. The run, although hard, was enjoyable almost relaxing even and physically Les felt on top of the world after he got cleaned up. He was beginning to come to grips with the situation at Blue Seas. Due to a certain amount of bad luck and no doubt his own negligence, he was stuck with an albatross around his neck. But somehow he'd work that out. He'd have to. He was going to lose money — there was no doubt about that — but no matter what, it wasn't going to break him. The scene in flat five was a different kettle of fish, however, and a nasty one. He decided it might be best if he made a phone call straight after breakfast, as soon as Isaac Steinberg and Marvin Ringblum opened for business.

'Hello? Steinberg and Ringblum Real Estate,' said a polite voice.

'Yes, it's Mr Norton, the owner of Blue Seas Apartments. I'd like to speak to Mr Ringblum, please.'

'Mr Ringblum's not in at the moment.'

'Mr Steinberg then.'

'Mr Steinberg's just popped out for a moment. Can I take a message?'

'Yes. Tell him Mr Olsen's gone and I'll be doing the caretaking and maintenance from now on.'

'All right, Mr Norton.'

'And tell him the tenant's moved out of flat five, and not to bother re-letting it at the moment as I want to paint it and re-carpet it.'

'I'll see that he gets the message. Anything else, Mr Norton?'

'No. That's all.'

'Thank you. Bye.'

Norton stared absently at the phone for a few seconds. That was another bloody thing. While flat five was empty it was costing him more money. So the sooner he did get it cleaned up and repaired the better. He drummed his fingers on the table. But a few more days wouldn't make much difference. In the meantime, he mused, I am the caretaker. So I imagine I'd better do just that. Caretake. He got into an old pair of jeans and sweatshirt he used for cleaning up round the house or working on the car, got a few things from the kitchen and the ghetto blaster from his bedroom and headed for Randwick.

Old Hoppy hadn't left the small flat in too bad a condition — it was a bit dusty maybe, but there were no rings in the bath and no lumps of fruit chutney stuck around the sides of the toilet bowl. But you could bet your life there'd be no shortage of fleas and cockroaches and various other forms of suburban wildlife hanging around. With the ghetto blaster going in the background, Norton Baygoned all the cupboards and Pea-Beaued all the carpets and poured bleach down the bath, both sinks, and the toilet bowl. The old gas heater above the kitchen sink caught his eye. He gave a good, long burst of Baygon underneath it, and all round the back. It was only a matter of seconds and it looked like the old heater was being hit by an earthquake. Then out they came. Cockroaches. Only little ones mainly, but there were virtually millions of them, coughing and spluttering, almost carrying suitcases and their furniture as they staggered out of the heater and fell down the wall into the sink.

'*Aiee*!!' cried Les. 'The evil ones!' He poured the Baygon into them. 'Die, evil ones. Die!' A bigger one staggered

46

across the sink; Les crushed it with a rolled up newspaper. 'Go to your grave, miserable cur.' Another big one got the same treatment. 'Feel my blade, craven dog. Let death be your reward.'

Parodying the voice of Conan The Barbarian, Les got stuck into the army of cockies, spraying, swatting and scooping them into the sink. Unexpectedly there was a knock on the door.

'Hello? Who's this?'

He opened the door and gave a double blink. Standing there was a dumpy little bloke of about sixty, wearing a brown skivvy and blue trousers. Perched on his head was a blue beret and a pair of fat, round sunglasses sat on a fat round nose set in a fat round face. It was all Norton could do to stop from bursting out laughing. The bloke looked almost like Benny Hill dressed as that stupid Salvation Army officer; all that was missing was the arse-about salute. He had a white cane in one hand and on a lead on the other was a pie-eyed, yellow Labrador bitch with a dopey, sloppy grin, a fat backside and a sagging fat stomach. If ever two 'people' were made for each other, it was this pair.

The Beret stared straight through his sunglasses into Norton's chest. 'That's not you is it, Hoppy?' he said.

'No, mate,' replied Norton. 'I'm Les. I'm the new caretaker.'

'Oh!' Beret shoved out a hand hitting Norton in the chest. 'I'm Burt,' he smiled. 'I live in number three.'

'Hoppy told me about you,' answered Les, shaking his hand. 'I'm pleased to meet you, Burt.'

'And this is Rosie.'

'Hello, Rosie.' Les reached down and patted the old dog on the head. It gave a whine of delight, sensing Norton was all right. Wiggled its ample backside and wagged its tail.

'Well, I suppose we'll be seeing a fair bit of you now, Les. When did Hoppy go?'

'Yesterday.'

'Oh!'

47

'So I'll be looking after the place from here on in.'

Burt stared oddly at Norton, 'You're a big lump of a lad, aren't you, Les?'

'It runs in the family, Burt,' smiled Norton. 'I take after me mother.'

There was a short silence with Norton still trying to contain his laughter, then Burt spoke.

'Okay, then we'll be off. We have to do our shopping. Come along, Rosie. I'll see you again, Les.'

'For sure, Burt. Anything you want, just knock on the door.'

'Good lad. Good lad.'

Norton had to laugh as he watched Burt tap-tap-tapping his way to the door with Rosie at the lead. He even followed them to the door and watched them cross the street. Bloody hell, he chuckled to himself. What a classic. Still laughing, he went back inside and resumed his attack on the cockroaches.

Considering he wasn't getting paid for it, Les didn't do a bad job on his first day as caretaker of Blue Seas Apartments. After he'd cleaned out his flat, he went upstairs and downstairs with the yard broom, swept the side passages and the backyard then cleaned out the laundry and the storeroom putting all the old papers, tins and bottles in the Otto-bins. The old push-mower didn't seem in too bad a condition, so he gave it a couple of squirts of oil and mowed what little grass there was out the front. There were a few people in the street and he could hear noise coming from the girls' school, but the only movement at Blue Seas was two women with long, scraggly brown hair and long flower print dresses and sandals who came out, got in the old kombi and drove off in the direction of the hotel. They didn't return Norton's gaze and somehow they didn't look like rock musicians, so Les figured they must be part of the team in flat six.

Christ! What a time to be going off the piss, he thought to himself as he watched the old blue kombi putter smokily around the hotel corner.

The Royal Hotel, Randwick, was one of the best hotels in the Eastern Suburbs and the food and beer there was always the grouse. He squinted at the sun and wiped some sweat from his brow; it was getting bloody hot now and he could just about taste a schooner from where he stood. Oh, well, he sighed, we'll just see what eventuates. He finished the front yard and put the mower back in the storeroom. Seeing as I'm in an outdoors mood, he smiled to himself, I may as well go out and do a bit of gardening in that magnificent landscaped area at the back. Might see about putting a fountain or a couple of marble statues out there.

She had to be one of the best sorts Les had ever seen in his life, hanging out pairs of jeans on the small clothesline. She was about five feet nine, somewhere in her twenties, with long, reddish blonde hair done in a plait that hung halfway down her back and wearing tight, black bicycle shorts, Reeboks and a white T-shirt with a leopardskin print singlet over the top. She had great boobs, great legs, a sensational backside, and her only make-up was some bright red lipstick on a wide, full mouth full of perfect white teeth. There was nothing around her eyes but a healthy glow and pure sex appeal. Bloody hell thought Les, almost falling in the garden. Who the fuck's this?

She caught Norton's eye and gave him a quick, confident smile.

Les smiled back and began to make a pretence of being interested in what there was of the garden. 'Not a bad day,' he said tentatively.

'Yeah. It's getting nice now,' replied the girl taking a peg from her mouth.

Fuck the garden, thought Norton. He stood up and just ogled her till she turned around. 'I'm Les, anyway,' he said. 'I'm the new caretaker.'

'Oh,' replied the girl. 'What happened to old Hoppy?'

'He's gone up to Newcastle to live with his sister.'

'Oh.' The girl seemed to reflect for a moment or two. 'I liked old Hoppy. He wasn't a bad little bloke.'

'No. He was all right.'

The girl looked at Les and seemed to be quickly sussing him out. 'I'm Sandy,' she said. 'I live in flat three.'

Ahh, so you're Sandra Jean Garrett, the famous artist, eh? mused Les. Wouldn't I like to get my hand on your palette! 'Nice to meet you, Sandy,' he said, throwing in his number one smile.

'You too, Les,' she replied brightly.

Norton watched her peg out another pair of jeans as he went back to making a pretence at gardening. 'How long have you been living here, Sandy?'

'About three or four years.'

Four years? Christ! Why would a doll like you want to spend four years of your life in a dump like this? 'You must like it here?'

Sandy shrugged. 'It's okay. It was better. But it's cheap, plus I've got a lot of friends are artists who live across the road and ... a friend who's a doctor at the hospital.'

'Hoppy told me you were an artist.'

'Did he?' smiled Sandy. 'What else did he tell you?'

Norton shrugged. 'Not much. Just you were an artist, that's all. And he told me a bit about old Burt and the others who live here. I only spoke to him for a while before I drove him to the station.' Norton watched her peg out the last pair of jeans. 'So how is the art world? You doing okay?'

'I get by.' She flashed Norton a smile of pure ivory that made him feel like smashing up all the bricks holding Blue Seas' excuse for a back garden together. 'I also sell T-shirts and things up at the Paddington Markets on Saturday.'

Hello, another bloody dropout from the Paddo stalls. 'So between the two you're not starving, Sandy.'

'No, I'm not starving. What about you, Les? How come you finished up here?'

Norton looked at the tall, sexy redhead for a moment. Sandy, he thought, you've got to be one of the best sorts I've come across, but somehow at this stage of the game I don't think I should be telling you too much.

50

'I've only been down from Queensland a little while and this came up. It's free rent with a few bucks thrown in and ... well, it ain't actually the Burma railway.'

'So it looks like you'll be the live-in caretaker for a while Les?'

Live here in this cockroach castle? thought Les. Not fuckin' likely. But then again, with a honey like you living just across the hall, why not? 'Yeah,' he drawled easily, 'it sure looks that way. I reckon I might even get to like it.'

'You'll love it, Les. This place has got character.'

Norton reflected on the two million or so cockroaches he'd just killed and the blood-spattered walls of flat five. 'It's sure got something,' he answered.

Sandy hung up the last pair of jeans and straightened them out.

'Okay, Les,' she smiled. 'It's been nice talking to you, but I have to be off. I'll probably see you again.'

'Sure, Sandy. Anytime you need something, just give me a yell. You know which flat it is.'

She gave Norton another smile that made the Macleans girl's teeth look like a row of bombed-out houses, then walked out the front. Les watched her climb into an old white Holden utility and drive off in the same direction as the blue kombi. Sandy bloody baby, where did they find you? He watched the old ute disappear around the hotel corner and shook his head. Cockroaches, bed bugs, giant rats — I don't give a stuff. I'm gonna move into that shithouse of a flat. For a while anyway — until about the first night I get into your tight-fitting pants. Then, Cinderella, I'll let you know it's really Prince Charming in flat one come to take you away from all this. He pottered around a bit longer, trying to get interested in what he was doing but the main thing on Les's mind was what was living just across the hall in flat three. After a while he locked up the storeroom and his flat and headed back to Bondi, stopping to get a barbecued chicken on the way.

Warren was still looking all bright eyed and bushy-tailed

that night, when they got into the chicken with a bit of salad and baked potatoes. He was going on about how he could stay off the piss forever and wondering whether Les could do the same. He made a big deal of drinking another glass of mineral water with a slice of lime in it and looked up from his plate at Les.

'So, what have you been up to today, landlord?' he asked.

'Not much,' replied Les. 'Put the car in for a grease. Had lunch with a couple of old mates. Went for a walk around town. Just enjoyed my leisure time. What about yourself? How was the pickle factory?'

'Flat out. We're up to our necks in a big promotion for a travel company at the moment.'

'You're not looking for a male model, are you? I could do with a quid. I am out of work, you know.'

Warren took another sip of mineral water. 'Male models, yes. Semi-housetrained orang-utans — no.'

Norton smiled. 'You going out tonight?'

'No. What about you?'

Les shook his head. 'To tell you the truth, I'm just starting to enjoy these early nights. I feel tops.'

'Me too. In fact while I'm off the piss, I might stay celibate too.'

'You may as well. All the sheilas have been giving you the arse lately. The word's finally got out that you're a dud bash.'

'Pig's arse,' snorted Warren. 'I am known throughout the advertising industry in Sydney as "the man".'

'Yeah. The man who can't get it up. Listen, mate, I've seen you on the nest in there some mornings and you're hopeless. It's like watching a pigeon trying to fuck a paper aeroplane.'

'Bollocks! At least I do bring a few good sorts home. Better than those cheesy old mutts you drag through the door.'

Les smiled and conceded Warren the point. You won't be saying that when I bring Miss Picasso back for coffee and ted at chez Norton, you little shit, he thought.

Again they watched another video of Warren's choice and again they were in bed around midnight. Warren had a big day at the office the next day and had to make an early start. Norton had other plans.

Their paths crossed briefly in the morning with Warren wishing that he didn't have to go to work seeing it was such a nice day. Les just said stiff shit and went for another run in Centennial Park. When he returned home his flatmate was long gone.

Naturally Norton had been reflecting on Blue Seas Apartments during his training session, not so much about the predicament he was in, more about who was in flat three. Sandra Jean Garrett, unbelievably spunky artist. To have any chance with her, he was going to have to be pretty cool about it. He'd also have to be Johnny on the spot, and that meant moving his swag into Blue Seas, which he could handle for a few days until he gained her confidence. But winning the fair maiden's hand and then taking her back somewhere decent to get her pants off without letting her know he was the landlord was going to be a tricky business to say the least.

Les was pondering on this as he sorted out some blankets, pillows, shaving gear and other odds and ends after he'd showered and had breakfast, when the phone rang. It was Billy Dunne.

'Billy! What's doing, mate?' said Les brightly.

'Not much,' replied Billy. 'What about yourself? What have you been up to?'

'Not a great deal, William, to tell you the truth. In fact I've been rooting around with that old block of flats I own over at Randwick.'

'The Waldorf Astoria,' chuckled Billy.

'You got it, mate. Hey, while you're there, do me a favour, Billy? Don't mention anything about the place to anybody. About me working there and that. Not even to Price.'

'Sure, mate. No worries.'

Billy understood. He and Les were very close now

53

and there were certain things they said and did that were strictly between them and nobody else. Nobody. Though Billy did think it a little curious that Les didn't want Price to know, particularly as it was Price who had talked him into buying the old block of flats in the first place.

'Have you seen Price lately?' asked Les. 'I rang a couple of times but all I got was the answering service. And I've been out during the day.'

'That's what I'm ringing you about,' said Billy. 'He's opened up the club again.'

'What!!'

Billy laughed. 'He hasn't actually opened it. He's just up there playing cards at night with a bit of a team. You know the blokes I mean. They talk shit, drink piss and play five hundred all night for a hundred bucks a point.'

'Jesus! He can't help himself, can he?'

'You're not wrong. A fair bit of money changes hands and they're all half pissed so he's got me up there just to keep an eye on things. You don't need two of us. But I thought I'd ring you and tell you what's going on and see if you want to do it night about? It's money for old rope and I'm out of the place by one, one-thirty.'

Norton smiled and shook his head; there was no doubting Billy's honesty. 'No, don't worry about it, mate. You do it on your own. Get yourself a few extra bucks. But if ever you want a night off or need a hand, give us a yell.'

'Righto, mate. As a bean.'

They yarned for a while about different things; what they'd both been up to and that. Les reiterated that Billy wasn't to say anything about Blue Seas to anyone then he hung up saying they'd have to get together over the weekend sometime for a good training session.

After he'd hung up, Norton stared at the phone for a moment. While I'm here, he thought. I may as well ring Whittle. Leave a message that I'm stuck with those flats and to get his finger out with my tax return. He

54

again expected the answering service but was surprised to hear the polite, measured voice of his accountant.

'Hello, Des. It's Les Norton.'

'Oh, hello, Les. How are you?'

'All right. How's my tax return going?'

'Very good. I've almost got it completed. I think I should be able to get you back almost two thousand dollars.'

'Just enough to cover how much I'm in the red over that stinking block of flats.'

'Well, I imagine that is one way of looking at it, Les.'

'I pissed that caretaker off. I'm looking after the place myself now.'

'That's very good, Les.'

'Hey, did you know the fuckin' joint's not even insured?'

'I beg your pardon, Les?'

Norton quickly explained how he'd gone through the documents and found the bogus insurance policy. 'So that arsehole of a fuckin' lawyer's got a bodgie insurance rort going as well.'

By the tone in his accountant's voice Norton could almost sense him shaking his head in despair as he replied. 'No, Les,' said Whittle, slowly and methodically. 'It's not like that at all. The property is fully insured until March next year. For a hundred and fifty thousand, I think.'

'Oh!'

'If you had just taken the blood — if you had just examined the document a little more closely, you'd have found it's not ERIN. A Insurance Company. It's ERINA. They're an insurance company on the Central Coast. I do quite a lot of business for my clients with them. They're a very scrupulous and honest firm.'

'Erina, you say, Des?'

'That's right, Les.'

'Oh!'

'Anyway, look, Les. I have to leave for the city now. I should have your tax return completed by next week. Why don't you call me then?'

'Yeah, righto.'

'And in the future, Les, do examine any documents or papers appertaining to this a little more meticulously.'

'Yeah, righto, Des. See you later.'

This time as he stared at the phone, Norton felt like a prize wally. Due to his usual impetuosity and bull-in-a-china-shop approach to things he'd completely missed that detail. Funny, though. It didn't look like it. But in the state he was in at the time it could have looked like anything.

He went to his room and pulled the insurance policy from the pile of papers. Sure enough, Des was right. But at the end of the N in ERINA was a speck of fly shit or something and it did look like a full stop. Though if he hadn't been in such a shitty mood and had taken his time to read through the rest of the form he would have got his facts right. However Norton being Norton, he picked up the phone and dialled long distance.

'Hello, Erina Insurance,' came a girl's soft voice.

'Yes, hello. My name is Marvin Ringblum from Steinberg and Ringblum Real Estate in Randwick, Sydney. I'm just ringing to see if the insurance on one of our blocks of flats, Blue Seas Apartments in Aquila Street, Randwick, is ah...up to date.'

'Could you give me the policy number, Mr Ringblum?'

'Certainly. H1009845DA.'

'Just one moment.'

Norton could just picture her staring at a computer screen after she'd pushed the appropriate keys.

'Yes. That policy is valid until March the twentieth next year. For a hundred and fifty thousand dollars.'

'Thank you very much, miss.'

'You're welcome.'

Well, what do you know? mused Les. The old dump's insured after all. Les shook his head and stared at the phone. But it still doesn't get me out of the shit I'm in. He returned the policy to the file in his room and continued packing.

With what he thought was enough to keep him going

56

for a while, Les was at Blue Seas around ten; parking behind Sandra's utility which was behind the old blue kombi. He put the stuff in the flat, made a cup of coffee and had a think about things. The main thing he was thinking about was across the hall. Well, he thought, gazing from the gloomy old kitchen into the back yard, I won't find her sitting in here; her car's out the front so she's got to be around somewhere. So he rinsed his cup, got the broom out of the storeroom and went outside to do a bit of caretaking.

Norton figured she'd have to come out to her car sooner or later so he stuffed about in the small front yard then swept it till the front of Blue Seas Apartments almost shone. After a while there was movement; but it wasn't Sandra.

The four hippies Les had met on the roof the day before came out, accompanied by what must have been their girlfriends or wives or whatever. The men, still scraggly and unkempt, looked more like Neil out of The Young Ones than ever, the girls were just as scraggly and had earth mother, hunza pies and bean sprouts written all over them. If they noticed Les they didn't let on and seemed to play him pretty wide. I must have upset the children of the rainbow on the roof yesterday, mused Norton. I wasn't that awful to them, was I? The Manson Family clambered into the old kombi, which started after about the fifteenth time and spluttered off, destination unknown. Peace, love and tofu, thought Les and continued sweeping.

There was still no sign of the artist and Norton was thinking of continuing the charade in the back yard when a car backfired in the street like a gun going off. Momentarily startled, Les looked up as a fair sized, transit van swung into the street, backfired again, then did a U-turn and parked where the hippies had just pulled out. The van was a bilious green; painted down the side in black, Apocalypse Now type of writing, edged with orange and purple was: *The Harlots*. No need to guess who this is, mused Norton.

The driver switched off the motor and got out. He was about six foot six, lean, and very wiry, with thick black hair pulled back into a ponytail. He wore black jeans, red, ten-hole Doc Martens boots and a sleeveless, Violent Femmes T-shirt. There was a look of anguish on his already gaunt face. Steve Hoy's 'Break Up Fallout' was howling from somewhere inside the van, abruptly cutting out as the driver swung the side door open. Norton leant on his broom and double and triple blinked as what was inside stumbled out and whoever or whatever they were, their cup of happiness was nowhere near running over and the object of their avalanche of abuse was the driver.

First out was a tall, sexy, leggy thing with flowing black hair, wearing a low-cut gown that barely covered a massive cleavage and a split up the front that showed plenty of a sensational pair of legs. She wore thick, blue lipstick, blue nail polish, blue eye shadow — and if she couldn't have got a run in an el-cheapo vampire movie, she could have been Elvira's stand in, right down to the tassels hanging from the elbows of her gown. She stretched her legs and ripped into the driver.

Next out, refusing the driver's hand, was another tall, leggy piece only with a shock of teased, blonde hair, tinged with purple, green and red that matched her make-up. A pair of faded, frayed cut-off denim jeans ate into her crotch over a pair of thick, black stockings; pieces of metal flashed from a pair of black Doc Martens. Clinging to a pair of healthy white boobs was a black cotton singlet with a white cobweb design all over it. She immediately joined in abusing the driver.

Following her was another tall, dark-haired girl in thick, black stockings and red high-heels wearing a black leather, micromini covered in pockets with about the same number of thin, studded belts wound around her slim waist. Her hair was long and straight pulled beneath a red beret covered in badges, pretty much like a New York Guardian Angel. Like the others, she wasn't badly stacked either and all that covered her boobs was a purple top that looked like it had been made from an old string shopping bag. Two nice, pink nipples poked through the holes and somehow she'd managed to pin a James Dean badge to the top without doing herself too much damage. That made three abusing the driver as another got out. Christ, thought Norton. What next?

Next was taller than the others with an explosion of copper-coloured hair tinged with red, white and blue that matched her make-up and silver glitter around her eyes. Somehow she'd managed to get into an incredibly tight pair of faded jeans that had been given the death of a thousand cuts with a razor blade and sat nicely over a pair of red stiletto heels. What remained of her jeans was held up by a pair of wide, red braces covered in badges and other odds and ends, over a loose white T-shirt with Marilyn Monroe on the front. As soon as she'd finished stretching her legs she too joined in the payout on the driver.

Last out was a dumpy, short blonde in a school tunic, white shirt and school tie, school hat, black stockings and white Adidas running shoes. For some reason she didn't join in abusing the driver.

'Look, Fran, I'm really sorry,' pleaded the driver to the Elvira lookalike.

'Get fucked, Syd,' was the blunt reply. 'You're a dead-set fuckin' goose. Hand me my bass and piss off.'

'Okay, Fran. But I am —'

'Ohh, blow it out your arse, Syd,' said red beret. 'Just hand us our gear and fuck off.'

'All right, all right.' The driver got inside the van and began handing out various instruments, including a slide trombone.

'Running out of petrol,' cursed the one in shorts. 'We should've been home six fuckin' hours ago. I'm fucked.'

'That gig was a mother, too,' said the one in the lacerated jeans. 'Now this on top of it. You cunt, Syd!' she yelled into the van.

'I said I was sorry, Riona,' came a voice from inside the van.

59

'In your arse.'

'This is fucked. Absolutely fucked,' said the one in the shorts, as she took a guitar. 'And so am I. I'm going to bed for about five days. And don't come around before I wake up, Syd,' she howled into the van, 'or I'll take you to Taronga Park and feed you to the fuckin' yak! You cunt!'

'Don't worry, Isla. I won't,' answered the voice in the van.

The girls picked up their various instruments and, except for the one in the school uniform, gave the driver another last torrent of abuse before storming past Les into the flats. If they took any notice of Norton they didn't show it. Somehow they managed to glare at him and ignore him at the same time. Norton leant on his broom and watched in amusement and amazement as they click-clacked past him and up the stairs in their high heeled shoes.

'Don't worry about it, Syd,' said the one in the school uniform who had remained behind. 'The girls are just tired.'

'Yeah, but Franulka's really upset,' replied the driver. 'I've never seen her like that.'

'She'll be okay. See you, Syd.'

'Okay, Gwen. See you. And I'm sorry about what happened.'

The one in the school uniform smiled over her shoulder at the driver, gave Les a brief one as she went past and followed the others up the stairs. The door slammed and that was that.

After the avalanche of abuse that still hung in the air, it was uncannily silent out in the street. Norton watched the dejected driver light a cigarette, then run a hand across his face and through his hair. Curiosity got the better of him and still holding the broom he walked across to the van.

'So, how's show biz treating you, mate?' he asked, with half a smile.

The driver gave Les a disinterested once up and down

60

and took a drag on his smoke. 'Unreal, man,' he said tightly, 'Un-fuckin'-real.'

Norton made a bit of shuffle with the broom. 'Well, you know the old saying, mate: it's a long way to the shop if you want a sausage roll.'

The driver didn't seem too impressed at all with Norton's weak attempt at a joke and continued to drag away at his cigarette. Les had met a few roadies over the years and knew they were a tough bunch in general, not used to taking much shit. Up closer, this one was even wirier, and dangling off his long, sinewy arms were a pair of hands that looked like two baseball mitts. Christ, thought Les, I wouldn't fancy getting those wrapped round my throat. Yet somehow he seemed to have 'mug' written all over him.

'Anyway, mate. I'm Les. I'm the new caretaker.' Norton offered the driver his hand. 'I only just started this week.'

The driver looked at it for a second then took another drag on his cigarette. 'Syd. Good to meet you, Les.' Syd's grip was like sticking your hand in a wool press.

'So what's your story, Syd? Are you the band's driver, or roadie, sort of thing?'

'That's me. And Mr Fixit and bouncer thrown in.'

Norton made another little shuffle with the broom. 'If you don't mind me saying so, Syd, that wasn't a bad blast they just gave you. You could hear it down at Coogee. What did you do? Get caught with your hand up the schoolgirl's dress?'

Syd looked at Norton and almost smiled. Apart from the one in the school tunic he'd copped nothing but abuse. Here was someone, a bit of a battler like himself, who didn't seem like too bad a bloke and maybe a shoulder to cry on. He took another drag then flicked the butt into the gutter.

'We've just been touring Canberra. Five full-on gigs in five days. Last night's was a complete bummer. Brawls, drunks... I had five fights keeping the pissheads away from the girls. It finished up an all-in with the bouncers

61

all getting into it. The pigs came and closed it down; which suited us. We were paid and out by one-thirty and would have been home by four.' Syd made a helpless gesture with his hands. 'But in all the confusion I forgot to fill the tank and we ran out of juice six ks past Goulburn. I had to thumb it back to Goulburn with a can. Thumb it back to the van. Then drive back to Goulburn and fill up. The carbie got full of shit and we've been spluttering and farting all the way back to Sydney. The girls have been stuck in the back for nearly ten hours, so you can imagine how they feel. And on top of five shit gigs.'

Norton took a peek in the back of the van. There were speakers, amps, mixers, a drum kit, tools, wires and more junk. Even allowing for three girls in the front and the stuff they'd just taken out, Hitler would have given the Jews more room on a train to Auschwitz in 1942.

'So what's doing, Syd?' asked Les. 'You want a hand with the rest of this stuff?'

'No, that's all right, thanks, Les. I live with me brother over at Maroubra; he's got a big double garage and I leave it all there.' Syd looked evenly at Les for a moment. 'But I'll probably come over tomorrow and see how the girls are. Take Franulka out somewhere.'

'Franulka?'

'Yeah. The one in the black gown with the blue make-up. Fran's my girl.' The way Syd looked at Les as he spoke it could possibly be interpreted as a hint for Les to keep his eyes off her.

'Okay,' smiled Norton. 'I'll more than likely be here. Call in and we might have a beer or something. I'm in flat one.'

'Righto, Les. I might even do that.' Syd gave Les a goofy sort of smile. 'You don't seem like a bad bloke.'

'Ohh, don't worry, Syd. There's heaps of blokes round worse than me.' Norton couldn't help but grin. 'This time I might even tell you my troubles.'

Syd's goofy smile matched Norton's grin. 'Fair enough.'

62

Les watched Syd slam the door and then get behind the wheel. After a bit of coaxing the motor started and the van backfired and sputtered down Perouse Road, through The Spot and in the direction of Maroubra. Well, how about that, he mused. I've finally got to meet all my tenants. I wouldn't mind rooting any of those tarts in the band. Especially that one in the leather mini. As for Elvira? Syd's just a little on the large, strong side; he can keep her to himself. I'd stick it up that one in the mini, though. Les continued to fiddle around in the front yard and again his thoughts returned to Sandy, clouded slightly by thoughts of sex with those horny members of the band. He was concentrating on this when he felt something soft and wet gently probing around his backside. Les turned round to find Rosie with her nose fair up his date. Standing behind her, holding the lead and wearing the same clothes he had on the day before, was Burt.

'Is that you there, Les?' he said.

Norton felt like giving Rosie a quick backhander, but she looked up at him with such an affectionate, sloppy grin he patted the old girl's head instead. 'Yeah, how are you, Burt?'

'Good.' Burt gave a little chuckle. 'Rosie must have recognised you.

'Yeah,' agreed Les. 'She's certainly got a good nose for faces.'

'That's my girl all right.' Burt again peered oddly through his sunglasses at Norton for a moment or two. 'Anyway, we have to do a bit more shopping. Come along, Rosie. See you later, Les.'

'Yeah. See you, Burt. Have a good day.'

Norton leant on his broom for a while as he watched them disappear round the hotel corner then went back to sweeping the front of the flats. Well, I'm fucked if I know where the artist is he pondered. I've been hanging around here all morning like a stale bottle of piss and all I've met is some Dubbo roadie and had a dog stick its nose up my Khyber. I could be here all fuckin' day.

Norton's stomach suddenly rumbled and somehow he instinctively turned towards the hotel. He knew what was inside: cold beer, juicy steaks and crisp, fresh salads. There was still no sign of Sandra. Ahh, fuck this. I'm gonna go and have a steak.

There were a number of people seated on the white, plastic chairs and tables outside the hotel, taking advantage of the shade offered by the old colonial style verandah edged with iron lattice work and hung with gaslamps that ran around overhead. The beers on the tables looked almost irresistible and walking past after all that strenuous sweeping Norton was sorely tempted. No, fuck it, he thought. I'll have a lemon squash. He rounded the corner and went into the Saloon bar. A barmaid, in the hotel uniform of black dress and black and white striped collarless shirt caught his eye and a schooner of squash was on the bar and halfway down his throat by the time he'd got his change.

The old hotel was spacious and bright with ample chairs and tables and paintings and blown-up photos of old Coogee and Randwick on the walls. The Luminarie bar with its statue of 'The Thinker' amongst the indoor plants wasn't what Les was looking for. Another eating area painted pink and grey with comfortable, blue wicker chairs and tables, Quacks, was. Sipping his squash, he strolled over to the counter above which, several copper plaques said Starters, Soups, Main Courses etc. He studied the menu for a moment, changed his mind about a steak, and ordered roast beef with Yorkshire pudding. This was ready straightaway and after paying Les got some salad as well from a refrigerated servery then sat down next to an old, dark grey, marble fireplace just around from the bar.

Well, this is all right, thought Norton, ripping into his roast beef and pud. I can certainly think of harder ways to put in a day. After a couple of mouthfuls of food his lemon squash was gone so he got another one. But then again, that caretaking is bloody hard yakka; not to mention all the responsibilities I've got. So I deserve a break. He took his time eating, then leisurely checked out the clientele while he finished his second squash. Well, this establishment is very handy to my new place of employment, he mused. I should've come here more often. Finally, he quietly belched into his hand, got up and headed back to the old block of flats.

A bottle shop next to the bar in Perouse Road with Royal Hotel Vintage Cellars made him hesitate and have a momentous, five-second struggle with his conscience. It was just too hard to resist. Ahh, fuck Warren, he thought. What he don't know won't hurt him. He bought a dozen cans of Fourex to put in the fridge of the old flat — just in case. On the way back he was disappointed to see the old white utility gone. Shit, he cursed. Missed her! How's my fuckin' timing?

Norton made a cup of coffee and gazed moodily out the window of his flat. Well, he thought, as Roger Miller almost put it, I've had about four hours of pushing broom, and I'm still stuck in this eight by twelve, four-bit fuckin' room. Don't know where the beautiful Miss Picasso is and it's much too good a day to be stuck in here like a battery bloody hen with the didgeridoo string quartet about ready to start up on the roof. I doubt if I'll see Elvira and the rocking vampires before midnight and I don't particularly feel like going out the front again and getting Rosie's snotty nose wedged into my blurter. No. You can stick this joint in your arse. I'm going down the beach — Coogee.

Norton did just that. He found a parking spot not far from Gales Baths and, although Coogee wasn't his favourite beach, spent the remainder of the day on his banana chair swimming, reading *Penthouse* and perving on the beach girls. For a poor, battling caretaker, trying to get over his divorce, he was doing it very cosy indeed. It was late afternoon when he went back to Blue Seas Apartments and got under flat one's dribbly, but warm enough shower.

After he'd slipped into a T-shirt, jeans and sneakers, Les decided to walk down to The Spot and get the paper and something else to read. When he walked out the front the white Holden utility was parked near the corner and his hopes rose somewhat. But sank just as quickly when he noticed the girl of his dreams standing across the road next to a dark green Ford Fairlane with a tallish, good style of a bloke in his thirties with a neat, brown moustache. They weren't exactly locked in a 'passionate embrace' but the way they were holding onto each other said that he and Sandra were definitely more than just good friends. Not wanting to be caught rubbernecking, Norton took a quick left in the direction of the shops, slowing up once to take a peek over his shoulder to see the bloke drive off as Sandra waved daintily but enthusiastically.

So that's what I've been hanging around for all day, he grumbled to himself. Miss Picasso appears to have herself a bloke. And not a bad style either. And I think if she had a choice between his car and the Nortonmobile I'm sure I know which one she'd take. This could be a bit trickier than I thought. I might even have to play my right bower early and let her know who the landlord is. Anyway, we'll see what happens. While he was at the shops Les got some fish and chips which he took back and ate in the luxurious surrounding of his caretaker's flat, washed down afterwards with a cold can of Fourex. It was the first one for almost a week and Les couldn't believe how good it tasted. It tasted that good he had another one almost straight after it which seemed to taste even better. In fact the taste lingered so piquantly and tantalisingly in Norton's mouth that, after sitting around reading and listening to the radio till almost nine, he decided to go over to the Royal and fill up completely.

Leaving the building, Norton was right on time to see the girl of his dreams, this time wearing an ultrashort blue minidress and an embroidered denim top. Only this time she was getting into a maroon Jaguar and the new squeeze had dark hair, no moustache and an expensive looking sports coat. She noticed Les out of the window and gave him a smile and a wave as the Jaguar cruised easily off up Perouse Road. Norton had time to wave back before he was left standing like a shag on a rock in a wisp of expensive exhaust fumes. Christ, he thought, Sandy baby sure doesn't let too much grass grow under her feet. But see her in that mini. A top sort like her; what would you expect? And they sure ain't calling round in FJ Holdens. Shit, this certainly is going to be trickier than I thought. Thumbs jammed into the pockets of his jeans, Les strolled thoughtfully to the hotel.

The Royal was a much different place at night; more people, more noise and the crowd spilled out onto the footpath. They were all fairly well-dressed and appeared to be mostly in their mid-twenties and early thirties. The men didn't actually look like yuppies, but Les couldn't picture any of them leaning on a shovel for the local council either. The girls were attractive, well-groomed, and laughing away over their mixed drinks. Norton guessed that most of them would have been either nurses or staff from the hospital across the road. But there were no Sandra Jean Garretts amongst them. Les chose the saloon bar opposite the park and ordered a schooner of Brown Old which he drank out on the footpath while he checked out the punters and did a bit of thinking.

Two schooners later, Les switched to middies; the first beers in a week were already starting to give him more than a glow. But he was feeling good and wouldn't have minded having a mag or cracking a joke with someone, though so far he hadn't seen a soul he knew. After a while, his thoughts started drifting back to Blue Seas and the lovely Sandra Jean, but whether he'd get her in the end or not, the old block of flats was losing him money and there had to be a way of cutting costs.

He took a notebook and biro from his back pocket and, leaning against one of the wrought-iron poles out the front with his beer resting on an adjacent windowsill, Les started doing a bit of adding and subtracting. But the more he added and subtracted, the more it came up a no result. Norton was floundering around in a morass of boring facts and figures, getting more depressed, when he noticed an attractive woman doing pretty much the same thing barely a metre or so away. She looked about thirty years of age, and was wearing a black, woollen skirt, floppy, ankle length denim boots and a loose-fitting, red drawstring cotton top. She had brown shoulder length hair parted in the middle, and a pair of inquisitive blue eyes darted around the hotel above a pert nose and a wide, sensuous mouth. She was carrying a small clipboard on which she'd scribble furiously for a few seconds, then look around, then scribble some more. Somehow she caught Norton's eyes and paused momentarily as she noticed him scribbling away too.

Revved up with beer Norton was now in a gregarious, if not cheeky, mood. 'Are you from the gas company too?' he asked her.

'I beg your pardon?' replied the woman.

'I'm with the local council. I've come here to read the gas meters. I thought you might be doing the same thing.'

Norton's stupid grin brought a twinkle to the woman's eye. 'I'm certainly not here to read the gas meters,' she said, then took a sip of her drink and placed it at the edge of a nearby table.

'You're a health inspector then. Either that or the police.'

The woman smiled. 'No, I'm not a health inspector. And I'm not a cop either.' She took a peek at the notebook in Norton's hand. 'And don't give me any of that shit about reading gas meters. If anybody around here's a cop, it's you.'

Norton couldn't help but roar laughing. 'Yeah, that'd be right,' he chortled.

'To be honest,' said the woman. 'I'm a writer. I'm here researching a book.'

'Fair dinkum?' Norton was impressed. He'd never met

68

a writer before. A few pisshead, lowlife journalists, the odd gossip columnist and an editor or two — but no writers. Especially not a woman writer. 'What sort of books do you write?'

'Crime stories mainly. Murders, fraud, drugs, gambling — all that sort of thing.'

Christ, thought Les, have you ever come to the right place at the right time. 'I thought you might have been more into romance novels. You know, trembling young virgins, torn bodices. All that sort of thing.'

The woman shook her head slowly and gave Les a tired look. 'No, not this little black wood-duck. I leave all that sort of thing to Barbara Cartland and the other girls. Though I do throw plenty of good old-fashioned sex in my books. A decent root doesn't go astray every now and again,' she added evenly.

'I'll drink to that,' laughed Norton and raised his glass. 'What's your name, anyway?'

'Nola. Nola Lloyd.'

'I'm Les.' They shook hands briefly. 'Where are you from Nola?'

'Balmain.'

Hello, thought Norton. A bloody feminist writer from right in the very heart of enemy territory. I can sure bloody pick 'em. Oh well, who gives a stuff? She doesn't seem like a bad scout.

'What about you, Les? Where are you from?'

Norton nodded towards Perouse Road. 'Just across the road.'

'Handy.'

'Yeah. I suppose it is.' He finished his beer and made a gesture with the glass. 'Can I get you a drink, Nola?'

Nola thought for a moment. 'Yeah, okay. Scotch and lemonade. Can you make it a double?'

'Sure,' smiled Norton.

'You want some money?'

Les dismissed her offer with a smile and disappeared in the crowd towards the bar. He was back shortly with Nola's Scotch and another middy of old for himself.

It turned out Nola was a writer, a popular one, and she'd had four books published. Norton thought that he'd seen a couple of the girls from the club reading her books down the beach. She didn't make millions, but between her novels and other things she was doing all right and was in the process of selling the rights to one of her books for a telemovie. She shared a house in Balmain with another writer and a cartoonist for one of the newspapers. She came to the hotel on her own to do a bit of research for the book she was writing now: *Ten Milligrams of Murder*. It involved nurses, a large hospital, a murder in an old block of flats and a search for missing jewellery, amongst other things. Nola said she always researched her books meticulously no matter how trivial the subject or location involved. In fact, getting drunk and researching her books was a lot more fun than the actual writing; almost as much fun as the royalty cheques that came in twice a year.

Les couldn't help but like Nola Lloyd. She was full of chat, jokes and cheeky observations of the other drinkers, and she spoke exceptionally well with a deep, throaty chuckle thrown in. She also had the peculiar trait of letting her eyes zap around all over the place, taking in everything else as she spoke to Les, yet not diverting any of her attention away from him. It got Les in. It was almost as if she were two people in one. Others might find it annoying, but it intrigued Norton delightfully.

A few more drinks and they were getting on famously, with Les starting to roar just a little. He couldn't be bothered making up any stories and figured she'd only catch him out anyway. He told her what he did, where he worked and what he was doing here, though he didn't let on that Blue Seas was a financial lemon and he was doing his arse over it. Nola continued to scribble more notes as she spoke to him and as Les got oiled up she started to get very horny-looking somehow. Her smile seemed to get wider, her waist got thinner, her boobs bigger and her hair shinier. Getting on towards eleven and an unknown amount of beer and Scotches later, an idea formed in Norton's half-drunk mind.

'I'll tell you something Nola,' he grinned. 'This book you're researching now. You said there's a murder in an old block of flats and a search for some missing tomfoolery. Is that right?'

'Yeah. That's part of it, Les.'

'Well, if you want to come over to where I'm staying, I might be able to show you something that could help you with your book. Something very fishy in the state of Denmark.'

The woman novelist from Balmain gave Norton an amused if not quizzical look. 'This isn't some insidious ploy, is it, Les? To get me back to your manor, where the evil squire rips open my bodice and, ignoring my anguished sobs and cries for help, forces me onto the bed and has his reprehensible and dastardly way with me. Is it, Les?'

Norton blinked at her. 'I don't even know what you're talking about. I just want to show you something that might suit that devious writer's mind of yours. Besides,' he added, 'do I look like an evil squire?'

'No. You look just like a typical Australian jock half full of beer who'd root a goanna with a festered arse if someone would hold its head.'

Norton angled his head towards one shoulder, poked out his bottom lip and tried to look hurt.

'Oh, don't give me any of that little boy lost shit, Les. Come on. Let's go and have a look at what you're on about.'

'If you want any more to drink, there's nothing back there but beer and coffee.'

'Doesn't matter. A beer'll do fine.'

Nola put her clipboard in her bag and they headed towards the old block of flats with the novelist from Balmain falling against the caretaker from Randwick for support on more than one occasion. When they got there, Norton noticed the maroon Jaguar was parked out the front. Hello, he mused, looks like the artist is

71

doing a little entertaining. Then again, maybe he's just sitting for a portrait. Yeah, that'd be right. More like her sitting on his face. Oh well.

'So this is your sumptuous apartment is it Les?' said Nola giving the caretaker's flat a very laodicean once-over. 'Looks nice. Who had it before you. Burke and Hare?'

'A little ex-jockey with a crook leg,' answered Norton.

'He'd certainly have a crook something after living here.'

'You want a beer?' asked Les, going to the fridge and pulling out two cans of Fourex.

'Thanks.' Nola had a quick sniff around the kitchen. 'Don't bother about a glass. I'll drink it straight from the can.'

Norton flipped off the ring-pulls and handed Nola a can. 'Cheers,' he said, with a smile.

'Yes. Cheers, Les.' Nola took quite a healthy pull for a dignified writer and had another look around the tiny flat. 'So this is part of your fabulous Blue Seas Apartments, eh, Les?' she said, with just a hint of sarcasm in her clear, soft voice. 'It's really nice. It's got... it's got depth of character.' She raised her can. 'Here's to the depth... to the deep Blue Seas.' Nola took another good glug of Fourex.

'Yeah. To the deep Blue Seas,' replied Norton, matching her drunken grin and taking a good slurp of beer himself. 'Anyway,' he said. 'I didn't bring you here just to show you my fifteen thousand dollar, Customtone dream kitchen. Grab your clipboard, Agatha Christie, and follow Hercule Norton to the scene of the crime.'

The light in the hallway of flat five was the only one that worked but after Les fumbled around and switched it on it was enough to cast an eerie glow over the inside of the flat and the carnage littering the floors and rooms to make it look more like the scene of some horrible crime than ever.

'My God!' gasped Nola. 'Whatever happened here?'

'You tell me — you're the writer,' replied Les. 'But

72

I'd reckon someone was in here looking for something, wouldn't you say? Like missing jewellery?'

'Christ! They've practically destroyed the place.'

'Yes. They were certainly efficient, weren't they?'

Nola blinked around the flat in disbelief for a few moments then the Robert Ludlum or something suddenly came out in her. She dropped her beer on a shelf in the kitchen, grabbed her note pad and biro and began furiously scribbling away. She seemed to almost ignore Les as she flicked over the pages. He could hear her breath coming in short gasps; it was almost as if the whole macabre scene was turning her on.

'Oh, this is fucking fantastic,' she cried.

'Madam, please. Mind your language.'

'Fuck my language, sunshine. I've never seen anything like this in my life.' Nola stopped to take another healthy slurp of beer then began scribbling away some more.

'You want a murder scene, Ms Lloyd? Have a look at this.'

Les took her into the smashed-up bathroom and showed her the dried blood spattered around the bath; the sickly light coming in from the hallway gave it a dull, rusty sheen. It was sinister and gruesome to an extreme and Nola was loving every second and every detail of it.

'Oh, Les,' she almost shrieked. 'This is unbelievable!'

'I'm glad you like it,' replied Norton.

'Like it? I love it!' Nola threw her arms around Norton's neck and kissed him full on the mouth. 'You're a doll, Les. Thanks.'

'My pleasure.'

Norton stood sipping his beer in the lounge room as Nola skipped from room to room taking notes. She toed through the wreckage on the floor, picking up pieces of torn and shredded clothing. She ran her hands over the smashed furniture and ripped bedding almost as if she was caressing it. Every now and again she'd let out a little squeal of delight. If Norton wasn't mistaken it almost sounded as if the sensuous novelist from Balmain was starting to come to the boil. Finally, she returned to the kitchen, put down her clipboard and had a very lengthy and unladylike pull on her can of Fourex, almost draining it. She noticed Les watching her, and walked over to him and put her arms around his waist.

'Oh, Les,' she sighed. 'What can I say? This is perfect. It's ... it's just breathtaking.'

Norton put his arms around her, stroked her hair and massaged the small of her back. 'See, the Aussie jock wasn't having you on. I told you there was something in here you'd go for.'

She snuggled into his chest. 'Mmmhh, you're not wrong.'

Norton continued to rub her back as Nola's breathing turned into a kind of rasping purr. Before long Les could feel her grinding herself against him. She angled her head up as Les looked down and in the half-light from the hallway he could see a sheen in her eyes almost as if they were glazing over. She ran her tongue lasciviously over her lips. Norton tilted his head to the side and down and kissed her; and the lady writer from Balmain knew how to kiss. Richard Burton knew what he was talking about when they asked him what was the first thing he looked for in a woman. And he said she must be at least thirty.

Nola's lips were soft and warm and pure delight and the tip of her warm, sweet tongue played havoc with Norton's. He squeezed her into him and she ground harder against his pelvis. Les ran his hands up over her ribs and across her small but firm boobs enclosed but in no way supported by a delicate, white lace bra. He brought his hands down and began squeezing the cheeks of her neat backside, edging her skirt up at the same time. Nola started kissing him with more passion and hunger than ever; scrabbling at his hair and grabbing his T-shirt. Les kissed her neck and a tongue darted into his ear.

'Why don't we go downstairs to my flat?' he said. The sheen in her eyes had disappeared and all that was there now was the pure devil.

'What's wrong with right here?' she breathed.

'You're the boss lady.'

Flat five wasn't exactly Norton's idea of a romantic setting and there wasn't much in the way of furniture except for the half-smashed lounge with the stuffing and springs sticking out in parts. He eased Nola onto it, removed her denim boots and slipped off her dainty white knickers, leaving the woollen skirt on. He got out of his jeans and sneakers and no sooner had his Speedos off than Nola reached up and started working on his old boy like it was a big, juicy banana paddle-pop. Les went cross-eyed and he could feel the veins round his temple pumping as his knob swelled up like a balloon. That Richard Burton was no mug, all right. Oh well, thought Les. What's sauce for the goose is sauce for the gander. He spread her legs and decided it was time for a big face full of crime writer's ted.

Nola bucked and squealed as the big Queenslander went to work with his teeth and tongue. Moaning and groaning, she clawed at his hair and the neck of his T-shirt. It was a lot of fun but Les was getting too horny; he had to have her. He lifted up Nola's knees and started to slide in. Nola let out a choking moan that seemed to come from somewhere down near her toenails, she shuddered, shook her head and clawed at his back till Les was all in, then away they went.

Nola knew how to make love. She wriggled, kissed Norton's neck and screamed with joy. Les felt like he was Errol Flynn. If Nola was making some noise while he had a face full, now she sounded as if he was chopping off one of her legs with a blunt axe. Christ, thought Les. I hope those walls are double brick, or those poor bloody hippies'll think there's another murder going on. The beer kept Norton a little restrained but he couldn't last forever; Nola's ted was too warm, firm and moist and already he'd felt her go off under him twice. Ahh, fuck the neighbours, he thought. He lifted her ankles almost up under her chin and away he went, putting in the big ones. Nola shrieked louder and Les felt as

75

if his brain was going to burst out of his ears. He felt her go off again, just as Les exploded himself; he rode it out, then came to a shuddering, panting halt.

They lay there holding each other for a while, but if the old lounge was okay for screwing on it definitely wasn't made for pillow talk. Les suggested it might be an idea if they got their gear on, went back to his flat and got cleaned up and maybe have another beer. Nola agreed.

'Well,' said Norton, raising his can and giving her a kiss on the cheek. They were cleaned up now and Les had his ghetto blaster on softly in the background. 'Here's to *Ten Milligrams Of Mayhem*, or whatever you call it. Did you enjoy your research?'

Nola put her arms around Les and gave him that throaty chuckle again. 'I told you research was a lot of fun, didn't I?'

They sipped their beers and sort of jigged around to the tune on the radio. Bang The Drum's 'Only You'.

'Hey, Nola?' said Norton.

'Yes, Les.'

'This book you're writing?'

'Yes. What about it?'

'You feel like researching another chapter?'

Nola looked up at him and out came another throaty chuckle. 'Why not?' she answered. 'Another paragraph or two wouldn't go astray.'

Number two was pretty good but it didn't quite have the lust or spontaneity of upstairs; maybe it lacked atmosphere. There was still nothing wrong with it though and both were more than happy with a warm glow planted in their cheeks when they finished. However, if the old lounge upstairs was uncomfortable, the night-and-day in Norton's flat wasn't quite meant for honeymooners either. Before long they were both dressed again and Les was walking her out the front. As they stepped out into Aquila Street, Les noticed that the maroon Jaguar was gone. Wonder what'll be parked there tomorrow, he mused. A Maserati? A Mercedes SLE?

Les apologised to Nola that he couldn't drive her home, but he'd poured quite a bit of beer down his throat that night and if a booze bus pulled him up and put a bag on him he'd probably blow the thing to the other side of the moon. He'd have to shout her home in a cab. Nola said that was all right. She'd got a lift out and was expecting to catch a taxi home, anyway. At least that's something blokes can thank the wallopers and their breathalyser for, thought Les. It certainly takes the stigma out of putting sheilas in a cab to save driving them home after you've got pissed and done the business.

Nola actually thanked Les for a splendid evening and she was quite sincere about it. She gave him her phone number and said to ring her in a week or so if he wanted to, after she'd got back from visiting her family in Adelaide. They kissed goodnight and the last Les saw of her was her smiling face as she waved out of the back of a Legion cab heading towards Randwick Junction.

Norton couldn't help but chuckle to himself as he ambled back to the old block of flats. It had been two crackajack roots, and one a very unusual one. Nola was a top lady plus he'd broken in the old flat the first night he'd been there. He was still keen to get onto Miss Picasso, though all those blokes hanging around her had taken some of the elan off it. Still, a couple of slices off the loaf shouldn't make that much difference.

When he got back to the flats Les suddenly found himself absolutely busting for a leak. He decided to piss down his side passage facing Aquila Street. If a man couldn't piss all over his own block of flats in a democracy, what could he do?

Norton was hosing away at the fence when a grey BMW pulled into Aquila Street and parked almost where the maroon Jag had pulled out. Ohh no, thought Les. This couldn't possibly be — not at this time of night. A wiry sort of figure got out of the BMW and, although it wasn't all that cold, he was wearing an expensive-looking beige trenchcoat and a hat pulled down over his eyes. In the dark the figure couldn't see Les and likewise Les couldn't make out the figure's face. But there was something in the figure's mannerisms and the way he walked that Les could almost swear he'd seen him before. The figure looked up and down the street and walked into Blue Seas Apartments. Ohh, no, thought Les. This isn't real. He zipped up his fly and peeked into the main entrance of the flats through the door. Sure enough, the figure was knocking softly on flat three. I don't fuckin' believe this, thought Les. The figure wasn't there more than a second or two when he went inside leaving Les blinking into the gloomy light. Well, I'll be stuffed, he thought again. Why doesn't the moll just hang a red light out the front and be done with it? He shook his head, went inside, cleaned his teeth and hit the sack. His disappointment in Miss Picasso lingered in his mind for a short while, along with the odd mannerisms of her last boyfriend, but he soon put it out of his mind. Even if the old night-and-day was a bit hard and his pillow a little lumpy, after two solid roots and a gut full of beer Norton was soon in the land of nod.

Ahh, how sweet it is to be back in hangoverville thought Les, when he woke up around eight the following morning. All those things he'd been missing after almost a week off the piss: the wonderful, throbbing headache, your mouth tasting like Jabba The Hutt had crapped in it; grainy eyes; lethargy — and no box of Warren's little prescription pills to ease the suffering. Actually Norton's hangover wasn't the full-on, industrial strength type and luckily he'd stuck to drinking beer all night. But a week of having a clear head made it seem a lot worse. The ghetto blaster was on the table near the bed; he switched it on and listened to some music as he lay there and suffered. He could hear the front door open and close a few times, and knew he was eventually going to have to make a move himself. There was only one way to get rid of this feeling: a crap, a run and a feed. He got up, put the jug on and slowly began to organise himself. After a mug of coffee and a dump, he got into his shorts, T-shirt and Nikes and went out the front.

It wasn't too bad a day; there were a few clouds around, a light breeze, sunny without being too hot. Les did a few stretches against the front fence, wrapped an old sweatband around his head and took off, not going anywhere in particular, just burning up forty minutes and as much toxins and stale booze as possible. He trotted down past Randwick Boys High School, turned left into Rainbow Street then up and down a few hills around Coogee and Randwick. While he ran, his thoughts alternated between last night's sexual romp with Nola, his disillusion with Sandra and the old block of flats in general. But mostly his thoughts were on the run and the shape he was in; the hangover had the big Queenslander doing it tough. Somehow he made it back to the flats and somehow he was able to grunt out a hundred sit-ups and agonise over the same number of push-ups. He was sitting against the inside of the front fence, trying to figure out whether he felt better or worse, when Sandra came out of the flats carrying a carton of different coloured T-shirts. She noticed him in his running gear covered in sweat and gave him her Macleans smile.

'Hello, Les,' she said cheerfully. 'You're looking very fit and healthy this morning.'

She was wearing a pair of faded jeans that were so tight it was a miracle they hadn't given her gangrene and a khaki T-shirt with Christian Dior across the front in white, probably a sample of what was in the carton.

'G'day, Sandra,' puffed Norton, trying his best to return her smile. 'To tell you the truth, I'm trying to run off a hangover.'

'Oh. Bit of a naughty boy last night, were you?'

'Yeah,' nodded Les. 'I finished up in that pub across the road. It was good while it lasted. But, Jesus, I'm crook now, I can tell you. What about yourself? What did you do?'

'Went out for dinner with a friend, the one I was

with when I waved to you. Then had an early night watching TV. Not like some other lucky people round here — I have to work this morning,' she added with a grin.

Lying bitch, thought Les. He nodded to the carton of T-shirts. 'You haven't got much stuff there for a busy day at the Paddington Bazaar.'

Sandra shook her head. 'This is just some stock I brought home from the studio. The rest is in a friend's garage at Edgecliff.'

'Yeah. I don't suppose it would be too safe in here.'

The artist shook her head again. 'We've had a few break-ins. Same with my paintings. I leave nearly all of them at the studio too.'

'Fair enough. Would you like the nice caretaker to come over and change the locks for you?'

'I tried that and the bastards stole the locks too. It's good living in the Eastern Suburbs.' Sandra took another hold on the carton of T-shirts. 'Anyway, I'm off to work. I'll see you later, Les.'

'Yeah, righto. See you, Sandra.'

From where he was sitting, Les heard the old ute start and shortly after take off towards the hotel. He sat there for a few more minutes and was about to get up when the door opened again and out filed the hippies carrying their didgeridoos, a carton of absolute junk, a couple of rolled up mats and dressed as if they were on their way to join the chorus line in a remake of *Hair*. They couldn't miss Les sitting where he was but his vibes must have been bad or he was giving off bad karma or maybe he just looked uncool or really, incredibly freaky, or vibes to that effect so they ignored him. Norton was pretty shattered. Off to the Markets for another day of didgeridoo massaging are we, smelly ones? he thought. A few minutes later the old Kombi wheezed and coughed into life and headed off in the same direction as Sandra had. Have a really cosmic day guys, mused Les. Well, that's two lots of my tenants gone. All I need now is ...

Sure enough, the door opened again and the next thing Les knew, Rosie was slobbering all over him, tail banging away as she licked the sweat off his arms and face. It was like being attacked by someone with a soggy paint-roller.

'Is that you there Les?' Burt had the lead in one hand and his walking stick in the other. He had on his usual beret and a pair of dreadful fitting, cheap blue jeans.

'Who else?' replied Norton.

'By golly, the old girl's really taken a shine to you, you know.'

'Yeah. I've always had this fatal attraction for women, Burt. They can't resist me.'

Burt laughed and stood there as Rosie continued to slobber all over Les. Les felt like giving the old Labrador a quick left hook. But what could you do?

'It looks like a nice day, Les,' he said.

'How would I know?' replied Norton. 'All I can see from down here is tongue.'

The old blind man laughed again. 'Anyway, we have to do our Saturday shopping. Come along, Rosie. See you later, Les.'

'Yeah, see you, Burt. Look after yourself.'

Norton sat there for another minute or two as the tap-tap-tapping of Burt's cane disappeared up the street. Oh well, he chuckled to himself, at least I don't need a shower now. But I'll have one just the same. Still undecided whether he felt better or worse, Norton hauled himself to his feet and went inside.

After a shower and a huge drink of water, Norton did feel decidedly better. He still had his headache and he badly needed a feed; but at least he'd sweated most of the stale booze out of himself and he did feel alive. He got into a pair of jeans and a clean T-shirt and strolled down to The Spot where he got some T-bones, eggs, a packet of Codral Reds and a few other odds and ends.

Half an hour later, the pills were working and a big feed of steak and eggs was sitting on the table next

81

to a mug of coffee and the morning papers. Don't know who said life wasn't meant to be easy, mused Norton, hacking off a piece of T-bone, but it sure wasn't me. Before long that was all washed down with another mug of coffee and Les was figuring out what to do with himself for the rest of the day. I s'pose I should ring Woz and let him know I'm still alive. No, fuck the little weasel, he chuckled. He's always wanting to know every detail of what I'm doing. Let him sweat. He heard the front door open and close a few times and figured out that the Heathen Harlots had finally surfaced. But after the pay they gave poor bloody Syd, Les wasn't all that sure whether he wanted to meet them. He finished the papers then removed the racing section. Yes, that's what I'll do. Have a stroll around Randwick Junction then make a few careful investments on the punt. I might even have a hair of the dog back at that pub and maybe another feed later on. Whatever I do, it's going to be a nice leisurely day all round. I've got no phone, no one to annoy me and no one knows where I am.

The stroll amongst the shoppers in Randwick Junction was okay but it didn't enthuse Norton all that much. As he strolled past the Steinberg Ringblum Estate Agency, he noticed the Sadducees were hard at work, but violating the Sabbath in the eyes of the Yaweh didn't appear to be bothering Marvin and Isaac one little bit. Have a nice day in the temple, boys, he mused. Before long Les found himself back at the Royal with a middy of white old in one hand and his form guide in the other. There was a PUB-TAB, the crystal clear sky channel was beaming the race meetings in from all over Australia, and Les decided that was where he would spend the afternoon.

Four or five middies later, Les was immeshed in earnest conversation with several other astute judges of horseflesh and starting to get the taste for more, knowing that if he did, he'd end up doing another job on himself. He was also about $375 in front and knew if he didn't pull up he'd put that back, plus. He put some more bets on, finished his beer and after reluctantly bidding his new-found friends adieu, he went back to the flat. A mug of coffee and a couple more Codral Reds got his head back together and had him realising it was much too nice a day to be inside. The beach and a swim would be the go. Then for some strange reason Les felt like doing a bit of caretaking — on his block of flats. Yes that's what I'll do, thought Norton, in his slightly, spaced-out state. I'm the landlord. I'll run the broom over my block of flats, then I'll go for a swim.

Norton took off his T-shirt, got the broom from the storeroom and started sweeping around the side passage and the front, picking up any rubbish or leaves and putting them in one of the Otto bins. For some odd reason he was whistling and even appeared to be enjoying what he was doing; probably because he was a bit boozy and light-headed from the headache pills. Ahh, this old block of flats ain't all that bad, he thought. Like Sandra said, it's got character. Yeah, all the weird characters that live here and all the characters that are rooting you. He did the laundry and the backyard, noticing a bit of underwear and some jeans and things on the line. Some of the underwear was pretty classy and sexy. Hello, he mused, maybe Elle McPherson is living in here somewhere and I don't know it. She's probably in there shacked up with Burt and Rosie. He began on the stairs knowing it was best if he started at the top and worked down. He climbed the stairs and was about to start sweeping, when the sound of music coming from the roof made him hesitate; and it wasn't the sound of didgeridoos either. If Les wasn't mistaken it was an old Richard Clapton number, 'The Universal'. Well, I am the owner, he thought, I'd better go out and investigate. Also in my capacity as caretaker and cleaner it's my duty to sweep the roof as well.

Holding the broom, Les stepped out onto the roof, straight into the po-faced stares of five girls. Even without their outrageous clothes and make-up, one look at their bodies and hairstyles told him who they were. They were all wearing sunglasses and various types of shorts. Two wore men's singlets, two were topless and the dumpy blonde, whom Les recognised as the one in the school uniform, was wearing a plain blue shirt open at the front. The two topless ones were on banana chairs drinking wine coolers, the other two were seated cross-legged on a blanket playing backgammon and smoking a hash joint; the dumpy blonde was reading a Jackie Collins. There was a large ghetto blaster between the two banana chairs and next to it an esky full of ice, wine coolers and what looked like long-neck Tooheys Dry. It was warm on the roof, with a nice summer breeze blowing. The Heathen Harlots were obviously taking advantage of a pleasant, reasonably secluded Saturday afternoon in Sydney.

There was a sort of pregnant pause as the girls continued to stare expressionlessly at Les, while he, a little bemused, stared back at the girls. Finally, Norton spoke.

'Hello, girls,' he said, with a bit of a lopsided grin. 'How are you goin'?' There was a general muttering of 'hello' and 'hi' and a slow, deliberate nodding of heads. 'You must be the girls in the band?'

The one Les recognised as the Elvira lookalike raised herself up on her banana chair, sucked in a lungful of air and poked out a massive pair of boobs. 'Well, we certainly ain't the *boys* in the band, handsome,' she said huskily, à la Mae West.

This brought a bit of a titter from the girls, then the one with blonde and purple hair on the other banana chair spoke.

'Who are you?' she said. 'Weren't you leaning on that same broom when we came in yesterday morning?'

'Yeah,' nodded Norton. 'I'm Les. I'm the new caretaker.'

'New caretaker?' said the copper-haired one who was playing backgammon. 'What happened to little Hoppy?'

'He went mad and the police shot him.'

'What!!?'

'No,' grinned Les. 'He's gone to live in Newcastle. I started here this week.'

'Gone to Newcastle.' Copper-hair turned to the one reading. 'Did you hear that, Gwen? Your boyfriend's split for Newcastle. Looks like you missed out again.' Gwen gave a half smile and continued with her Jackie Collins.

Rather than stand there perving, Norton made a pretence of sweeping around the roof. Not that he wouldn't have minded perving — the girls looked just as good, if not better, in their civvies than they did in their stage outfits. 'Anyway, don't mind me,' he said. 'I'll just give this a quick once over, then I'll leave you in peace.'

'No, you're right,' the Elvira lookalike said slowly. 'Just take your time.'

The bit of broom pushing downstairs had given Norton's torso a sheen of sweat, and stripped to the waist there was no shortage of muscles bulging out around a rock-hard stomach. If Norton was having a sneak perv, the Heathen Harlots were straight out ogling him from behind their dark glasses; especially the Elvira lookalike. The dumpy blonde, however, seemed more interested in reading *Rock Star*.

'I hear you had a bit of bad luck coming back from Canberra,' said Norton, running the broom towards the edge of the roof.

'Who told you that?' said one of the backgammon players.

'I got talking to Syd out the front,' replied Les. 'After you'd finished with him,' he added with a grin.

'Fuckin' Syd,' said the blonde on the banana chair. 'I could've kicked the big dork right in the nuts for that. Fuckin' idiot. What a prick of a night.'

'Oh, it wasn't entirely his fault,' said the one looking up from her book.

The blonde stared at her for a second or two but didn't say anything.

'So you're going to be our new caretaker, eh?' said the Elvira lookalike. So far she'd barely taken her eyes off Les.

'Yeah, it sure looks that way,' replied Les, continuing to push the broom.

'Well why don't you tell us a bit about yourself, muscles. Do you want a beer?'

Norton looked at the esky full of icy cold Tooheys Dry and his mouth watered. 'Yeah, righto. Thanks a lot.' He got a bottle, squeezed off the top and held it towards the girls. 'Cheers.'

'Yeah. Cheers,' was the general reply.

Les gave them more or less the same story he'd told Sandra the artist, but said he'd come down from Townsville. It was easy money to him and he hoped to get more work soon. That would do them. He regretted blabbing so much to Nola Lloyd the writer and now wished he'd never shown her the murder scene.

It turned out the girls came from Melbourne and Adelaide. The Elvira lookalike on the banana chair was Franulka; she played lead guitar and sang. The blonde with the purple tint next to her was Riona, she played saxophone and bass. The copper-haired one playing backgammon was Isla, the group's drummer. The other dark-haired one was Alastrina; she played rhythm guitar and keyboards. And the one reading was Gwendoline, who did the mixing. They'd formed the group in Melbourne about eighteen months ago and although they hadn't actually set the world on fire they had quite a cult following south of the border and had been on 'Hey Hey It's Saturday' and 'The Big Gig' twice. They'd released a single which had laid an egg but were about to do another one and if it fired, they might even get to do an album. They'd been in Sydney about three months when ironically they met Syd. They lived in Blue Seas because even though it was a dump and cramped, it was super cheap, handy to a pub and transport — and when they arrived in Sydney they scarcely had a pot to piss in. Life on the road was hard. The most they could get for a gig was between one thousand and fifteen hundred dollars; split five ways, after agent's commission and paying their roadie plus not to mention a myriad of other expenses and tax, didn't exactly give them the life style of Dire Straits or INXS. But they supplemented their income with the odd TV or radio commercial and a bit of back-up vocals and other things now and again. They enjoyed performing and, like all up and coming rock 'n' roll bands, were hoping for that one big break, a hit single or a best-selling album. Till that happened they'd just keep going as best they could. In the meantime, apart from a gig at the Revesby Round-house next Wednesday they had almost ten days off before they started touring the north coast.

'So that's life on the road, Les,' said Riona. 'And you know the old saying...'

'Yeah,' cut in Norton. 'It's a long way to the shop, if you want a sausage roll.'

'Hey, you got it,' beamed Alastrina.

By now Norton was more than halfway through his second beer. He finished it and put it in a garbage bag the girls had brought with them. He wouldn't have minded another one, or even another three, but drinking in the sun on top of his hangover and the headache tablets had Les half-pissed already. So he thought it might be best if he got on the toe before he brought himself undone. There'd be plenty of time to see the girls again; and even if they did swear like bullock drivers and seem more than a little weird, they weren't a bad bunch.

'Well, thanks for the beers, girls,' he said. 'But I got a few other things to get done this afternoon. And you know that other old saying: a caretaker's work is never done,' he added with a wink.

There was a general muttering of 'goodbye' and 'see you later'. He was told to call round anytime and have a cup of coffee or a drink or a joint or whatever. Les replied that, if ever the girls needed him for anything, just knock; he'd be there most of the time. He picked up his broom and left. If Norton wasn't mistaken, as he closed the door to the roof behind him he got a very heavy once up and down from Franulka; and a heavy sideways and back too.

The water at Coogee was absolutely beautiful and just what Les needed to clear his head late in the afternoon. He splashed around in the nonexistent surf and lay around the beach for the best part of an hour and a half, after which he had a shower on the beach and two cappuccinos in a beachfront coffee lounge. It hadn't been too bad a day, really, and was made even better when he called into the TAB to find that, although two of his bets went down he'd picked up another $150 on a quinella in Brisbane, which made him around four and a half hundred in front on the day. And he didn't have to go to work busting heads in The Cross that night.

He returned to his sumptuous apartment, had a shave, then got into a clean T-shirt and went in search of a Chinese restaurant he'd found earlier and filled up on prawn cutlets and chicken in mushroom sauce with almonds. After that it was back to the Royal for a couple more beers and a few bourbons and Coke.

The Royal was a little quieter that night, which suited Les, as he wasn't actually in a raging mood. In fact, by ten, the Chinese food, the booze, the sun and the remnants of the previous night's hangover were starting to catch up on him. He finished his last drink and went back to the flat, looking forward to an early night. In his own, almost childish way, Les was having a bit of fun secreted away in the old block of flats at Randwick. The next day he intended making a start on the horrible mess in flat five. He'd also have to decide what to do about the disappearance of Jimmy the bikie. He couldn't just leave that as it stood and by rights something like that should be reported to the police; if only to protect his own hide. He now wished more than ever that he hadn't blabbed about that to Nola Lloyd when he was pissed. Christ! Wouldn't it be lovely if she started blabbing to some of her journalist mates?

Norton was having a last can of Fourex as he listened to the radio while he thought about this when there was an unexpected soft knock on his door. Hello, I wonder who this is?

Les opened the door and there stood Franulka, wearing high heels and a tight, shoulderless black dress that buttoned all the way down the front except for the top four buttons, which were undone and showed enough cleavage to lose your arm in. Her pitch black hair was loose and shiny and she had 'fox' written all over her carefully made-up face.

Almost mesmerised, Norton just stood at the door and blinked. 'Franulka,' he finally spluttered. 'What's...?'

'Hello, Les', purred the Elvira lookalike. 'I heard the radio going so I thought I'd pop in.' From behind her back she produced a chilled bottle of Houghtons Cabernet Rose, already opened. 'You are going to invite me in?'

'Yeah, sure. Right... come in,' replied Les.

He closed the door behind her as she walked in, had a quick look around and placed the bottle of Houghtons on the table. Norton, besides being a little mystified, also felt a bit self-conscious having to bring a top sort like her into a dump like this and wished he had her back in Cox Avenue with the stereo, the lounge and a few more home comforts.

'Welcome to the penthouse suite at Blue Seas Apartments,' he said.

Franulka smiled at him as she gave the flat another quick peruse. 'It's no worse than ours.' She nodded to the bottle of wine. 'You got a couple of glasses?'

'Sure.' Les dropped what was left of his can of Fourex in the kitchen tidy and rinsed two glasses. He placed them on the table, filled them up and handed one to Franulka. 'Well, here's to the breezes that blows through the treeses,' he grinned.

'And lifts the girls' dresses up past their kneeses,' answered Franulka.

'And shows us the things that teases and pleases.'

'And gives us diseases. By Jesus.'

'You know that one too, Franulka?'

'I learnt that one at school, Les.'

89

They each took a good sip of the light sweet wine and stood for a moment looking at each other. All of a sudden Norton's tiredness and hangover cleared up and he felt a sudden rush of fresh blood flow through his body, especially around his loins. Franulka looked good enough to eat, clothes and all, and Les felt like putting a headlock on her and spearing her straight onto the old night-and-day. She sure as hell didn't come round to complain about a blocked-up sink. But whatever was on the big horny thing's mind, he was still going to have to be a little cool.

'So, what's doing, Franulka?' he said, taking another sip of wine. 'Just having a quiet night, were you?'

'Yes. Two of the other girls have gone out. The rest of us were watching TV and I thought of you down here all on your own, new in town and not knowing a soul. So I just thought I'd call in and say hello.'

Norton gave her a wink. 'Yeah that's me, Franulka. Lost and alone in this big heartless city. It's . . . it's almost frightening in a way.'

'Ooh, I don't think you'd frighten too easy, Les. It might be the other way around if anything.' Franulka gave her head a quick toss and her raven hair danced almost magically across her shoulders.

Les made a gesture with his hands. 'There's not much in the way of furniture. But why don't you sit down?'

'Okay.' Franulka had a quick look around then sat on the night-and-day and kicked off her high heels.

Oh well thought Norton, after all this is my bloody flat, so he sat down next to her on the night-and-day too. He finished his glass of wine and smacked his lips. 'Hey, this wine's all right,' he said. 'You want another glass?'

'Sure.' Franulka finished hers and Les topped up both their glasses.

They sat there, chit-chatting about nothing much in particular with the radio playing softly in the background. Norton kept cracking the jokes and Franulka kept laughing and before long the bottle of Houghtons was gone. Franulka now appeared to be in an extremely relaxed mood and FOX was blinking on and off above her head in bright neon lights; Norton felt like kicking in one of the walls. It was time to make some sort of a move.

'I'll tell you what, Franulka,' he smiled. 'That's not a bad dress you're almost wearing. Do you wear that on stage?'

'This old thing?' Franulka gave her boobs a bit of a shake. 'It wouldn't last the first two bars of our opening number.'

'No, I don't suppose it would.'

Les reached across and undid the fifth button. Franulka smiled at him but didn't say a word. Les undid the next button and the next, till the whole of her dress was open, revealing those unbelievable, round, firm breasts that just sat there jutting out towards him with two delicious, big pink nipples in front. The dress fell away some more to show that Franulka was wearing a pair of black satin knickers that came up on the sides with a V-shaped satin flap around the front. The tiniest wisp of hair ran from the top of her knickers up to her navel. Norton felt like tearing the knickers and her dress off and eating them right there and then. He ran his hand over her shoulder and the dress fell away. Norton couldn't remember the last time he'd seen or had his hands on a body like this. He ran his hands over her breasts and softly massaged the nipples as Franulka heaved and panted. He put his hand round the back of her neck and drew her towards him as Franulka did precisely the same thing to him.

Their lips met. Norton couldn't remember ever kissing a woman like this — it was almost as if someone had tipped a spoonful of molten lava into his mouth. She fairly sizzled. Her tongue found his and it was like a red-hot razor blade slicing into his emotions. Les ran his tongue over her neck and ears and across her breasts and nipples and heard her moan softly in his ear. He massaged her breasts and nipples and the flat of her stomach then ran his hand over her ted which felt warm, moist and delightfully slinky beneath the black satin.

Franulka scrabbled at his back and pulled Norton's T-shirt out of his jeans. He got up, kicked off his sneakers, pulled off his T-shirt and jeans and lay down alongside Franulka, caressing her beautiful body and kissing the boiling volcano that was her mouth. Franulka did much the same to Les, running her hands up and down his spine and scratching him lightly with her long, red fingernails. Christ! This is enough foreplay to last the next six weeks, thought Norton — his old boy was throbbing that hard you could hear it a block away. He got out of his Speedos, slid Franulka's knickers off and was about to slip inside her when she put her hands against his chest and softly, but firmly pushed him away. Norton blinked in disbelief.

'What's up?' he said.

'Do you know anything about Taoist Yoga, Les?'

'What!!?'

'Chinese Taoism, Les.'

Norton looked at her incredulously. He was that horny it was almost crippling him. If Franulka didn't liven up she'd find out about something called premature ejaculation. About four gallons of it.

'I don't know what you're talking about,' said Les. 'I had a Chinese meal earlier and I didn't see it on the menu. Jesus Christ! Don't stop now.'

'Get on your back, Les,' ordered Franulka.

'Huh?'

'On your back. Lay on your back.'

Norton looked at her for a moment then rolled over. Franulka climbed over his chest, got herself into position and straddled him. A shudder went through Norton's body as she lowered herself down. It was pure heaven.

'This is how we drive the elixir of immortality into the cauldron,' gasped Franulka.

'Sounds all right to me,' croaked Les. 'Go for your life.'

Franulka 'drove' for a while, then turned around and did it with her back to him.

'Now we plunge the spirit into the lower T'ien cavity.'

'Plunge all you like,' said Norton, holding her round the waist.

After that, Franulka and Les got into it in about six hundred different positions which had Norton not knowing whether he was coming or going. One minute she'd be on top, then on the bottom, the side and from the back. Legs and arms were going every which way and half the time Les couldn't work out who was screwing who. But it was certainly a lot of fun, and seemed endless which definitely stopped Norton from blowing his bolt too early.

Every time they'd change positions, Franulka would come out with all these strange phrases. 'This is called gathering the microcosmic alchemical agent,' she'd say. 'Clearing the eight psychic channels... Microcosmic orbiting... Driving the fire... The light and vitality at the mysterious gate... Formation of the immortal foetus... The egress...' Les didn't have a clue what she was talking about, but just about every time Franulka would change positions, she'd throw back her head, scream and get her rocks off.

Finally, in a lather of sweat, Les found himself on top with Franulka's knees somewhere up near her ears, so he started with a solid, steady stroke.

'Ohh, yesss,' groaned Franulka. 'The dragon and tiger in copulation. Leap into the great emptiness, Les.'

Norton didn't have to be told twice. Away he went, putting in the big ones. As he hit the vinegar strokes, the lead singer of the Heathen Harlots hit high C. Norton arched his back and drove it in faster and harder till finally he went off with an explosion that nearly blew his spine out. Franulka let out with a scream that virtually rattled the window panes and almost cracked every glass in the kitchen. Somehow they shuddered to a stop and lay there. Franulka was panting away, Norton's eyes were spinning around like a couple of well-oiled roulette wheels. After a while they both came back to earth.

'Well, Les. What did you think of that?' purred Franulka.

93

'What did I think of that?' answered Les. 'I dunno. But I reckon it'd beat tai-chi hands down.'

Franulka gave a throaty chuckle. 'You got a towel?'

'Sure.'

Norton got a towel and they both got cleaned up. They'd finished the wine so he got a couple of beers from the fridge. Franulka put her knickers back on and her dress, but didn't bother to do it up. Les decided he may as well put his jeans and T-shirt back on as well. If the Shao-Lin priestess, or whatever she fancied herself as, wanted to descend into the cauldron of immortality or something again he could soon get them off. They sat on the old night-and-day sipping beer, having a bit of a kiss and a fondle while the radio played softly in the background. Norton thought it would only be a matter of time before they were into it again, when there was a knock on the door. Only this wasn't a nice little tap like Franulka's. This was a dead-set knock which if it had been any louder would have taken the door right off its hinges. Oh oh, thought Les, I think I know who this might be. In the suddenness of Franulka's arrival and the gear she had on Norton had forgotten all about him. He looked at Franulka and opened the door.

Syd was standing in the doorway, his face a stone mask. In his jeans and tight-fitting Johnny Diesel and the Injectors T-shirt, he looked about half a metre taller and about five kilos heavier than when Les had met him out the front.

'Is Franulka in here?' he snarled at Norton.

Les was about to shake his head and give Syd a definite no, when a voice came from inside. 'What do you want, Syd?'

Syd charged past Norton and found Franulka sitting comfortably on the night-and-day, her hair all over the place and her dress still undone.

Syd's voice was almost piteous. 'Franulka. What are you doing in here?'

Franulka gave Syd a tired smile. 'Ohh, I'm in here

selling bloody encyclopedias. What do you think I'm doing in here, Syd?'

His gaunt face now a portrait of anguish, Syd stared at Franulka. 'Franulka! How could you?' Then the anguish turned to pent-up rage as he swung round to Norton. 'What did I say to you out the front? You... you... *aaarrghh*!!'

Norton more or less knew what to expect, but he didn't think Franulka would be so blunt and the suddenness of Syd's attack took him off guard. With a scream of hatred and jealousy the huge roadie threw himself at Les, forcing him against the wall and those two monstrous hands Norton had noticed holding the cigarette on Friday went straight to Norton's throat. Les barely had time to gulp in some air before Syd started choking the life out of him.

Les couldn't believe the strength in Syd's hands and fingers — it was like two steel bands clamped around his neck. Les banged his fists down on Syd's elbows, that didn't work. He brought his arms up; that didn't work either. Syd was as strong as an ox and a grief-stricken lover to go with it. Les tried to knee him in the balls but couldn't seem to get any leverage. His head was starting to swim now, after the best part of an hour's solid screwing this was all he needed; some crazed fifteen-stone roadie choking the life out of him. He knew he didn't have much time left before he blacked out. Syd's grip only seemed to get harder when Les brought his arms up and jammed his thumbs into Syd's eyes — he didn't just stick them in, he gripped the sides of Syd's head and began doing his best to gouge them both out. Syd screamed and jammed his eyes shut but Norton didn't have a bad grip either and if Syd was going to choke him, he'd be blinded in the process.

With a shout of pain, Syd finally let go. Les shoved him away and gulped in some air. He barely had time to massage his throat when Syd was on him again, raining punches. Les copped one on the eye, the nose and another in the mouth; Syd knew how to put them together and they all hurt. Les belted a couple of left hooks into Syd's face, busting up his mouth. A short right mashed up his nose. The punches were doing plenty of damage but they didn't seem to be stopping Syd all that much. Norton covered up as another torrent of punches slammed into his arms and the top of his head. Out the corner of his eye he saw Franulka sitting cross-legged on the night-and-day. She wasn't screaming or horrified at the sight of two big men punching and gouging the life out of each other. It was almost as if she was enjoying it.

Les and Syd fought and swore across the room smashing the table and the wardrobe as they went. Norton was getting more punches in but they still didn't seem to be hurting him. Syd was a hard man but he was in too much of a wild state of mind. Les kneed him under the ribs and head-butted him, splitting open Syd's eye. A big roundhouse right slammed into Norton's ear. Then they crashed into the kitchen, sending pots, pans and dishes everywhere. Before Les knew it, Syd had his massive hands around Norton's throat again trying to choke him, and Norton knew that if he didn't do something drastic, Syd would more than likely kill him. Besides that, the big Queenslander was starting to run out of steam. Norton's hand went into the sink on top of an old cake of Sunlight Soap slopping on a plate that had been soaking. He grabbed the cake of soap and smashed it into Syd's face, squashing plenty into his eyes. The enraged roadie screamed with pain as the soap blinded him, and clutched at his burning eyes. This gave Les time to set himself and drive probably the best uppercut he'd ever thrown in his life up between Syd's elbows right on to the point of the chin. Les smiled to himself as he felt Syd's jaw crack under his fist like a dry biscuit. The roadie screamed some more as a follow-up left hook smashed out half his front teeth and another big right crushed his already battered nose. The tide of battle had finally swung in Norton's favour. Syd started to slide as Les grabbed him by his ponytail and speared him from the kitchen, face down into what was left of the lounge room. He wrapped his left forearm around Syd's throat jamming his wrist into his Adam's apple. Gripping his left hand with his right, Les then stuck his knee behind Syd's neck and started squeezing the lot together.

'Now,' hissed Norton, 'see how you like being choked. You big cunt.'

Les could feel the blood and spittle bubbling out of Syd's mouth and face running over his arm. The big roadie made a futile grab at Norton's arms, then after a few nervous kicks began to go quiet. Norton still didn't let up; he was going to crush the life right out of Syd and, if need be, tear his head right off his body.

The next thing he knew Franulka was banging on his back shouting at him.

'All right, Les. For Christ's sake, don't fuckin' kill him!'

'Don't kill him?' retorted Les. 'What do you think the prick was trying to do to me?' Norton continued crushing Syd's Adam's apple.

'Fuck off, will you, Les? He's got to drive us to Revesby Workers' Club on Wednesday night.'

'What?' Subconsciously Norton started to slacken his grip.

'He's got to drive us to the gig on Wednesday night. Christ almighty!'

Norton looked up at Franulka and suddenly let go. Syd gurgled in some air through the blood and smashed teeth then passed out. At least he wasn't dead.

'Ohh, Christ! Have a look at him,' cried Franulka. 'How's he gonna drive the fuckin' truck on Wednesday?'

Norton crawled to one side of the room, trying to get his breath back. He continued to stare at Franulka. Here was their roadie or her boyfriend or whatever the poor sap was, smashed to a bloody pulp, half dead and all she could think about was whether he could drive their stinken purple truck through the week. Blues singers could have written a thousand songs about Franulka.

She might have been a top sort and an unbelievable screw but she was the original Hardhearted Hannah from New Orleans.

Naturally, all the noise and shouting brought the girls down from upstairs; Syd must have called for Franulka and they'd've told him where she was. Wearing their tracksuits Gwen and Isla stepped cautiously up to the door and looked in. They saw Franulka and then Syd, covered in blood, lying at her feet.

'Oh, God!' shrieked Gwen. 'It's Syd! What happened?' She ran to Syd's side, cradled his head and began wiping away the blood.

'Christ!' said Isla, and did the same thing.

'Oh Syd, Syd,' Gwen seemed to be almost grief-stricken with tears streaming down her face, she looked accusingly at Franulka. 'What happened?' she wailed.

'He had a fight with Les,' she replied, a little indifferently.

Gwen and Isla glared at Norton. 'You bastard,' said Gwen. 'What did you have to do this for?'

Norton thought he was hearing things. 'What did I do that for? To stop the big moron from doing the same thing to me. That's all.'

'Ohh, no! Syd, Syd.' Gwen continued to hold Syd's head and mop his face with the front of her tracksuit.

'Come on! We'd better get him to a hospital' said Isla. She gave Norton a steely look. 'Bastard!'

'No sweat,' said Franulka. 'There's one across the road.'

Norton shook his head in disbelief. They couldn't miss the blood on Les, the poor bloody caretaker, yet not a word of sympathy, no apology, nothing. It could easily have been him lying there, not Syd. And only a lucky thing it wasn't. And it wasn't even his fault.

'Well, come on, Les,' said Gwen. 'Don't just sit there. Give us a hand.'

Give us a hand. Norton was just about to tell the three of them to get well and truly stuffed when there was the noise of a taxi pulling up out the front. Norton's timing to make a big hit with the girls in the band couldn't have been better. Alastrina and Riona walked into the hallway carrying three pizzas. They couldn't miss what was going on in Norton's flat. Next thing they too were standing at Norton's door in a state of shock.

'What happened?' gasped Alastrina.

'Bloody Les did it,' said Gwen.

The two latest arrivals glared at Les. 'Bastard,' they chorused.

Norton shook his head and didn't move. To a general chorus of bastard, cunt, prick and a string of other vile names all directed at him, the girls somehow managed to get Syd to his feet and carry him to the door and out into the hallway, leaving Franulka behind.

Franulka picked up the three pizzas, moved towards the door then stopped and looked at Les, 'What can I say?' she shrugged.

From the floor Les gave her an expressionless once up and down and a sideways and back too. 'How about goodnight?'

Franulka shrugged again then joined the others out the front.

Alone in the flat now Norton began to feel around his face through the pain and blood. He was going to have a black eye, a fat lip and a swollen nose in the morning and was bruised and scratched. But nothing was broken; it could have been a lot worse. He went to wipe some blood out of his eye, forgetting about the smears of soap still on his hand.

'Oww, shit!' he cursed.

Les dragged himself to his feet and went to the bathroom where he filled the sink with water and wiped the soap from his eyes. While he was at it he checked himself out properly in the mirror. It was like he thought; plenty of bruising, a bit of bark missing, but nothing broken. But his genuine American George Strait Tour T-shirt was completely stuffed.

Back in the lounge room the wardrobe was smashed along with the table, but his ghetto blaster still worked.

99

The old night-and-day never got a scratch. Yeah, that'd be right, thought Les. Trust her not to get a mark on her. The devil Goddess or whatever she thinks she is probably put up some aura around her, or a vibe or some bloody thing while Syd and me were trying to smash each other to pulp. In fact if you ask me, this whole fuckin' joint's starting to get one giant, bad vibe about it. Something else kept nagging at Les about the old block of flats too but he just couldn't seem to put his finger on it. He needed someone to talk this over with. He looked at his watch which had also managed to survive the fight. It wasn't too late to ring a good friend.

The phone box across the road from the all-night garage opposite the flats was well-lit and not vandalised. Les jangled the coins in the slot, dialled and subconsciously turned back towards the old block of flats while he waited.

'Yeah, hello?' came a voice he was sure he recognised.

'Hello, Billy?'

'Yeah.'

'It's Les!'

'Les! G'day mate. How's things?'

'All right. Sorry I'm ringing a bit late.'

'That's okay. We're almost ready to go home anyway.'

'Sounds like you're gettin' it easy.'

'It's a bludge, like I told you. The front door's closed, I just sit up the top of the stairs near a phone and keep an eye on things. Don't even wear a tux. There's only Price and George and about six of his mates in here. Drinking wine, talking shit and trying to take each other's money at five hundred. I'm even reading books.'

Norton laughed. 'Listen, Billy. What are you doing tomorrow?'

Billy noticed the tone in Norton's voice. 'Not much. Nothing I can't get out of. You're not in any strife, are you?'

'No, no, nothing like that. But do you reckon you could meet me somewhere tomorrow?'

'Sure. Where?'

'You know The Royal Hotel at Randwick?'

'Yeah.'

'How about out the front at twelve o'clock?'

'Yeah, no worries. I'll be there.'

'Thanks, mate. And Billy...'

'Yeah?'

'Don't tell Price or anyone I called.'

'Okay. If they ask me who it was I'll say it was me missus.'

'Good on you, mate. I'll tell you all about it tomorrow.'

'See you tomorrow, Les. Twelve o'clock.'

Les strolled slowly back to Blue Seas Apartments, noticing that the old white utility was back. Jesus! They sure come and go in here, he thought. But at least she missed all the drama. He made a cup of coffee, put the radio on and tried to think. He was tired but at the same time his nerves were on edge. He switched off the light, lay back on the night-and-day and did his best to get to sleep; managing after a while to half doze off. He'd been that way for three-quarters of an hour or so when the noise of the front door made him open his eyes. There were hurried footsteps, then a discreet tap on Sandra's door. Hello, thought Les, one of Ms Garrett's late night lovers. Next thing I'll be getting pinched for having premises for the purpose of.

He dozed off when not long after the door opened again. This time the voices told him it was the girls in the band back from the hospital. Les couldn't hear Syd's voice. Thank Christ for that, he thought. I wouldn't have answered the door to those sheilas anyway. Les glanced at his watch. He'd been there just over an hour. Again he half dozed.

Again the noise of the door opening woke him up. That and his neck. The old pillow from home wasn't all that good at the best of times, but tonight with his neck the way it was it was worse. There was an old cushion in the car he used on the front seat, he decided he'd get that for a bit of extra support. Somehow he

101

dragged himself up from the night-and-day and walked sleepily out the front. As he stood there, he noticed the same grey BMW he'd seen the previous night and the same figure in the hat and trench coat getting into it. Only this time the figure had the back door open and was placing what was obviously a painting wrapped in brown paper on the seat. Norton stepped back into the shadows and watched with something a little more than just curiosity. The figure got the painting in, closed the door then got behind the wheel and the next thing the BMW cruised off towards Randwick Junction.

That's all it is, Les thought sarcastically. He's an art dealer. Sandra's just selling all these blokes paintings. And to think I should have such a dirty, suspicious mind. Les shook his head and spat in the gutter. Yeah, that'd be right.

He got the cushion from the front seat and went back inside. Ahh yes. That's better. More support. This time Norton did manage to get to sleep. Like a log.

It was after ten when he climbed out off the night-and-day and cleaned himself up. Cleaning his teeth in the mirror, Les could see his left eye had coloured up nicely overnight and it looked like he'd swapped top lips with Mick Jagger. His throat was sore but the bruises weren't all that bad and could almost have passed for love bites. Apart from that — okay.

He got into a T-shirt and jeans and walked out to get the Sunday papers. It had turned out another nice, sunny day. Sandra was out the front standing in front of an easel, daubing at an oil painting. She couldn't have missed Norton coming out the front door but she didn't bother to look up from what she was doing.

'G'day, Sandra,' said Les pleasantly.

'Huh!' Sandra barely shifted her eyes away from whatever she was painting. 'Oh. Hello, Jim.'

Norton frowned slightly. 'Jim?'

'Oh, Len, Les. Whatever.'

Terrific, thought Les. I really have made a hit with

her, haven't I? The bitch can't even remember my name. Moll. Slightly miffed, Norton was about to walk on, then changed his mind. 'What are you painting?' he asked.

'Not much,' was the whimsical reply.

'Mind if I have a look?'

Sandra shrugged a reply that was neither a yes, or a no. Oh well, thought Norton, maybe artists are a bit funny like that. He moved around and had a look at what Sandra was painting. It was Blue Seas Apartments at night. Sandra might not ever get anything hung in the Louvre, but she'd managed to capture the old block of flats in a sombre, night mood of mainly blues and yellows. Coming out the front of the flats was, of all things, a figure in a trench coat and hat. The face, like the rest of the painting, was very abstract, but there was an uncanny familiarity about it that Les couldn't help but stare at.

'Hey, that's not bad Sandra,' he said, after a moment or two. 'It's the block of flats, all right. Who's the bloke coming out the front door?'

'Just a friend.'

'A friend?'

'That's right.'

Norton was about to say something and changed his mind. 'You're quite good, Sandra. Do you sell many paintings?'

Sandra continued to daub away. 'A few,' she replied absently. 'My friend buys most of them.'

'He's got good taste.' Yeah, for a Bulgarian, Norton thought to himself.

'Thanks.'

'Does it take you long to do a painting?'

Sandra shrugged. 'I hope to have this finished by next Saturday. It's going to be a birthday present to myself.'

'Is it your birthday next Saturday?'

Sandra nodded without looking up from the painting. Norton did a little mental arithmetic.

'November fourteenth?' Sandra nodded again. Norton

103

thought for a moment. 'Isn't that Prince Charles' birthday too?'

This brought a slight smile to Sandra's face. 'That's right. If he ever becomes king, there'll be a public holiday on my birthday.'

'And right royally so,' smiled Les. Norton was going to carry on the conversation, but he somehow sensed Sandra didn't seem all that interested. 'Anyway, I'll see you later.'

'Okay.'

Norton left her and walked off to get the papers. The painting played on his mind all the way down to the shops — especially Sandra's 'friend'. No, he thought, shaking his head. It couldn't be. I'm seeing things. Then he stopped in mid-stride. Or fuckin' am I?

On the way back he gave Sandra a brief smile and got pretty much the same back in return. He went inside, poached some eggs and went through the Sunday papers while he listened to the radio. Before long it was around quarter to twelve. Sandra was packed up and gone from out the front and so was her utility.

Les walked across to the hotel and found a table near the Perouse Road entrance. A few minutes later, Billy's station wagon pulled in front of the hotel opposite the park.

Norton almost didn't recognise Billy when he came walking towards him. Like Les he was wearing jeans and a T-shirt but he looked about a stone lighter and almost ten years younger than the last time he'd seen him. Billy saw Les staring at him and grinned.

'Hello, mate. How are you?'

'Good. Jesus, you're looking well Billy.'

'Yeah.' Billy pulled up a seat then noticed Norton's face and his grin got bigger. 'Hello, what happened to you?'

Norton grinned back and shrugged. 'What do you reckon?'

Billy shook his head. 'Well, if you've copped that, I'd hate to see the other bloke.'

Still grinning, Norton gestured with his thumb. 'He's in the hospital across the road if you want to see him. Anyway, you feel like a beer?'

Billy shook his head. 'Just a mineral water'll do, mate.'

Les went to the bar and came back with two bottles of Hepburn Spa, and middy glasses full of ice and slices of lemon.

'Well, cheers, Billy,' he said, raising his glass.

'Yeah, cheers, Les. Good to see you, mate.'

Norton couldn't help but stare at his workmate. 'I just can't get over how well you look, shifty. What's going on?'

Billy smiled as he drank his mineral water. 'Well, I've been off the piss. I haven't had a drink since we wrote ourselves off last Saturday night.'

'Can't say I blame you.'

'And with all this extra time I've got and the early nights, I've been training twice a day. Running in the morning and sparring down Clovelly Surf Club in the afternoon. And fuckin' hard. I've ripped off nearly a stone. I'm punching like Mike Tyson. Fair dinkum, I've never felt better in me life.' Billy grinned and shaped up to Les across the table. 'I might even make a comeback.'

Norton smiled back at Billy. 'You do look extra good,' he conceded. Then his eyes narrowed. 'But there's something fuckin' else.'

Billy ran a hand through his hair. 'You noticed the Barney, did you, mate? Lyndy cut me hair the other day and stuck some Redken or something in it. And away went all those distinguished touches of grey.' Billy reached over and punched Les in the arm. 'Fair dinkum. I was walking down the street yesterday and some sheilas in a schoolbus started whistling me. They thought I was George Michael.'

Norton roared. 'George Brennan'd be more like it. You fuckin' larrikin.'

'Just don't tell anybody, will you?'

They laughed and continued on their spa waters.

'So what's doing, Les? What did you want to see me about? I rang a couple of times but you weren't home. Warren said he didn't know where you were.'

Norton nodded behind him to Blue Seas. 'I've been holed up in my old block of flats.'

'I figured it'd have something to do with that.'

Les stood up. 'I'll get us another couple of spa waters and I'll tell you what's going on. I just want to get some of it off my chest.'

Norton returned with the drinks and gave Billy the whole smear. How the place was losing him money. The state it was in. What old Hoppy had told him. The estate agents. The weirdos that lived there. Flat five. His night with Nola. How he'd met the Heathen Harlots and the rest of them. Syd. The fight. The fuck with Franulka. And more. By the time Les had finished they were on a third bottle of spa water and Billy didn't know what to think.

'Yeah. It's been a lot of fun, Billy, I can tell you,' said Norton.

'Bloody hell!' Billy had to shake his head. 'You sure packed it into a week, didn't you?'

Now Norton had to shake his head. 'Fuckin' prick of a joint. I wish I'd never bought it.'

'I remember when you did. I was nearly gonna say something, but I thought, no, fuck it. It's none of my business. No wonder you never talked about it.'

'Yeah,' sighed Les. 'Anyway, finish these, and I'll take you over and give you a guided tour.'

'You reckon those sheilas in the band might be up on the roof?' hinted Billy.

'If they are,' replied Norton, 'I'm certain they won't want to talk to me.'

'Who said anything about you? I'll go up and tell 'em I'm the new caretaker.'

'You're a happily married man, remember, Billy.'

Billy Dunne grinned and ran a hand through his thick black hair. 'I'm too young to be married.'

'Get out you fuckin' thing.'

Laughing and joking they crossed Perouse Road. Seeing Billy and having a good talk was just the tonic Les needed. His blues from the night before and the other things weighing on his mind were starting to lift already. It sure was good to see his old mate again.

'So, this is your penthouse suite, is it?' said Billy, looking around the caretaker's flat. 'Nice, isn't it? You'd get a grand a week for this during the season.'

'What? The duck season?'

'Christ! Have a look at the wardrobe.' Billy toed at some pieces of wardrobe and table that had got smashed the night before plus some clothes and other things which Les hadn't bothered to clean up. 'You and your mate Syd sure had a good time in here last night.'

'I was having a terrific time until he turned up. Come on, I'll show you the rest of the joint.'

Les gave Billy a quick tour of the flats: showing him the backyard, the laundry, pointing out the hippies' old kombi-wagon. He didn't bother to show him the dusty old storeroom and he was glad there was no one around when he took him up to the roof.

'Yes, it's a real nice place, Les,' chided Billy, gazing over towards Coogee. 'Let me know when there's a vacancy and I'll move in.'

'You wouldn't be that crooked on yourself, would you? Now, come down and have a look at this. See what you make of it.'

Norton took Billy down to flat five, closed the door behind them and gave him a quick look around then stood with him in the lounge room. 'Well? What do you reckon? Nice, isn't it?'

'Bloody hell!' Billy Dunne could scarcely believe his eyes. 'What a fuckin' mess!'

'They did a good job, didn't they? And I've gotta clean it all up.'

Billy shook his head in astonishment. 'And you porked that writer in here?'

'Yeah. Right on the lounge.' Norton grinned and gave

107

what was left of the sofa a pat. 'It got her all fruity. Plus my good looks, of course.'

'Of course.' Billy shook his head again. 'Listen, I might have a bit more of a look around. This is unbelievable.'

'Go for your life,' shrugged Norton. 'I'll try and figure out the best way to clean the shit up.'

While Billy nosed slowly around the flat, Les tried to figure out what cleaning and repairing the place was going to cost him. Besides the actual labour, he was going to need paint, carpet, tiles and light-fittings. He'd also need a carpenter for the kitchen, and probably a plumber and a bloody tiler as well. Christ! It was going to cost a lot more than he thought. Billy was in the front bedroom and Les was still in the kitchen pondering and wondering what he'd ever done to deserve all this when the vroom-vroom-vroom sound of five big motorbikes pulling up in the street below drifted up past the window.

The window was closed and Les was deeply engrossed in thought so he didn't take a great deal of notice. He did a few minutes later, when the front door opened and closed and the sound of heavy footsteps and gruff, humourless voices came down the hall.

'It's in here somewhere. It's fuckin' gotta be.'

'Yeah, but where? We just about wrecked the fuckin' joint last time and we still couldn't find it.'

'Well, this time we *will* wreck the joint. I ain't leavin' here without it. Even if we gotta take the fuckin' joint apart brick by fuckin' brick.'

From back in the kitchen, Les managed to get a good sight of who had just walked in. They were five bikies — big, mean and hairy. Two looked Australian, the other two could have been Maoris or Islanders of some description and the other was swarthy with a mop of curly black hair and a big, droopy moustache, suggesting he might have been Greek or had a bit of Arab in him. They were all wearing standard bikie gear: greasy T-shirts, Levis and boots and Levis jackets minus the sleeves. The Arab-looking one had his back slightly

108

turned and Les noticed 'Rat Manners Motorcycle Club' embroidered on his jacket, around a drawing of a rat with an eye patch. The one doing most of the talking was an Australian about six feet three and as he spoke, he emphasised his words with a pinch bar he was carrying in his right hand. So, thought Norton, you're the young gentlemen that wrecked my flat and are going to cost me a lot of money. How jolly decent of you to call back.

'Okay,' ordered the tall one carrying the pinch bar. 'Gazza, you and Chin start in the lounge room. Pull it to fuckin' bits. Jacko, you and Monk go through both the bedrooms. I'm gonna tear this kitchen apart. But we ain't leavin' till we find it, even if we're here all fuckin' night.'

'Righto, Mick.'

Eyebrows bristling and his adrenalin starting to pump, Norton decided it was time to make a move. He stepped up to the kitchen doorway.

'Hello, fellas,' he said pleasantly. 'Looking for something, are you? Maybe I can help you.'

All five bikies swung towards the kitchen doorway, annoyed someone was there more than startled. They glared at Les, exchanged a brief glance with each other for a moment before the tallest one spoke.

'Who the fuck are you?' he said, in a demanding sort of snarl.

'Who am I?' replied Norton. 'I'm Mr Smith, the caretaker. I'm the poor mug that's got to clean up all this mess that you and your mates left here last time.'

There was a bit of a silence as the bikies exchanged mystified looks.

'I have to admit, I was a bit upset at first, but it looks like you've come back to give me a bit of a hand. How thoughtful of you.' Norton looked evenly at the tall one with the pinch bar. 'And to think that for a while there I thought all bikies were dirty, rotten low cunts. I do apologise.'

The bikies looked at each other, then at Les like he

109

was some big, poncey idiot and they couldn't quite believe what they were hearing. Whatever their thoughts, they certainly weren't in the realm of niceties.

'Listen, Shithead, or Smith, or whatever your name is,' said the tall one holding the jemmy. 'There's something in this flat belongs to us. And we ain't leavin' till we get it.'

'Oh dear,' said Norton.

'So, Smith — why don't you just fuck off till we're finished?'

'Yeah. Go and sweep up out the front. Or clean out the shithouse,' said one of the Maoris.

'Yeah. And come back in about a week,' added the other one.

If the bikies had Les rattled he certainly wasn't showing it and they could have been a bit curious as to what he was smiling at. But the bikies didn't see Billy slipping his watch off as he came quietly down the hall. Les did. He also caught Billy's eye and got the look they'd perfected between them at the Kelly Club. A sort of a code. Les knew exactly what to expect; and even though he was still a bit sore from the previous night it was exactly what he was looking for.

'Can I help you gentlemen at all?' enquired Billy.

The bikies swung round at the new voice. Two glared at him, the other three kept their eye on Les.

'And who are fuckin' you?' said the tall one again.

'Me?' answered Billy. 'I'm the other caretaker.'

The bikies were slightly taken aback, but only for a moment. Billy and Les weren't your average punters, but they were just as big, if not bigger, plus there was five of them and they had a pinch bar.

'Yes,' continued Billy, still smiling sweetly. 'I'm a caretaker with Bachman Turner Overdrive.' He turned to one of the Maori bikies on his right. 'And you know what we like to take care of?'

For some reason the Maori bikie shook his head dumbly.

'Business,' said Billy. Before you could blink, Billy

110

threw a left hook that caught the dumb bikie flush on the mouth. Billy had said he was training a lot and punching harder than ever, and Les didn't disbelieve him. He couldn't remember ever seeing a punch like it. The bikie's face seemed to disintegrate in a spray of blood and teeth. His knees buckled, his arms went limp and as his eyes rolled back, all sixteen stone of him slumped down on his backside. Before he hit the deck Billy belted the bikie on his left with a short right to the ear, a left hook and a right uppercut that nearly took his head off. Norton could hear the bones breaking across the other side of the room before he joined his mate on the floor. Jesus you are fit Billy, thought Les. Oh well, can't let you have all the fun on your own. Now it's my turn.

There were three bikies facing Les. He crouched low and drove a vicious, short right, straight into the one on his left's balls. It was a dirty punch and Norton smiled to himself as he heard the bikie scream. It was a good thing he ducked down because the tall bikie swung the jemmy in a backhand arc at Norton's head. It missed but almost took the entire side out of the door jamb — if it had landed it would have crushed Norton's skull. Les straightened up slightly and where the biggest bikie had left himself open smashed a short left up under his floating rib. He grunted with pain as Les slammed a short right into his temple that spun his brain around in his skull. Les followed this with a right backfist that crushed his nose and two quick, right elbow shots that ground what was left of it into bonedust. As he dropped the jemmy and started to slide, Norton kneed him in the spine. On the other side of the room Les could see Billy going toe to toe with the bikie with the droopy moustache. It was no match. The bikie was getting in one or two ineffectual hits, but Billy was in a crouch like a professional fighter, landing ten to the bikie's one, and literally chopping him to pieces and it looked like Billy was loving it; the week of solid training had turned him into a dynamo. The bikie dropped his hands and

111

Billy clamped his hands around his head, brought it down and rammed his knee up into his face leaping up off the floor as he did. It was a move that would have brought the crowd to its feet at Lumpinee Stadium in Bangkok.

This left one bikie standing. Somehow he made a lunge at Les. Les just stepped inside and headbutted him, moving his nose about two inches across his face. He was about to give him another one when the bikie yelped with pain and seemed to jerk towards him straight into another headbutt. Instead of going down the bikie seemed to jerk towards him again. Then behind him Les could see Billy ripping lefts and rights into his kidneys. He let him go and Billy jerked his head down by the hair and kneed him in the back of the head. The bikie hit the floor with a thud.

That should have been it, but Billy now had blood in his eye. 'Well, that was all right, Les,' he grinned, still shaped up and still rocking around on the balls of his feet. 'But what about a bit of Balmain folk dancing? Give the cunts something to remember us by.'

Norton thought about the one that had almost decapitated him with the pinch bar. 'Okay, Billy,' he shrugged. 'If you insist. Why not?'

The members of the Rat Manners Motorcycle Club were lucky that Billy and Les were wearing running shoes, because for the next five minutes they kicked them from one side of the lounge room to the other.

In the end Les had to pull Billy off or he would have still been kicking them when the sun went down. 'Righto, Billy. Don't kill them, for Christ's sake.'

'Why not?' replied Billy, trying to kick the one with the moustache's kidneys almost out of his back.

'Because then we've got to cart them away. Leave them so they can drive themselves home.'

'Yeah, fair enough.' Billy stopped kicking and grinned at Les. 'Well, that was a bit of fun, wasn't it?'

Norton looked at the battered, moaning bikies. 'I'm glad you think so, Billy.'

'I told you I've been getting into the training.'

'I believe you, mate. I believe you.' Yeah, I wouldn't fancy fighting you myself, thought Norton. 'Well, come on. Let's get 'em out of the place. Their bikes should be out the front somewhere. They'll be able to get themselves home sooner or later.'

Billy grinned at Les. 'No worries, mate. It's downhill all the way. Just open the door.'

Les had seen Billy in this sort of mood before and knew what to expect. Jesus you're a sadistic, low bastard, Dunne, he thought. But I'm sure glad I've got you for a mate. He opened the door and Billy began flinging the bikies down the stairs as though they were sacks of onions. Eventually they got them down to their bikes, leaving a trail of blood and other stuff down the stairs for the poor cleaner to get rid of later.

The bikies were lying on the footpath next to their Harleys, not in too good a shape. Norton went to the laundry and came back with a bucket of cold water, which he threw over them. Even though they were battered, they were still tough, hard men with probably a bit of 'go fast' running through their systems, so the water brought them around. Somehow they managed to get on their bikes and glare at Les and Billy through bruised and bloodied eyes. Norton produced a piece of paper and a biro from his jeans and began taking down the registration numbers of their bikes.

'Now, you listen to me,' he said solemnly. 'I don't know who you gentlemen are, but I must warn you. Mr Scravortis here and I are the caretakers of this block of flats. And if there is any more of this outrageous behaviour from you, I will have no alternative but to call the authorities. I have the numbers of your bikes and if I see you around here again, I will not hesitate to inform the constabulary. As far as my friend and I are concerned you're a disgrace to the fine motorcycle club you represent.' The bikies glared at Les like they could have boiled him in oil. 'Now let this be a lesson to you. Violence only begets violence. My friend and

I are good Christians and we won't tolerate this behaviour. Now, go on. On your way before I call the police.'

The bikies didn't have to be told twice. Somehow they got their bikes started and after a few muttered curses, and gobbing up some blood they rumbled off towards Avoca Road.

'Jesus, you're a mug, Les,' grinned Billy. 'Good Christians. Piss off.'

'Well, I am.'

'So was Nero. Listen, come back upstairs to that flat. I want to show you something.'

'What? Is there a bikie left in there you want to kick?'

'No.' Billy was serious. 'There's something in there I want to show you.'

'Okay,' shrugged Les. 'Whatever.'

As Les took Billy back to the flat he was surprised to see no one around after all the ruckus. Then again, the fight didn't last all that long — barely a few minutes — and the only noise when they tossed the bikies out was a bit of laughing and swearing from Les and Billy. The five 'Rats' didn't say a great deal at all.

'In here,' said Billy, after Les closed the door. 'In this front bedroom.' Les followed Billy into the litter-strewn bedroom. 'On the wall next to the bed. I reckon someone's tried to write something in blood.'

Norton's eyebrows knitted. 'Turn it up, Billy.'

'No, I'm fair dinkum. I remember something like this years ago. I had a ten-rounder at Marrickville RSL. The young bloke in one of the prelims before me copped an awful hiding. He was a mess. And I remember him saying to me he was never going to fight again. They couldn't get his nose to stop bleeding and they put him on this rubbing table. And I remember to this day, him writing on the wall in his own blood, Boxing is a Bastard. Now look at this.' Billy pointed to some scrawls and smears of blood on the wall next to the bed which had dried a rusty kind of brown; if you looked at them in a certain way and used your imagination they did look like letters.

114

'Look at this,' continued Billy, running his fingers over the smears. 'There's a B. And an S. And that looks like an A. There's another B and an A and that's a T. And I don't know what that is. It looks like an N or an M or two N's or something. I reckon he's tried to write Bastards bashed me or something, before they've either sprung him or he passed out.'

Les was about to tell Billy he'd been reading too many cheap detective novels when something about the blood smears on the wall hit him between the eyes like a piece of four by two.

'Jesus Christ, Billy,' he said. 'Have another look. That is a B an S and A, all right. It stands for BSA. And the N, the T, and the M and the rest of it. You know what he's written?'

Billy looked blank.

'BSA Bantam.'

'BSA Bantam?'

'Fuckin' oath.'

'Why would he write that?'

'Come on and I'll show you.'

Fit and all as he was, Billy had trouble keeping up with Les who was taking the stairs six at a time to the storeroom.

'I didn't bother to show you this before,' said Les, as he opened the door. 'I didn't think it was worth it.' Billy blinked around in the dusty gloom of the storeroom as Norton pointed to the old motorbike standing near the wall. 'There, Billy. What's that?'

'Jesus! An old BSA Bantam. Where did that come from?'

'It belonged to Jimmy, the bloke in that flat. Old Hoppy told me he was restoring it. Whatever those five mugs wanted is in that old motorbike.'

'Christ! You could be right, Les.'

'Fuckin' oath I'm right. That crowbar's still upstairs. I'll go and get it and we'll rip the thing to pieces.'

Norton was about to make a beeline for the door when Billy grabbed him by the arm. 'Hold on. Before you go charging off like a bull at a gate, have a look at something.' He turned Les back to the motorbike. 'Notice anything?'

Norton gave the little old BSA a once-over, wiggled the handlebars and ran his hand over the seat. 'It's covered in dust is about all.'

'Yes, Watson. But notice where there's no dust.'

Les had another look. 'Round the headlight.'

'Excellent, Watson. Excellent. That headlight has either been wiped clean or replaced.' Billy peered into the headlight. 'There's no bulb, but I'm certain there's something else in there. My dear fellow, whatever it is we're after is in that headlight.'

'You could be right,' smiled Les. 'But we won't bother trying to unscrew it.' There was a small piece of rusty pipe lying on the floor next to some old paint tins. Norton bent down and picked it up. 'Stand back, Holmes,' he commanded, then swung the pipe and smashed the headlight. Glass tinkled on the floor and inside the metal shell of the headlight. Les scooped the shards of glass out with the piece of pipe. 'You're right, Billy. There is something in here.' He pulled out a clear, plastic bag that had been folded around several sheets of paper inside then squeezed around the inside of the headlight. 'Shit! What do you make of that?'

Billy looked at the rolled up plastic bag. 'Dunno. But it's too dark in here. Let's have a look inside your flat.'

Les locked the storeroom and they went back to his flat, where he took five sheets of foolscap paper from the plastic bag and lay them out next to the kitchen sink.

'Well, what the fuck do you make of that?' asked Les.

Billy looked at the papers and shook his head. 'I'm buggered if I know,' he answered slowly.

The sheets of paper were numbered one to five and consisted of typewritten text and drawings and diagrams something like Les remembered from his futile days at high school when he tried to master chemistry and science

116

lessons. There were neat sketches of plastic tanks and tubes and something that looked like a moonshine still. Everything was numbered and seemed to be laid out in instructions.

Across the top of page one was printed in capital letters: PREPARATION OF BETA-PHENYL ISO-PROPYLAMINE IN 5 KILOGRAM AMOUNTS. On the pages were strange words like: isopropic acid, phen-ylamine, acetic acid and other things.

Norton peered at the pages and shook his head. Billy was doing much the same thing only he was scratching his chin.

'Well, what do you reckon, Billy?' asked Les.

Billy shook his head. 'Buggered if I know. It might as well be a Chinese newspaper.'

'Yeah. And what's Beta-Phenyl Isopropylamine?'

'Don't ask me. Sounds like a railway station in Wales.'

They continued to scan the pages of drawings and odd scientific-sounding names when Billy snapped his fingers and looked directly at Norton.

'Hey, Les! What do bikies like?'

'I dunno,' shrugged Norton. 'Gettin' pissed. Gettin' into fights and gang bangs. Onions or whatever they call them.'

'Yeah. And what else?'

Norton had to think. 'I know, they don't mind a bit of Lou.'

'That's right. Speed.'

'I reckon those blokes we just had the stink with were half full of Lou Reed,' agreed Les, ''cause they came good pretty quick despite the flogging we gave them.'

'Right. And did you see that thing on the news last week when the cops busted that bikie gang just outside of Melbourne? They nicked 'em in a backyard laboratory with twenty kilograms of home-made speed.'

'Yeah. It was on the "7.30 Report".'

Billy's eyes lit up and he gave Les a punch on the arm. 'That's what this is. It's a fuckin' chemical break-down of how to make speed! It's a recipe.'

117

Norton turned to the papers and went through page one again. 'You're fuckin' right, Billy. Look at that: beta, phenyl, amine. I'll bet that's amphetamine. You're a bloody genius, Billy.'

'That's why they killed that bloke. They were after this. And he's tried to leave a clue for someone else. This could be worth anything to those pricks. Hah!' Billy patted the papers on the sink. 'Looks like you've got yourself a recipe for making speed, old son. All you need now is an industrial chemist and you're in business.'

Billy went into the lounge room and sat on the night-and-day, leaving Norton in the kitchen staring at the five sheets of paper. What he was thinking was anybody's business.

'So, what do you intend to do?' Billy called from the lounge room.

'Dunno,' answered Norton absently. 'I'm buggered if I do.'

'I'd burn it if I were you. The less you have to do with that shit the better.'

'Yeah, you're right,' agreed Les. 'It is bad news. It's no better than coke or smack.'

'Yep. That's right.'

Norton continued to peer at the sheets of paper for a few more moments before folding them in the plastic bag and putting them in the back pocket of his jeans. 'You fancy another mineral water?'

Billy looked at his watch. 'No, I'd better get cracking. I promised Lyndy and the kids I'd take them to the pictures this arvo.'

'Okay. I'll walk back up to your car with you.'

Les didn't have to thank Billy for backing him up in the fight, as they laughed and joked their way back to the station-wagon; that went without saying. But he did thank him for coming over when he needed him, although that more or less went without saying either. Les said he'd be back home through the week, he'd ring him and start training with him. In the meantime, still

118

say nothing to anyone about where he was or what had happened here. Billy gave Les a wink. That went without saying also. Billy tooted the horn leaving Les standing outside the hotel.

Back in the flat Les got the sheets of paper out and had another look; it still may as well have been written in Sanskrit, but at least he now knew what it was. Something Billy had said rang a note on the ever present cash register in Norton's head. And it wasn't 'burn it'. Norton folded up the papers and hid them in some clothes in his overnight-bag. He looked at his watch. It was still too good a day to be inside. Coogee Beach would be much better.

Les spent the rest of the afternoon on his banana chair reading, swimming and perving on the girls while a lot of strange thoughts floated around in his head. He had a T-bone, salad and chips at The Coogee Bay Hotel, washed down with four middies of Powers. It was eight o'clock by the time he drove back to the flat, got cleaned up and made a cup of coffee. He was debating whether to pack up and go home but the middies had given him a taste and he remembered his agreement with Warren. There was a choice pub barely a minute's walk away; why not get pissed?

Norton was in his jeans and a clean T-shirt walking out the front door when who should come tap-tap-tapping his way down the street carrying a bottle of brandy, glasses crooked, beret all over his head but old Burt and Rosie. Oddly enough it was the first of his tenants he'd seen all day. As he stopped to hold the door open, Les noticed that Burt was a bit wobbly on his pins, when he got closer he smelt like a box of rum babas.

'Hello, Burt,' he smiled. 'How are you goin' there, old mate?'

Burt swayed to a stop at the door. 'Oh, hello there, Les,' he slurred. 'How are you, my boy?'

'All right, Burt,' replied Les, patting Rosie's head as the fat old Labrador wagged its tail and rubbed itself against his leg. Norton couldn't help but think the old dog looked just as pissed as its owner. 'Been having a few, have you Burt?'

The old blind man stuck his chest out. 'Just a little something for the spirit, my boy. For the spirit.'

'Good on you, Burt. We could all do with a bit of spirit.'

'Yes. And now Rosie and I are off to bed. It's... been quite a long day.'

'Okey-doke. I'll see you later then.'

'Good luck to you, my boy.'

Les stayed at the pub about an hour or so drinking steadily. It was Sunday, so it was a bit quiet; there were a few people around but nobody he knew. After a while, he could feel himself getting drunk and quite tired, so he decided to towel it. He'd drink what beer was left in the fridge, listen to the radio and have an early night. He wondered if the bikies would come back, but he couldn't see it. Not the ones they'd belted, anyway. Maybe through the week, but not tonight. If they did, he'd hear them pull up and he could hit the toe over the back fence, anyway. He finished his last bourbon and Coke and ambled very casually back the flats.

For some strange reason again, probably because he was eight parts elephant's trunk, Les decided to have another piss down the side passage of the flats. This time in the back garden. And this time he wouldn't be cleaning it up either. They could get another bloody caretaker for all he cared. Fuck 'em. Mr Norton was handing in his notice.

Norton was piddling away against the fence, not thinking about much, just enjoying himself in his drunken state when in the middle of it, he heard a strange howling sound. It was long and low and seemed to rise and fall, then stop and start again. It was one of the weirdest noises Les had ever heard, it sounded like a dog, but unlike anything he'd ever heard before. He cocked up an ear, it was coming from somewhere inside the old block of flats. Les listened for a moment or two more. It appeared to be coming from old Burt's flat. He finished what he was doing, zipped up his fly and walked quietly round the side passage to flat two.

The light was on and although the curtain was drawn there was still enough room at the edge of the window to see inside old Burt's bedroom. It was about as sparse as his: an old, wooden double bed on a rug, a chair, a wardrobe, an equally old dressing table and a few cheap paintings on the wall. Old Burt's white stick was hanging on the end of the bed and there was a pair of trousers over the back of the chair. It was what was on the bed that made Norton's eyebrows furrow.

Rosie was on her stomach, tail up in the air, ears pinned down and her eyes darting towards the back of head. Her front paws were tied to the front of the bed with cord. Half drunk, Norton stared mystified at the old Labrador. Then, from somewhere in the bedroom, Burt materialised into view wearing his dark glasses, a shirt and nothing else. He climbed up on the bed, knelt behind Rosie then after shuffling around the howling started up again. 'Owooo-ow-ow-owooo-owooo-woooh!'

This time Norton's eyes almost bulged out of his head. He gasped in a deep breath then had to look away. Ohh, no! I don't believe it, he said to himself, almost in a complete state of shock. He had another look and quickly turned his head away as the howling continued. Norton could believe it, all right. You dirty, filthy, old bastard, Burt, cursed Norton, the soft howling now ringing in his ears. You lewd, rotten, disgusting old prick. You complete arsehole. '*Owooo-ow-ow-owooo*!'. The howling continued.

Norton had another quick look then tremulously tore himself away from the window. No, bugger this, he cursed, I'm not copping that in my block of flats. He strode towards the hallway, determined to bang on Burt's door and put an end to it. Then he stopped. What could

121

he really do? Kick the old blind bloke and his dog out? Ring the RSPCA? Get in touch with the Guide Dogs Association? Maybe this sort of thing went on all the time. And what was that thing he and Warren had read in the paper the other week? Someone had caught a fieldhand in Zimbabwe having sex with a cow and the judge gave him three months. And some crazed disc jockey had read it out on air and some bloke had rung him up complaining about the severity of the sentence, and asking what was wrong? The disc jockey never knew when he might get cold himself one night and feel like slipping into a Jersey. What would he say about old Burt? Pretty much the same thing. How many people go out and get drunk, then get into a Blue? Norton was stumped. He shook his head, ran a hand across his eyes and went inside.

He had one more beer before going to bed — after that he needed something. When he finished he crawled onto the night-and-day and jammed his head into the pillow, positive he could still hear Rosie howling. Considering everything, he managed to get to sleep all right.

Eight-thirty the following morning found Les with the car packed, sitting on the wall of the garage opposite Blue Seas, sipping an orange juice. He was staring at the old block of flats and reflecting on the whole shitty, rotten scene of the last few days. What was going through his mind wasn't actually turning him on either. The bottom line was that his million-dollar investment, Blue Seas Apartments, was a dog all round. The only thing it had going for it, Sandra the artist, the girl he fancied and was going to sweep off her feet, hardly knew he existed. Besides that, she was pulling more tricks than Mandrake the Magician. There was a team of soapy hippies living on a pittance who wouldn't give him the time of day, plus an old blind drunk who was porking his guide dog. Norton gobbed towards the gutter and took another sip of orange juice. There'd been an obvious murder in one of the flats and by not reporting it to the police and giving them the information he had, he could be charged with withholding evidence and conspiracy. That was a definite worry. Then he'd let himself be bonked by some sheila in a band who had to be the most cold-hearted moll he'd ever come across and he was lucky her boyfriend or whatever he was hadn't killed him. And then the rest of the band had turned on him like he was the greatest cunt in the world. On top of that, the place was falling down around his ears; he'd lost money already and was losing around another four hundred or so a week. But there was something else about the old block of flats he just couldn't quite put his finger on. Something very fishy — very fishy indeed. He took another mouthful of orange juice and continued to stare balefully at the old block of flats.

No, it was a sad fact of life — Blue Seas Apartments had to go, and the sooner the better. But how? Well how was pretty obvious. The block would have to be hit by Jewish lightning. Or what about a nice Lebanese stocktake. But those two particular things were a bit passe and old hat. What's wrong with a Romanian midsummer clearance? And Norton knew just the person to organise it. He was owed a favour, a big one, and it was time to pull that favour in. He finished his orange juice, tossed the container in the nearest bin and started walking over to his car. Halfway across the road, he patted the pocket which contained the recipe he and Billy had found in the old BSA, looked up at the sky and grinned. Yes, boss, Norton said to himself. There just might be a way out of this yet. He kicked the old Ford over and headed towards Bondi.

Christ, I wonder what I'm going to tell Woz, Les smiled to himself when he pulled up in Cox Avenue and saw his flatmate's red Celica still parked out the front of the house. I s'pose I'll think of some bloody thing. Norton was smiling and whistling to himself as he opened the front door — yes it sure was good to be back home again. The decent shower, his own double bed with a

123

proper mattress, stereo, TV, and to be able to cook a steak on a decent stove. If Les was whistling and smiling when he opened the front door, it abruptly stopped when he walked down the hallway into the lounge room. He propped and gave a double, triple blink as his jaw dropped. There were empty bottles and glasses all over the place; plus records, tapes, ashtrays half full of cigarette butts, chip packets and a host of other odds and ends.

In the kitchen Warren was sitting hunched over a cup of coffee in his white shave-coat, looking like death warmed up.

'Hello, Les, how are you?' he said.

Norton blinked at Warren almost in disbelief. '"Hello Les, how are you?"' he echoed. 'Hello Les. Don't fuckin' "hello Les" me, you cunt. What the fuck's been going on here?'

'I had a bit of a party.'

'You had a bit of a party. A party. I'm not out of the place five minutes, and you're throwing parties. In *my* fuckin' house.'

'Well, I didn't know where you were. You left no message. You didn't ring. Knowing the life you lead and the people you run with, I thought you were dead.'

'You thought I was dead, eh?' Les went to the lounge room and came back with an empty Jack Daniels bottle. 'And what happened to going off the piss for a week?'

'Well, that's what started it. When I thought you were dead, I was gripped with remorse. And I hit the bottle again.'

'You rotten, lying little toerag.'

Norton picked up his overnight bag and the ghetto blaster and went to his room.

He was back almost before he left glaring and pointing an accusing finger at Warren. 'Somebody's had a fuck in my bed. You low, dirty cunt, Warren Edwards.'

'Nobody's had a fuck in your bed,' groaned Warren. 'And please, Les. Do you have to shout?'

'Well who's been in it? Don't say it was the cat, 'cause we ain't got a fuckin' cat.'

124

'It was the girl I was with last night. She . . . she didn't want to sleep with me 'cause I was too drunk. And it was late, so she dossed in your bed. She left about half an hour ago.'

'Hah!' snorted Norton. 'I see nothing's changed since I've been gone. Party or no party. You still can't get a root, you poor silly cunt. You're hopeless.'

Warren stared into his coffee mug for a moment, then decided to go on the offensive himself. 'So where have you been anyway, you prick? The least you could have done is rung. And what happened to your face and your bloody neck? You come in here abusing me in my time of grief for practically no reason at all. You've got a bit of explaining to do yourself, you fuckin' big dope.'

Norton went to the sink and switched on the electric kettle. Warren's sudden attack flummoxed him a bit and he had to try hard not to smile. 'Well,' he said, as he fossicked around getting a mug of coffee together. 'the reason I didn't ring, is because I've been shacked up with a married woman while her husband was overseas. And as you know, Warren, that's not my go.'

'Hello. The Queensland sex symbol's got himself into a bit of scandal, eh?'

'Sort of. She's only young and she's married to this rich old bloke. I knew her from the Kelly Club. She's always been chasing me — she rang me, so I discreetly went over to her place for a few days and hung round the pool. She's got a big joint over at Seaforth.'

'And what happened to your head?'

'Well, one morning I heard this noise and I thought it was her husband coming home, so I leapt out the window into the garden and hit my head on some rocks.' The kettle boiled and Les poured his coffee. 'But it was only the caretaker come round to fix a leaky tap in the kitchen.'

'Hah! Serves you right.'

'And these,' Les pulled the neck of his T-shirt down, 'they're love-bites. She was one hell of a lover, I can tell you that, Warren, me old mate.'

125

'Christ! It looks like she tried to strangle you.'

'She did. With her tongue.' Norton took a sip of coffee and smiled at his flatmate. 'Unlike you, dry-balls, I have been getting my end in. In fact Warren, I'm convinced that after your recent run of outs, the only way you're ever going to get laid is to crawl up a chicken's arse and wait.'

'Ha-ha-ha! Very bloody droll.'

'Anyway, Woz, to cut a long story short: Rosie's husband was due home this morning, so here I am. The landlord's back in town. Sober and not hungover like some pisspot too, I might add.'

'How wonderful.'

'Yes. And don't get too comfortable sitting there, soupbones. You've got a lot of cleaning up to do before you bundy on at the pickle factory.'

'Don't shit yourself. I don't have to be at the office till lunchtime.'

Norton took his coffee into the lounge room and surveyed the evidence of the previous night's festivities. 'And if there's one fuckin' scratch, one tiny scratch on any of my Hunters And Collectors albums...' Norton's eyes narrowed as he turned to Warren, 'your future in the cosy warmth of Maison Norton could be very bleak, old son. Very bleak indeed.'

Warren shook his head and stared into his coffee. 'Why couldn't that woman's husband have stayed away another week? It was just starting to get good.'

With Norton helping as much as berating, they were able to get the house cleaned up and Warren off to work by eleven-thirty. Les wanted to get into Warren a bit more about having parties behind his back, but after a nice shower and a change of clothes, being back at home after that flophouse in Randwick had him in too good a mood; plus the look of remorse on Warren's face mixed with the misery of his hangover was satisfaction enough. Warren was gone about ten minutes when Norton made another cup of coffee, got a clipboard and a biro and sat down on the lounge near the phone.

126

He made a few notations on the clipboard and fixed the six sheets of paper from the old BSA plus the number-plates of the gang's motorbikes he'd taken down on there as well. The notations and tiny drawings looked almost like a plan of battle. What he was going to try and pull off, a very dubious earn and get rid of his old block of flats, was not something you took lightly. In a way, it was a battle campaign, and Les would treat it as such. He made a few more notations, did a bit of adding and subtracting and had a think. After a while, Norton gave a grunt of satisfaction and decided it was time to make some phone calls.

'Hello, George. How are you, mate?' said Norton. 'It's Les.'

'Well, if it isn't the boy wonder from the deep north,' replied George Brennan cheerfully. 'How are you, shifty?'

'Not bad, George. How's yourself?'

'Terrific. Did Billy tell you what's going on up at the club?'

'Yeah. I saw him down the beach on Sunday. He said you're all getting it pretty easy.'

'Easy? Without you up there to annoy me, it's almost like a paid holiday. It's beautiful. Price tried to ring you to see if you and Billy want to do it week about. But you've never been home.'

'No. I've been running around with this sheila I met. I've been staying at her place.'

'Where did you find this one? The Taxi Club?'

'No, outside the Matt Talbot. I shouted her a flagon of sweet sherry.'

They chitchatted away for a while, with George doing his best to rubbish Les and Les happy to feed the jovial, fat, casino manager a string of lies. Then they got down to the business at hand.

'So, what can I do for you anyway, Les, me old currant bun?'

'You still got that nephew working out the Roads and Traffic Authority?'

'Yes. The bludging little arsehole is still there.'

127

'I got the number of a motorbike. I need to find out who owns it.'

'No worries. Give it to me. I'll ring Shithead up and get straight back to you.'

'Good on you, George.'

Les consulted the clipboard in front of him, circled the numberplate he assumed belonged to the leader of the bikies that day, gave it to George then hung up. George rang back in around ten minutes.

'Fuckin' cunt,' was the first thing he said. 'He just tried to snip me for five hundred dollars. The little prick.'

'Did he have any luck, Uncle George?'

'None. Anyway, here's the bloke you're looking for. That bike belongs to Michael Ryan Sutton, 232 Carinyah Road, Bonnyrigg.'

'Christ! That *is* out west,' said Norton, writing the address down.

'I assume you're going out there to bash this bloke, Les. What did he do? Steal your one pair of socks off the line?'

'No, George. Warren sprung him knocking off a bottle of milk out the front.'

'That'd be a good enough reason for you.'

They joked on the phone for a few more minutes then Les hung up, saying he'd call into the club one night and have a drink.

Norton looked at the name and address and drummed his fingers on the clipboard. Michael Sutton — that would be right, because he remembered the other bikies answering to him as Mick. Well, if Mick was the boss, he'd almost certainly be in the phone book. Les picked up the White Pages and looked under S. It was there, all right. He wrote it down on the notepad, circled it, and had a quick think. What was that old saying? Strike while the iron is hot. Yes, there's certainly no time like the present. He dialled again and this time a nasally whining woman's voice answered.

'Hello,' it drawled.

'Yes. Is Mick there please?'

'I dunno,' replied the voice carefully. 'I'll have a look. Who'll I say it is?'

Norton had to think for a moment. If he said he was anyone to do with the old block of flats Mick probably wouldn't come to the phone. Bikies generally all have nicknames like Jacko, Davo, Oily, Smelly, Greaseball... He lifted one cheek of his backside off the lounge and farted.

'Tell him it's Stinky,' he said, waving at the smell with the clipboard.

Les could hear footsteps, a TV going in the background, some dogs barking, then more heavy footsteps. Then someone picked up the phone.

'Yeah, this is Mick. Who's this?'

'Hello, Mick, me old mate,' replied Norton happily. 'It's Mr Smith here, the caretaker of those flats at Randwick. I met you on Sunday.'

Sitting painfully in his weatherboard Bonnyrigg cottage, with six broken ribs, a couple of teeth missing and stitches and bruising all over his head, Mick wasn't ready for or wanting this. Norton had to hold the phone almost a foot away from his ear at the bikie leader's reply.

'What the fuck do you want?!!! How did you get this fuckin' number?!!'

'I wrote down the number of your motorbike, Mick. Easy.'

'Why you! Go and get — '

'Now hold on, Mick,' cut in Les. 'Don't be like that. I've rung up to help you.'

'The only way you could help me, you cunt, is to —'

'Yeah, I know,' interrupted Norton 'fall into a vat of boiling sump oil. But the thing is, Mick, I think I've found what you and your friends were looking for.' This slowed the big bikie up and stopped him from slamming down the phone. Les could hear his angry breathing and picture the look on his face. He smiled to himself as he recollected pulling a stroke something like this

129

before and moved the point of the biro across page one of the recipe. 'Does "Preparation of Beta-Phenyl Isopropylamine In Five Kilogram Amounts" mean anything to you, Mick?' Norton swore he could almost hear the bikie's face screw up and his eyes click over the phone. 'What about, "Acetic Acid in a two litre induction flask, heat to 280° fahrenheit"?' Norton flicked through the pages. "Benzol-Pschyloprine, Sodium Iso"... Shit! There's six pages of this stuff here and I can't even pronounce half of it. But it's all here. Retort stands, ketones. And I'm pretty certain it's what you're looking for, Mick.' Norton waited for a moment. 'Are you there, Mick?'

'Yeah, I'm fuckin' here,' hissed the big bikie. 'Listen, where did you get that?'

'Where? In that flat. Where do you think?'

'You fuckin' —'

'Now hold on Mick. It's no good getting the shits. The thing is, it's a recipe for crank. I've got it and you want it. And I'm more than willing to let you have it. But like I told you on Sunday, Mick, me and my mate are very religious people. And before we give it to you, you're going to have to make quite a considerable donation to the church.' Norton could sense the bikie's rage over the phone at the almost futile position he was in. Now it was time to really stir the pot. 'You can have it back for a hundred thousand dollars.'

'*What*!!! You know what you can fuckin' well do.'

'No,' chuckled Les, 'but I can imagine. A hundred grand, Mick. I'll ring you tomorrow morning at ten sharp. You got that?' The bikie didn't reply but Les knew he was still on the line. 'A hundred grand, you get your recipe back — I don't give it to the cops and I don't take them up to flat five and tell them what I think happened to Jimmy. It'd be a good bust for them, Mick. They'd love that, on the news and everything. I'll ring you tomorrow morning, ten a.m.'

Norton hung up and couldn't help but laugh out loud. Well, I reckon that might've put a cat amongst the pigeons, he mused. Or a cat among the rats — whatever the case may be. Norton got up, made a fresh cup of coffee, came back to the phone and once again studied the clipboard. So, that's phase one of Operation Blue Seas completed. Now, what about phase two? This time Les got the Sydney Yellow Pages. He let his fingers do the walking till he found what he was looking for: The Seven Gypsies Restaurant at Enmore.

Norton had met an unbelievable number of people since he came to Sydney from Queensland, mainly through working at The Kelly Club. Some he wished he'd never met, others he was glad he had. Grigor Ciotsa sort of fell into a grey area. Les first met him when he was driving a delivery truck for a meatworks in Ultimo. Grigor had not long migrated to Australia from Romania and he used to hustle Scotch fillets and rumps and stuff in the restaurant trade. This was just a temporary use so he could cement himself as a good Aussie citizen before getting into what he was best at: in Grigor's case, moving drugs, stolen cars, insurance scams and — his speciality — arson. Before he came to Australia, Grigor Ciotsa was a captain in the Romanian Securitate — an explosives expert. He must have read the writing on the wall and got out of Romania years before all the shit hit the fan there, with the fall of the Ceacescu dictatorship and got his brother Vaclav out to Australia not long afterwards.

Grigor got out of hustling meat long before Les got into football and working on the door at the Kelly Club, which was where he bumped into Grigor again. By now Grigor and his brother had well and truly established themselves in the Sydney crime scene and, like most crime figures, didn't mind getting into a bit of heavy gambling to wash away a bit of black money. And what better place to do it than the Kelly Club? It was well run, the mugs didn't get in, only the cream of Sydney's underworld frequented the place and whenever Grigor, Vaclav or their heavies lobbed up to splurge a few grand, Grigor's old compatriot from the meatworks was on

131

the door to greet them and send them straight up the stairs with a laugh and a joke thrown in. For all his rotten villainy, Les didn't mind Grigor, even if he was one of those schizoid types who could laugh and joke with you one day, then think nothing of it if he had to blow your head off the next. But there were two things that really cemented Les to Grigor and his brother, and they happened barely a month apart.

On the first occasion it wasn't all that much. Grigor's brother left the club early one night, leaving Grigor to punt on almost to the death and head home very drunk with about fifteen grand in his kick. Les and Billy offered to put Grigor in a taxi but, full of piss and bravado, he said he was going to have a meal and a coffee with some friends. After the club closed, Les and Billy walked to their cars. As was usual at that time of the morning Norton was feeling a bit peckish, so he decided to walk back up to the Cross and get a lamb yeeros. It was lucky for Grigor he did, because just before he got to the main road he saw the Romanian ambling drunkenly towards him with four young hoods right behind like a pack of wolves getting ready for the kill. They pounced on Grigor and even though he wasn't doing too bad, considering how drunk he was, his luck was fast running out until Norton lobbed on the scene. Between Les and Grigor, who was now on his feet, the four hoods were wishing they'd never been born, let alone come up the Cross that night — particularly when Grigor pulled out a knife and wanted to cut their throats. But this time Les bundled him into a cab and wouldn't take no for an answer.

The following night, Grigor was back at the club with a couple of his heavies, and two thousand dollars was shoved in Norton's hand whether he wanted it or not.

Helping someone out in a fight is a pretty good favour, but for a bloke like Les it was almost taken for granted — he'd done it that many times he'd lost count. But the thing that really cemented Norton to the Ciotsas happened two or three weeks later.

132

It was a late-summer Sunday afternoon on Bondi Beach with not all that many people around. Norton was walking arm in arm along the water's edge with some British Airways hostess he'd met somewhere, doing his best to act the romantic lover with the sun going down, the waves breaking on the sand, and the seagulls in the air. They just happened to be at the south end of the beach at the same time as Vaclav, who was there with his wife and four year old son. Vaclav had walked up to the car for something, leaving his wife on the beach. She turned her back for barely a second and kids being kids, the little boy jumped in the water, and was washed out by a wave into the rip that always forms at South Bondi between the rocks and the baths. Norton saw the woman screaming and the kid's head bobbing out to sea in the rip. The nearest boardrider was fifty metres away so, without thinking, he plunged in, drifted out with the rip, grabbed the terrified kid, got him up on the rocks and carried him back to his mother. Vaclav was walking back and heard all the commotion and could scarcely believe his eyes when he saw Norton carrying his son back to his wife who was yammering away in Romanian at the top of her voice. Really it was no big deal. Lifesavers and beach inspectors did more spectacular things hundreds of times every weekend and barely got thanks, let alone any recognition for it.

But to Vaclav and his wife, both non-swimmers, it was the most heroic deed they'd ever seen, and to them Norton was Indiana Jones, Tarzan and The Man From Snowy River all rolled into one. And when Uncle Grigor, the Don Corleone of the Romanian community, found out that Norton had not only saved his neck, but his loving nephew's life as well, it was a different matter altogether. It was almost a ceremony when he and Vaclav called round to the Kelly Club to thank him through the week. Les refused to take the money they offered, but the way Grigor put it, Les was now almost part of the family, and if he didn't give the Romanian a chance to show his gratitude in some way at some time, it would be an insult to Grigor's standing in the Romanian community. In Grigor's words, he owed Les Norton a debt of honour in blood. A debt that must be repaid.

Les knew that Grigor worked out of his restaurant at Enmore, which was little more than a front for his nefarious deeds, and tipped that he'd be there early in the week. He laughed to himself as he dialled. Oh well, Grigor, old buddy, old pal, you want to repay a debt of honour? Norton's laughter turned into a shrewd smile as he heard the phone ringing at the other end. This could be your big chance. And honour is honour.

'Hello,' came a thick, guttural voice.

'Could I speak to Grigor, please?'

'I am not sure he is in,' the voice said carefully. 'I will look. Who calls please?'

'Tell him it's Les Norton from the Kelly Club.'

There were heavy footsteps, a door slammed, more heavy footsteps then a cheerful, foreign voice boomed down the phone. 'Les Norton, my friend! My very good friend. How are you, Les?'

'Pretty good, Grigor. How's yourself?'

'Excellent, excellent. One hundred per cent. I hear of the trouble you are having at the club. A bad thing this.'

'Yeah. It's a bit of a bummer, all right, Grigor,' agreed Les. 'But that's the way it goes.'

'I would like to think you are ringing me for a job, Les Norton. Straight away I can do something for a man of your calibre.'

'No, Grigor. But thanks for the offer.'

'It is my pleasure — as you know, my good friend.'

'Actually, Grigor, I wanted to see you about something entirely different.'

'Yes?' answered the Romanian slowly, starting to get the picture already.

'I'd like to call over and see you if I could.'

'That is no problem — I would prefer that. I am not a man who likes to discuss, shall we say, personal matters over the phone.'

'Yeah. Not these days anyway. Could I come over tomorrow?'

'Of course, my friend. What time?'

'Say... eleven tomorrow morning?'

'No problem at all. Would you like to join me for lunch? We do an excellent Chicken Dniester at my restaurant.'

'No, just a cup of coffee'll do, thanks Grigor.'

'Then I shall look forward to your visit tomorrow, my friend. You know where it is?'

'Yeah. Enmore Road. Just down from the pub.'

'Tomorrow at eleven, then, Les.'

'See you then, Grigor.'

Well, that's the start of phase two, thought Norton, staring absently at the phone after he'd hung up. For better or for bloody worse. Now what will I do for the rest of the day? Will I have a feed or a run?

No, bugger it. I'll have a run, then cook something for tea and annoy the shit out of that little bastard Warren when he comes all hungover and crook tonight. Parties behind my back... Sorry Les, but I thought you were dead — taking advantage of the landlord like that. What a hide.

Norton had a run along Bondi Beach and a swim then spent the rest of the afternoon deep in thought as he pottered around the house. By the time he'd got a corner cut of topside baked and the vegetables done Warren was home looking exactly how Les hoped he'd look: tired and still a bit seedy.

'So? said Norton, sitting in the kitchen sipping a can of lemonade. 'The Great Gatsby's home. What's doing tonight, Gats? Another party?'

'Please, Les,' replied Warren, heading straight for the fridge and the mineral water. 'I've had a cunt of a day at work. I'm totally fucked, and I'm not in the mood for any verbal repartee.'

'Yeah? Not like last night, when you were running round here like Jack the lad, wrecking my beautiful house?'

Warren ignored Les and poured himself a glass of Hepburn Spa.

'You hungry?' asked Les.

'Yeah, I am, actually.'

'Well I've got a nice roast of beef in the oven. Why don't you get changed and have a shower and shitty old Les the Landlord'll have it waiting on the table for you when you come out.'

Despite himself, Warren couldn't help but smile. 'Have you honestly been off the drink all week?'

Norton nodded and held up the can of lemonade. 'And I'm still off it too.'

Warren shook his head. 'Jesus! I wish I had your willpower.'

'Yeah, well that's it, ain't it? Some of us have, and some of us haven't. Go on, go and have a scrub before I change my mind and send you down for a pizza.'

They ripped into the roast beef, cleaned up and settled back to watch the Monday night movie. Ironically, the movie was an old John Wayne thing about Red Adair the firefighter. Norton could barely conceal his amusement and would have loved to have said something to Warren. Instead, he was in bed not long after Warren, around eleven.

Tuesday was warm, bright and sunny with the summer nor'easter barely rippling the ocean when Norton got out of his car at North Bondi for a run at seven o'clock. He wanted his head nice and clear for what he had to do that day, so he jogged eight laps of the beach deep in thought, had a swim, then a cold shower on the promenade.

He was home when Warren surfaced just after eight; and although the young advertising genius was in decidedly better shape than the previous morning, he still mumbled and stumbled around the house getting his shit together. Norton put on a clean pair of jeans and a T-shirt, got some eggs and coffee into Warren and had him ready for work by nine.

'Jesus! Roast beef for tea last night. Poached eggs this morning...' Warren smiled and jangled his car keys at Les, who was still sitting in the kitchen reading the paper. 'If you weren't such an ugly, miserable big cunt it'd be almost good having you back home.'

'Just remember what I said, Woz,' replied Norton, without looking up from the paper. 'One scratch on those Hunters And Collectors albums... Just one, tiny scratch...'

Warren blew Les a kiss from the kitchen doorway. 'I'll be home about five-thirty Mum. Don't burn my dinner.'

Norton cleaned up in the kitchen, made another cup of coffee and went through the paper again. Before long it was ten and he went into the lounge room to the phone. He dialled Bonnyrigg, recognising the voice at the other end. 'Is that you, Mick?'

'Yeah, this is Mick,' came the surly reply.

'I thought it was. This is Mr Smith the caretaker. How are you mate?'

'You can knock up with the fucking around, pal. Get to the point. What do you want?'

'Jeez, we are titchy this morning, aren't we? Okay, Mick. Like I said, a hundred grand.'

'There's no way we can come up with a hundred grand.'

'You can't? Jesus, what a lousy, low lot of bikies you bunch are. Well, how much have you got?'

'Fifty.'

'Fifty! Fuck off. It'll take fifty grand just to recarpet that beautiful home unit you ruined. Come on, Mick. Get fair dinkum.'

'Fifty. It's the best we can do.'

'Bloody hell!' Norton thought for a moment or two. 'I'll make it seventy-five. And that's the best I can do.'

'Jesus...'

'Come on, Mick. That's my last offer or I go to the wallopers. Like a good, concerned citizen should.'

There was heavy breathing on the other end of the line then a hand went over the phone and Norton had an idea Mick wasn't alone in the house.

'All right!' Mick's voice came back. 'Seventy-five.'

'Good man. Now, I'll tell you what we'll do. You know that garage on the corner opposite the flats?'

'Yeah.'

'I'll meet you there tomorrow morning at ten-thirty sharp.'

'All right.'

'How many of you'll be there?'

'Four of us. We'll be in a blue, 1967 Ford.'

'Okay. I'll be waiting on the corner at ten-thirty. And don't get too many funny ideas.'

'We'll see you in the morning. Ten-thirty,' came the inimical reply.

Well, that's that, thought Les, after he hung up. A bit of luck, and I should have a nice seventy-five in the bin tomorrow. He stared at the phone for a moment. But I trust those crankheads about as far as I could place-kick a dead walrus. Should I take some help with me? He drummed his fingers on the coffee table. No, the less people know about all this the better. I think I know what to do.

Norton glanced at his watch. It was about time to go and see his old mate from Romania.

Grigor's restaurant wasn't hard to find; Les got held up in the Enmore Road traffic just before the lights at the Enmore Hotel. Unlike the Romanian flag the place was all dark brown, edged with red and white. There was a solid, double wooden door on one side, a plate glass window on the other with a number of plants and palms on a ledge at the bottom. Above this was a sign in red saying The Seven Gypsies Restaurant and an image of a caravan and a man with an earring in one ear, a red scarf on his head, and a violin tucked under his chin. Norton took a left at the lights into Edgeware Road and found a parking spot on a lot behind the Enmore Medical Centre. The door to the restaurant was locked when Les walked back. Les knocked. When the door opened a minute or so later, the person standing

138

there wasn't Grigor and his nickname definitely wasn't Smiling Jim. He was about six feet twelve with oily, black hair, high cheekbones and typical jowly, Slavic features.

'Yes?' he said bluntly, looking down at Norton.

'Is Grigor in?' asked Les. 'He's expecting me. My name's Les Norton.'

'Moment.' The heavy closed the door and was back about half a minute later. But this time he was smiling. 'Please to come in,' he said, with a slight bow of his head and a gesture with his arm. 'Sorry you must wait, but —'

'That's okay, mate,' replied Les and stepped inside.

The restaurant was fairly dark and it took a moment or two for Norton's eyes to adjust. The ceiling was black and the carpet was dark brown. There were mirror tiles on one wall, paintings, murals and Romanian flags on the other. Three rows of chairs and tables led to the kitchen and a servery at the rear, square tables on the outside, round ones in the middle. Les was peering around, still trying to adjust to the darkness when a voice boomed out from a cubicle in the far right-hand corner.

'Les! Down here, my friend.'

With a friendly grin on his face and wearing a brown, check suit, Grigor was seated next to his brother. Like the heavy on the door, Grigor too had oily, black hair and the same, jowly Slavic features. A pair of bushy eyebrows topped a pair of dark brown eyes and a slightly broken nose. Unlike the heavy, Grigor was shorter and stockier with a barrel chest and a paunch. Between his days hustling Scotch fillets and being a restaurant owner, it was obvious that Grigor hadn't gone without too many feeds since he arrived in Australia. Sitting next to him in a dark blue suit Vaclav looked much the same only a little leaner and without the broken nose. They both stood up and Grigor offered his hand.

'Hello, Les. It is good to see you.'

'Yeah. You too Grigor.' Norton took the Romanian's strong, friendly grip and he did the same with his brother. 'G'day, Vaclav. How are you mate?'

139

'Excellent,' replied Vaclav. 'And may I say it is a pleasure to see you at our place for a change.'

'Yeah. And during daylight too,' agreed Les.

Grigor said something to the heavy in Romanian and turned to Les. 'You want coffee, Les? Good coffee.' Norton nodded, Grigor said something else to the heavy then motioned for Les to sit down.

'So, how is it to be out of work, Les?' asked Vaclav.

'It's a tough old world, Vaclav,' winked Norton. 'But I think I'll get by somehow.'

'I am certain you will,' chuckled Grigor.

They exchanged small talk for a while, the Kelly Club, their restaurant, old times at the meatworks etc, as the heavy returned with a pot of coffee and other things on a tray which he placed on the table before disappearing once more into the kitchen. They finished one cup of coffee and were started on another when the conversation began to settle down a little and Grigor decided to get to the nitty-gritty.

'So, Les, my good friend. Now what is it my brother and I can do for you?'

Norton took another sip of coffee then put the cup down and looked directly at the Romanian. 'Are you still handy with a box of matches, Grigor?'

The two brothers looked at each other for a moment then roared laughing. Grigor reached across and gave Norton a friendly slap on the shoulder that almost knocked him out of the cubicle.

'By golly, I like this man,' he laughed. 'Are we still good with the box of matches? Of course we are. We are the *best*! We are number one with the box of matches.' They both roared with laughter again, then Grigor continued. 'So, Les. Tell us your problem.'

Over the rest of the pot of coffee, Norton told them all about the block of flats. Where it was, the condition, how big it was, who lived there. What the council intended doing, how much the place was costing him and what he intended doing.

'So, that's it, fellas. The place is a complete fuckin'

lemon and I want to torch it for the insurance. I know you're the best. How much do you want to do it?'

Suddenly both brother's faces went very serious.

'What was that you just said Les?' intoned Vaclav.

'I said how much do you want do to it?' repeated Norton.

Grigor reached across the table and gripped Norton's forearm. 'You must never mention money to us, Les,' he said, slowly and deliberately.

'Your money is no good in this restaurant,' added Vaclav. 'Here or any place else where my brother and I are.'

'Well, I just thought . . .' shrugged Norton.

'Don't even think of money, let alone discuss it before we two Ciotsa brothers,' said Grigor.

'Okay, fair enough,' said Les. 'It's just — '

'You are family to us, Les Norton,' said Vaclav. 'We are the ones in debt to you.'

'All right. I'm sorry.'

'So you should be,' Vaclav nodded.

There was silence for a few seconds, then Grigor spoke. 'So, Les. You say this old block of flats is over at Randwick?'

'Yeah. Not far from the hospital, just near the Royal Hotel.'

Grigor turned to his brother then back to Les. 'What is wrong with us going there now?' He gave a shrug. 'We have a look. Then we know one hundred per cent what we are to do.'

'Righto. Suits me,' said Les.

'Where are you parked?' asked Vaclav.

Les told them where his car was. Grigor said to wait in it, they would get theirs and follow him back to Randwick, but just park a hundred or so metres down the street. Les said he understood then finished his coffee and the heavy opened the door with another smile and Norton stepped out into the busy street.

Well, that's all right, he thought, as he walked back to his car. The boys are going to do it for nothing.

141

I'm in front already. Just as long as they don't fuck up. Nah, I can't see it — not those two villains. And I reckon they might do an extra special job on this one. Norton grinned to himself. And why shouldn't they? After all, honour is honour. I almost drowned saving Vaclav's kid in those mountainous seas.

Norton was sitting in his car when a dark blue Mercedes saloon with tinted windows cruised into the parking lot. The driver's side window was down and Les could see the heavy behind the wheel. Norton gave him a nod and drove back out into Edgeware Road. Less than half an hour later they were parked just down from the garage opposite the old block of flats. Les waited in the car as the two brothers walked up to him.

'Is that the place on the corner?' asked Grigor, nodding in the direction of Blue Seas Apartments.

'Yeah, that's it.'

'You wait here, then. We shall not be long.'

Norton switched on the car radio and read the paper.

They were back in less than twenty minutes. Grigor got in the front, Vaclav sat in the back; both had smiles on their faces.

'Well? What do you reckon?' said Norton.

'It is, how you say?' said Grigor 'A piece of piss.'

'Yeah?' Norton was pleased and at the same time surprised that there was nothing to stuff things up.

'Those old wooden stairs,' said Vaclav. 'The tar roof, the gas coppers in the laundry. I am curious an old place like that has not caught fire on its own. It is a death trap. There were some women sunbaking on the roof too. But they did not see us.'

'Don't worry about them,' said Les. 'They live there.'

'I tell you one thing,' said Grigor. 'When it does go, nothing will stop it. She will be off like the rotten fishcake,' he added with a laugh.

'Suits me,' replied Les. 'I'm only sorry I bought the fuckin' joint in the first place. So what do you intend to do? Or should I just mind my own business?'

'That is all right,' said Grigor. 'Do you know something of explosives, Les?'

'I've used gelignite and I know how to make a home-made bomb.'

'Have you heard of Semtex?' asked Vaclav.

'Semtex.' Norton had to think for a moment. 'Isn't that what the IRA and the terrorists use on the planes?'

'Correct,' nodded Grigor. 'It comes from Czechoslovakia. What we use is the next grade up. RT–66.'

'RT–66?' shrugged Les. 'Never heard of it.'

'Nor should you. It is the new generation of explosive. I helped to develop it when I was in the army. Only four people besides my brother know the formula; and three of them are dead.'

'It is two explosives in one,' said Vaclav. 'Do you know of the toothpaste called Stripe? How it comes from the tube?' Norton nodded. 'This one is much the same in appearance. The two components, they are counteracting each other, causing the implosion rather than the explosion.'

'I think I get the picture,' said Les.

'We put it in the right places,' said Grigor. 'First comes like the small explosion. Then all the gasses build up and three minutes later a massive fireball will hit the tar-covered roof, comes one more explosion then the lot comes down on those old gas coppers... and that is it, Les. The whole rotten place will fall in. Three minutes at most. Insurance company will think gas explosion. Beautiful.'

'What about the people inside?'

'That is not our concern,' shrugged Grigor.

'When do you wish us to do it, Les?' asked Vaclav.

'Shit! I hadn't really thought,' replied Norton.

'We must know before the weekend,' said Grigor. 'On Sunday we take our families to Tasmania. My brother and I we go trout fishing.'

Christ! What a couple of nice blokes. Blow up a block of flats, too bad if almost a dozen people get killed — that wasn't their concern. Then go off trout fishing

143

as if nothing had happened. Shit! Just what have I got myself into? Les had to think for a moment.

'How about I ring you tomorrow afternoon?'

'Two-thirty at the restaurant?' said Vaclav.

'Okay,' agreed Les. 'Two-thirty tomorrow. I should know by then.'

Grigor slapped Les on the back and laughed. 'Then it is done.' He and Vaclav once again shook hands with Les to cement the deal. 'We go now and organise things. Give us a minute or two before you yourself leave.'

'Okay. Well, thanks, Grigor. And you too, Vaclav.'

'It is our pleasure. We hear from you tomorrow.'

They got back in the Mercedes. Les watched them leave then after a minute or two headed for Bondi himself. As he drove past the Royal he snatched a glance at the old block of flats in the rearview mirror. Jesus, just what have I got myself into here? he thought.

The ramifications of what he was about to do and the chain of events he was going to set in motion now began to weigh on Norton's mind. It had all more or less started out as a bit of a lark. Burn down the old block of flats, collect the insurance then have a drink and a laugh and a joke about it afterwards. The people that happened to live in the flats had scarcely entered his mind; except in rancour. If this thing went wrong eleven people could die, and he was now dealing with ruthless, hardcore men to whom killing meant little more than changing their socks. As Grigor quite succinctly put it, 'that is not our concern'.

If this thing soured, Les would be left to well and truly carry the can. He couldn't shelf Grigor and his brother. Forget about the honour and family bullshit; if it came to saving their own necks they would kill him with no more feeling than if they were swatting a fly. There'd be a police investigation and if the insurance company smelled a rat and he got convicted the wash up was he'd get life imprisonment and go down as one of the most notorious mass murderers in Australian history. It would be the Whisky Au Go Go all

144

over again. It wasn't too late to pull out, but then it would be back to square one with that dead albatross in Randwick around his neck again and Grigor and his brother thinking he was just another flip with big ideas who possibly knew a little bit too much about them for his own good. Shit! Norton was suddenly beginning to find himself stuck between a rock and a hard place.

This all weighed heavily on Norton's mind, even when he was down the beach in the afternoon, trying to enjoy a swim and a perv. It took the edge right off his appetite, which was why he didn't bother cooking any dinner at home that night. Warren noticed this when he arrived from work and made his disapproval known. 'Sandwiches! Fuckin' sandwiches. You expect me to come home after working my cunt out all day and eat rotten, fuckin' roast beef sandwiches. You got to be fuckin' kidding, haven't you?'

Seated at the kitchen table, Norton looked up impassively from a can of orange and mango mineral water he was sipping.

'You don't like sandwiches, Warren?' he said slowly.

'I . . .' Warren was about to say something but changed his mind. 'Fair dinkum, what would be the good of me saying anything. You'd only come out with some smartarse Stryne remark like, "Garngeddapizza", or "Donfuggineadem", or "Stiggeminyerarseyagund". So rather than put up with the thrust and parry of your brilliant, Queensland, verbal repartee, I'll eat the fuckin' sandwiches.'

'Good idea, Warren.'

Warren went across to the sink and put the kettle on to make a pot of tea. 'In fact, to tell you the truth, it's too bloody hot to eat.'

'That's precisely what I thought.'

'In fact, when I come to think about it, we do have a tendency to overindulge ourselves at times.'

'Yes, quite correct, Warren. And although it may not have occurred to you, you are developing quite a noticeable bay window. You're beginning to look like a little pepper pot.'

Warren patted his paunch with both hands. 'Yeah, you're right. In fact now that I'm back off the piss, I might start running with you in the mornings.'

Any other time, Norton would have burst out laughing and bombarded Warren with sarcastic remarks. His expression didn't change. 'What time would you like me to wake you up? Six-thirty? The last time I did, you told me to get fucked and threw a book at me.'

Warren thought for a moment. 'Yeah, we might leave it till Thursday. Give me another day or so to adjust.'

'I think that's another good idea Warren.'

Norton was still very quiet watching TV that night, so much so that Warren remarked on it. But Les replied that he was just feeling a bit tired from too much sun.

'If you ask me, the landlord's getting a bit of male menopause,' guffawed Warren.

'It's my prostate, Warren,' nodded Les. 'I probably need surgery.'

'Yeah that'd be right, too, you pissy, smelly, dribbly old thing. Fancy having to share a place with you, you fuckin' old sheila. No wonder they gave you the arse from the Kelly Club.'

Whatever Norton's mental or physical condition, it wasn't helped at all when the movie came on. Steve McQueen in *The Towering Inferno*. Warren was coming up with some choice one-liners about the acting and the special effects, but for some reason Les just couldn't see the funny side of it.

When he went to bed later on, he couldn't get to sleep, either and spent the best part of an hour staring at the ceiling. Once he dozed off he slept all right though.

Wednesday dawned a perfect, early summer's day; warm and sunny with just the lightest northerly wind to clear the air. Les was up around seven. He didn't bother to wake Warren before he had a coffee then went for a run and a swim at North Bondi. Warren was up and ready to go to work when Les arrived back home. Warren agreed it was a great day; too good to have

146

to go to fuckin' work. With various things on his mind Les wasn't in the mood for any verbal jousting with his flatmate, so he just said he'd see Warren when he got home, have a nice day and stop complaining — at least he had a job to go to, unlike the poor, unfortunate landlord.

After he showered and got into a clean pair of jeans and a T-shirt and had some breakfast, Norton had a good think over another cup of coffee. He was seriously thinking of pulling out of this deal with Grigor and his brother; being stuck with the old block of flats was a pain in the arse all right, but the thought of murdering eleven people and spending the rest of his life in prison didn't appeal to him at all. However, he was in a little deep now and had called in one of his markers with the Ciotsa brothers, who would definitely think he was half-full of shit and who would also definitely not be too keen on his knowing so much about their business.

Still, there were more pressing things on hand at the immediate present; the meeting with the bikies and the extraction of seventy-five thousand dollars for something that was theirs in the first place.

Norton was toying with the idea of ringing Eddie for a bit of back-up and tossing a few grand his way. But the less people who knew what he was up to, even his closest friends, the better.

He drummed his fingers on the kitchen table, then finished his coffee and went out to the toolshed in the backyard. It didn't take Les long to find what he was looking for; a marking-pen, a Stanley knife, a roll of Durex-tape and about half a metre of black conduit pipe. He dropped the various articles into an overnight bag, locked up the house then drove over to Blue Seas Apartments stopping on the way to get a large cardboard carton from the front of a supermarket in Clovelly Road.

Les parked his car down from the flats and was happy to see there was no one around when he walked through the foyer with his overnight bag and a carton. He ran quickly up the stairs and let himself into flat five. A

147

quick look in the litter-strewn kitchen confirmed that the kitchen window gave a clear view of the garage on the opposite corner.

Smiling to himself, Norton flattened out the cardboard carton in the lounge room, then drew the outline of someone's head and shoulders on it with a marking pen. Satisfied that it looked enough like a person, even down to the tousled hair, he cut out the shape with a Stanley knife and taped it to the kitchen window with Durex-tape. There was a kind of metal winder with a small handle that allowed you to open and close the window; Les opened it out a few inches and poked the piece of conduit out about a foot or so. With pieces of cardboard behind it, he got the conduit at the angle he required, then secured that in place with Durex-tape also.

Happy enough with that, Les dropped the Stanley knife into the overnight-bag, locked up the flat, then went down to the garage opposite to survey his handiwork from that distance. With the curtains billowing slightly around it in the breeze, the cardboard cutout could pass for someone standing at the window and from that distance, the piece of conduit did look like the barrel of a gun. Oh well, thought Norton, not much I can do now but wait. He bought an orange juice at the garage and sipped it while he waited a few metres down from the corner.

A few minutes after ten-thirty, a blue 1967 Ford with a noisy exhaust system and fatties came up Soudan Street and pulled up on the garage corner. Les recognised Mick sitting in the front but not the one driving, nor the two men in the back. But they were big and mean-looking and wearing much the same gear as Mick had on now and when Les first met him on Sunday. But unlike Mick, they didn't have two black eyes, bruised and swollen features and a number of stitches around their foreheads and lips.

Slowly and carefully Mick walked up to Les. 'You got those papers?' he said. He was unsmiling and decidedly unfriendly.

There was the hint of a smile flickering around Norton's eyes and that was about all. His adrenalin was pumping slowly but steadily. He nodded his head slowly but didn't say anything.

'The money's on the front seat of the car. Come over and get it.' Mick's voice was easy and steady but absolutely dripping with treachery.

'Mick,' replied Norton, 'before we do anything, take a look up at the kitchen window of that flat you wrecked.' The tall bikie looked up and Les noticed him stiffen. 'That mate of mine from Sunday's up there with an M-16 on rock 'n' roll and eighty rounds of armour piercing. Now I don't know what you and your mates have got in mind and you might get me. But when the ambulance gets here, I guarantee that all they'll find inside that old blue Henry is steak and kidney and crumbed brains.' Norton made a gesture like a small salute to the window. Mick looked up also just as the curtains billowed around the piece of conduit and if you didn't know, you'd almost swear the figure nodded back. 'So go and tell your mates what's going on. I'll wait right here.'

Mick walked back to the Ford and stuck his head in the window. There was a brief confab and a movement and twisting of bodies. Maybe it was the cut-out in the window, maybe it was Norton's casual, confident manner, but the next thing Mick was walking back, holding a white, plastic shopping bag.

'You're a real smart cunt, aren't you?' he said.

'Ohh, I dunno,' drawled Les. 'But I don't think I'd have to have much brains to be smarter than you or your mates. Mind if I have a look?' Mick opened the bag and Les didn't have to count it too thoroughly to know there was seventy-five thousand dollars in there. 'Yep. That looks okay.' He handed Mick the papers and dropped the money into the overnight bag. 'There you go, mate. Get that into you and you'll have your money back in no time.' Despite the drama Norton couldn't help but grin. 'Then you'll be just like that bloke

149

in the song: "Motor bikin', motor bikin', Zoomin' down the Hume Highway, lookin' like a streak of lightnin'".'

Mick took the papers, gave Les one last filthy look then turned to walk away. As he did, he turned back. 'Hey, just out of curiosity, where was the thing? We turned that fuckin' joint inside out.'

'Underneath the welcome mat,' smiled Norton.

Mick's jaw almost hit the footpath. '*What*!!!?'

'Underneath the welcome mat outside the door. We went round to clean the place up. The first thing I did was sweep round out the front, and there it was.'

'Ohh, Jesus!!' Mick screwed his face up, shook his head in disbelief and walked back to the blue Ford. He looked like he'd shrunk by a foot.

The motor roared into life, and the car moved off down Perouse Road. As it did, Norton waved towards the kitchen window again, held the bag up and pointed inside; he was almost certain they'd be looking out the back window and in the rear-vision mirror. Once the car was out of sight, Les took a deep breath and let it out again. Some of the butterflies had settled down but there were still a few doing rumbas in his stomach. Well, I don't know about anything else, but after that I deserve a drink.

He walked up to the Royal, ordered a schooner of White Old, then found an empty table in the shade out the front.

The combination of the heat and his nerves meant that Les polished off the schooner pretty smartly, so he got another one. About a third of the way through that he started to settle down a bit. Naturally he was elated but he found that the beer plus the adrenalin that was still squirting around in his system kicked the old Norton grey matter into top gear. Seventy-five thousand dollars was a good earn in anyone's book — but robbing those bikies so smoothly with his only back-up being a cardboard carton and a piece of pipe — that was something else. Luck had been on his side though; if he'd walked over to the car, he would have

150

either got a knife in his throat or a shotgun blast straight in the face. Sure, luck had something to do with it. Plus a little something else. Norton looked up at the sky, winked and smiled a silent thanks.

So, he thought, taking his time over schooner number two. I'm seventy-five grand in front. I'll drop five of that in Billy's kick when the time comes and tell him all about it over a beer. Despite himself, Les still found his brain was revving at about a hundred miles an hour. His eyes kept drifting over towards the old block of flats and his mind kept returning to something Sandra the artist had said to him in their last conversation. It kept banging around in his head like a loose cannon and suddenly things began to fall into place like pieces of jigsaw puzzle. Yes, he thought, taking another swallow of beer. There just might be a way out of this mess after all...

It was a beautiful summer's day and due to an unfortunate accident that had happened to their roadie and driver, five members of a certain all-girl rock 'n' roll band wouldn't be playing the Revesby Roundhouse tonight. Norton swallowed the rest of his beer. On a lovely, warm day like this, I think I know just where those girls will be. He picked up the overnight bag and walked across to Blue Seas Apartments. He went into the caretaker's flat, took five thousand dollars out of the bag, put it in the pocket of his jeans and hid the overnight bag underneath the old night-and-day. Satisfied that no one would find it, even though he knew he wouldn't be all that long, Norton walked up onto the roof.

The Heathen Harlots were looking pretty much the same as they did last time Les had seen them up there: the same gear, the same two girls in their banana chairs, the other two playing backgammon and the little blonde one still reading *Rock Star*. The only difference this time was that the four hippie men were up there, and an old Rolling Stones track, 'Lean On Me' was playing on the ghetto blaster.

151

Norton wasn't actually given a royal welcome when he stepped out on the roof, if anything he was given no welcome at all, in fact, his sudden appearance on the roof went over like the proverbial turd in a bowl of punch. Franulka gave him a brief glance over the top of her sunglasses and that was about it. To the others, including the hippies, Les could have been invisible.

'Hello, girls. How are you?' Apart from music coming from the ghetto blaster, the silence was deafening. 'Not a bad day.' If anything, the silence got louder and Norton was beginning to think his coming up on the roof wasn't such a good idea after all. 'So, how's Syd?'

'Ohh, how do you think he is?' snapped Gwen. 'He's got a broken jaw, his neck's in a brace and his face looks like a Rottweiler's chewed it.'

'At least he's out of hospital,' Isla chipped in sullenly.

'Yeah? Well, have a look at my neck and face,' replied Les. 'It's lucky it's not me that finished up in the bloody hospital. Or the morgue.'

'Pity you didn't,' said Alastrina.

Norton gave each member of the band an even look. 'Just how much do you girls know about what happened on Saturday night?'

'Not as much as we'd like to,' snapped Gwen, exchanging a frosty look with Franulka.

'No. I didn't think you did.'

It was becoming obvious now to Les that there was a bit of melodrama in the band. Gwen obviously fancied Syd, who fancied Franulka, who, apart from being aware of his usefulness, didn't really give a stuff whether he lived or died. The fact that Gwen fancied him was made patently clear by the way she hung back and tried to comfort him when the others were abusing him after they arrived back from Canberra, and the way she screamed and went into a tailspin when she saw him after his fight with Les.

'Anyway, what's on your mind, Les?' said Riona. 'You've cost us a gig tonight worth fifteen hundred bucks, plus Syd's hospital bill. And we're almost broke as it

152

is. So unless you want to sweep the roof or something, why don't you just fuck off and leave us alone?'

Norton stood there nodding his head slowly. The girls continued to ignore him; the hippies avoided his eyes. 'That's lovely, isn't it?' he said. 'Just lovely. So I've cost you a gig worth a lousy fifteen hundred bucks? Big deal. How would you like one for five thousand bucks? And you don't have to go any further than the front of these flats.'

The girls exchanged glances, then Franulka turned down the ghetto blaster and looked at Les from over the top of her sunglasses.

'Did you say five thousand dollars, Les?'

'Yep. Exactly. Maybe even more.' Les fished into the pocket of his jeans, took out three thousand dollars and tossed it to Franulka. 'And there's three up front if you don't believe me. Go on, count it.'

The girls' eyes were rivetted onto the wad of money. The hippies' eyes stuck out like boiled eggs.

Franulka flicked through the money like a Mississippi riverboat gambler. 'Hey! He's right. There's three fuckin' grand here.' She gave Les a sugary, sweet smile. 'Why don't you tell us what's going on, Les?'

Riona snapped her finger. 'You know,' she said, 'when I come to think of it, Syd can be a bit headstrong at times.'

'Would you like a beer, Les?' beamed Isla.

'Yeah,' nodded Les. 'I wouldn't mind one at all.'

You rotten, low, mercenary bitches, he thought. There was a milk crate next to the hippies. Les brought it over, got a bottle of Tooheys Dry from the esky, opened it and sat down.

'You know what this Saturday is?' The girls shook their heads. 'It's November the fourteenth. Sandra in flat three's birthday — and Prince Charles's as well.'

'That big-eared wombat?' said Alastrina. 'What's he got to do with it? He talks about the environment and him and his old man go out and shoot about a hundred pheasants of a weekend.'

'Yeah, well, he's an upper-class pom. What do you expect?' Norton took a swig of beer. 'Anyway, forget that. The thing is, Sandra's got a rich admirer and he wants to throw a surprise birthday party for her this weekend.'

'Sandy's got a few rich admirers,' said Gwen.

Norton shrugged his shoulders. 'Well, I wouldn't know about that. Anyway, the thing is, he wants you to throw a street party out the front.'

'A street party?'

'Yeah. Evidently this bloke's got a mate with a film company who wants to video it.' The girls exchanged quick glances at the mention of the film company and video. 'The people in the flats across the road are all friends of Sandra's — you could organise it with them and block the street off.'

Gwen looked thoughtful. 'It wouldn't be hard. Aquila Street's only a little dead end as it is.'

'That's right,' agreed Les. 'It'd be as easy as shit.'

Alastrina looked quizzically at Les, then at the money in Franulka's hands. 'It all seems too good to be true. How do you figure in all this, anyway, Les?'

Norton took a sip of beer and made an open-handed gesture. 'I was out the front doing a bit of sweeping and this old bloke just come up to me and started magging to me about it and his mate with the film company. Being the caretaker, he probably thought I was in charge or something and he asked me if it'd be all right. He sounded like a Yank. And when he asked me how much the girls would want, I just said the first number that came into my head. Five grand.'

'Christ! You should be our agent,' said Riona.

'I also said you'd probably need another thousand for expenses with the council and that. And he didn't even blink. Just gave me the money — and Bob's your uncle.'

'You're kidding?' said Isla.

Norton shook his head and smiled. 'So, there you have it, girls. All you've got to do is put on a turn

154

right out the front. No travelling, no nothing. And no agent's fees. Call it the Prince Charles Birthday Bash.'

'For that kind of dough we'll call it the Second Coming of fuckin' Elvis,' said Alastrina.

'Just make sure Sandra's there. And old Burt and Rosie. And everybody else in the flats. Have a good time, get pissed and get paid for it.'

'How long do you reckon we'd have to play for?' asked Gwen.

Norton shrugged again. 'I dunno. Kick off, say, at nine and go till midnight. Whatever suits you. I can't see any hassle with the coppers if everyone in the street's involved. I won't be able to help you with your stuff. I start work at the ah... markets tomorrow unloading trucks and I'll be working late Saturday. But I'll be able to help you pack up.' Les nodded towards the four hippies who still hadn't said anything. 'But why don't you get the boys to give you a hand? Here's another five hundred towards expenses. Give them a drink out of that.' He fished in his jeans and came up with the appropriate amount and gave that to Franulka as well. 'He told me to give you the rest on Sunday morning.'

Norton grinned at the five flummoxed Heathen Harlots. 'Well, what do you reckon girls? Is it on or what?'

Franulka shook her head in disbelief. 'It's on, man. It's on like you wouldn't believe. Thank you, Les baby.'

'Yeah. Good on you. Thanks, Les,' was the general chorus.

Norton reflected sadly into his bottle of beer. 'And to think you girls called me a drop kick and told me to piss off.'

'Oh well, we didn't really mean it,' said Riona.

'No, of course you didn't,' answered Norton. He finished his beer, dropped the empty in the esky and stood up. 'Well, I've got a bit of running around to do, so I'd best get going. But I'll see you before Saturday. Okay?'

'Yeah, okay,' said Gwen. 'And thanks again, Les.'

Norton smiled and headed for the doorway.

Franulka called out just as he got there, 'Hey, Les! You're all right, you know.'

155

Norton turned round, gave her a wink and one of his best grins. 'There's heaps worse blokes round than me, Franulka. Don't worry about that.'

On the way down the stairs, Les stopped at flat five and removed the cardboard cutout and the piece of pipe from the window. Then he went back inside the caretaker's flat and got his overnight bag from beneath the old night-and-day.

Out in the street Les couldn't help turning around and smiling at the old block of flats. He stopped for a moment before he walked back to his car. You know, he thought to himself, all that lying's bloody hard work. I think I might have to go and shout myself another beer. Whistling softly, he strolled up to the Royal Hotel.

Norton ordered a middy of White Old and found another table out the front again; about halfway through his beer he was starting to feel reasonably pleased with himself. The dicey scam with the bikies had gone over as smooth as a billiard table and he was now seventy grand in front. The Heathen Harlots had come in like the proverbial Botany Bay mullets when he came up with that preposterous idea for the street party. It was an absolutely outrageous story and they fell for it; though Norton mused that for five grand those sheilas would fall for anything, and, no doubt, their pants with it. But the party should get everybody out of the flats, so he could now give Grigor the go-ahead to blow the place to smithereens and not make a dill of himself in front of the Ciotsa brothers.

Yes, he mused, taking another nice, cold sip of beer, I think I might just about have this thing by the nuts. Phases one and two of Operation Blue Seas are going swimmingly and according to the battle plan, I've got the money and I've cleared the beachhead. All I need now is an alibi, just in case being the owner of the said block of sumptuous apartments some flak should come back on me. Les took another thoughtful sip of beer and gazed absently at the few other drinkers out on the footpath. By rights, he shouldn't be anywhere near the place when it goes up; in fact, the further away the better. Like somewhere up the north coast. On the other hand, if I'm miles away at the time it could look just a little too... too obvious. What I need is to be somewhere doing something with witnesses around. It's a pity I'm not working. Les snapped his fingers. I'll swap a night with Billy at the club. No, that'd look just a little fishy because I told Billy he could have it all on his own. Norton was silently pondering this small, yet vital loose end, when his 'alibi' walked up to the table, pulled out a chair, and sat down.

'Hello, Les. What are you doing over this way?'

It was another bloke from the Eastern Suburbs Norton had got to know since his arrival in Sydney: Bob Quigley, the proprietor and chef of a small restaurant in Coogee called The Devlin Dining Room. Quigley was a lean, sallow-faced man of about thirty. He was roughly the same height as Les, with brown hair combed straight back off his forehead, a bony chin that always looked like it needed a shave and dull, brown eyes set in a grainy face that had definitely seen better days. He lived somewhere near Coogee but spent most of his time swimming or surfing at either North or South Bondi which was where Norton had met him and had somehow been talked into going to his restaurant with a bit of a side one night. The food was so-so but the service was even more ordinary — the waitress, Les remembered, was scruffy, half-pissed and stank of cigarette smoke. Norton never bothered going back. Quigley had been up to the club a few times and always struck Les as being a bit of a smartarse, much like the team he ran with. For the sake of being called a snob, Les always gave Quigley a friendly 'g'day' and 'how are you'. And if Quigley wanted to tell Les how good his restaurant was, and how great he was going and how many sheilas he was rooting, Les would also give Quigley his ear for a couple of minutes.

Still lost in thought, Norton stared for a moment or two at the figure, wearing a T-shirt and jeans pretty much like himself, who had just sat down opposite him. 'Oh. G'day, Bob. How's things?' he said.

157

'Not bad,' replied Quigley, taking a sip on his schooner. 'So what brings you over this way? This isn't your regular drinking hole.'

'No. No, you're right,' answered Norton, trying to think of an excuse. 'I've ah ... I've just been over the hospital having a chest X-ray.'

'All those late nights at the Kelly Club and hanging around the Cross starting to get to you, eh?'

'Yeah,' laughed Les. 'something like that. Anyway, I got the all clear so I thought I'd have a quick beer. It's warm enough.'

'Yeah. It is.' Quigley looked evenly at Les. 'I hear the cops closed the joint up,' he said, making the Kelly Club sound like a bit of a low dive.

'Yeah. Saturday before last,' nodded Les, already wishing that Quigley would piss off and leave him alone.

'So you're out of work?'

'Yeah. It sure looks that way.'

'What do you reckon you'll do?'

Norton shook his head. 'Dunno. See if I can get a bit of labourin'. If there's nothing around I'll probably have to go on the jam roll.'

Quigley looked smugly at Les for a moment or two and a shitty sort of smile flickered around his eyes. 'I'll give you a job if you like.'

'What?' replied Les.

'You want a job? I'll give you one. Kitchen hand.'

'What? At your joint?'

'Yeah. You ever done any kitchen work, Les?'

'Yeah,' nodded Norton slowly. 'At Easts Leagues Club when I was playing football.' Which was true. When Les had just come down from Queensland and signed up, the club offered him the world and put him in the kitchens, scrubbing pots and emptying garbage tins. Norton lasted about a month.

'All right,' said Quigley. 'You can start at my place tomorrow night. The bloke I had working for me, he, ah ... he got another job.'

Norton stared at Quigley and immediately realised

158

what was going on. The smartarse wasn't offering him a job as a favour. He was doing it to put Les down. He'd be able to go and skite to all his smartarse mates about how he had the big mug from the door at the Kelly Club working in his kitchen. It was all the dopey big goose was good for.

Norton couldn't believe his luck. 'Okay, Bob,' he said enthusiastically. 'I'll be in that. When do you want me to start?'

'Are you fair dinkum?'

'Bloody oath! I need the work.'

'Okay. Tomorrow night, five-thirty. You know where the place is?'

'Yeah, Devlin Place, Coogee. Just up from the beach. I had a meal there once. It was tops.'

'Okay. Work this Thursday, Friday and Saturday night. See how you go.'

'All right. Thanks a lot, Bob.'

Quigley suddenly finished his beer in a bit of a hurry, stood up and looked around him then looked down on Norton as if he'd just had a big victory. 'Anyway, I have to get going. I'll see you tomorrow night, Les.'

'For sure,' answered Les. 'And thanks again, Bob. I really appreciate it.'

Quigley had another look around, nodded at Les then hurried off in the direction of the hospital, where he more than likely had his car.

Well, I'll be stuffed, thought Norton, as he watched him walk away. I can't believe it. That's the perfect alibi. I'll work in his shitty, stinken restaurant for the next three nights — he can laugh his head off, for all I care. It's a low job, but three nights ain't the Burma railway. I'll just put my head down, keep my mouth shut, and nothing can go wrong. When I finish on Saturday night, this'll all be over. And I just won't be there the following week. Thank you, Bob Quigley. Another Eastern Suburbs smarty done me a favour trying to dud me. Norton grinned to himself and had another mouthful of beer. I wonder what the smartarse would have thought if he'd

159

got a little glimpse inside this overnight bag? Then Norton's grin faded and a frown crept over his face. The cunt never mentioned anything about money. Wonder what's he going to pay me?

It had been a very profitable and enjoyable day and Les was feeling more pleased with himself than ever as he stashed the bag of money behind the wardrobe in his bedroom. Satisfied it was secure Les made himself some sandwiches for lunch and a nice pot of tea.

At two-thirty, he rang the Seven Gypsies Restaurant in Enmore.

'Hello. Is Grigor there, please?'

'This is Grigor.'

'It's Les Norton, Grigor.'

'My friend.'

'That little matter we discussed. Can you fix it up at eleven-thirty this Saturday night?'

'Consider it done, my friend.'

'Okay. I'll see you later, Grigor.'

'Goodbye, my friend.'

Well, that's that, thought Norton, looking at the phone. For better or for worse. Everyone's out of the flats. My arse is covered. And when it does go up I imagine those sheilas will be running power from the flats and it'll look like they've overloaded the system. Lovely. Now, what will I do with myself?

Norton decided to spend the rest of the afternoon very low key down the beach. He walked down to Bondi and found a spot south of the pavilion where he propped; reading, swimming and watching the girls and the surfboard riders. If there was anything on his diabolical mind he certainly wasn't showing it.

When Warren arrived home about six he found Norton in the kitchen whistling and getting a Caesar salad together.

'So, what're we having for tea, landlord?' he said, getting a glass of mineral water from the fridge.

'Chops and salad. And I got an apricot pie from the Gelato Bar. We'll have that with a bit of ice-cream later. That suit you, oh magnificent one?'

160

'Sounds reasonable. But I'm going down for a swim first. I'm fuckin' boiling.'

'You do that, Warren,' replied Les. 'Enjoy your swim. Just leave me here to slave in this hot, stinken kitchen.'

After tea that night they were sitting in the lounge room watching TV and sipping coffee. Norton was in a much better frame of mind than the previous night and Warren noticed it.

'You're in a better mood tonight, ugly. Not like last night. What's going on?'

'I had a bit of luck today, Warren. I managed to get a job.'

Warren gave a double blink over the top of his coffee. 'You *what*!?'

'I got a job as a kitchen hand. In a restaurant over at Coogee.'

Norton told Warren how he'd bumped into Bob Quigley and that he'd offered him a job. He started tomorrow night at five-thirty.

'Kitchen hand?' said Warren. 'That's about the lowest job in the book. You're kidding.'

'Well, what else am I gonna do? I've got no trade. No brains. You've convinced me I'm just a Queensland hillbilly. I reckon I'm lucky to get another job. I just hope I can keep the bloody thing.'

Warren stared at Norton in disbelief. 'Do you really need a job that bad?'

Norton stared back at Warren in equal disbelief and his voice rose. 'Fuckin' oath I do. I got bills to pay. Rates. Insurance. I got to eat. I got to feed you, and you eat like a fuckin' horse.' Norton took a sip of coffee. 'Besides, I'm used to working of a night. What else am I gonna do? Sit around here pickin' my toes and looking at you for the next six months?'

Warren shook his head. 'I can't figure you out. You're un-fuckin'-real.'

'And I can't figure you out, Warren. One minute you're whingeing about having me here all the time.

161

Then when I get a job, you poke shit at me. You're a funny bloke.'

'I don't know why you don't shout yourself a decent holiday, you miserable big cunt. Surely you're not that broke?'

'Hah! A holiday. You'd love that, wouldn't you, you little weasel? More parties every night. More molls in my bed — or the way your luck's been running lately, it'd probably be some old poof in a dressing gown. No, Warren. It was either I get a job, or put your rent up.'

Warren stared at the TV. 'Take the job, Les. If anybody asks what you're doing, I'll say... I don't know what I'll say.'

'Just tell them it's a hard old world out there, Woz, and the landlord's doing his best.'

Warren was still shaking his head when he went to bed later that night. For Norton, it was all he could do to keep a straight face.

Thursday had clouded over with a light southerly blowing when Les rose around six thirty. This suited Norton. He decided to stick at home and lie low rather than hang around the beach for the next three days. The die was cast for Saturday night and although it all looked sweet, you could bet there'd be a glitch or two between now and when the balloon went up so it wouldn't hurt to keep his wits about him and keep the old thinking cap wedged firmly on his head. He had a run in Centennial Park and went over the whole thing in his mind — he could only think of two other minor loose ends, things he could quite easily attend to today.

Warren had left for work early when Les got home. Norton got cleaned up and the first thing he did was ring Grigor and arrange to see him at ten-thirty. As taciturn as ever over the phone, the Romanian said that would be all right and little else. Norton had breakfast, read the paper, got into a pair of jeans and a T-shirt and at ten headed for Enmore.

*

162

The same heavy opened the door of the restaurant, only this time he had a big smile and let Norton straight in. Grigor was seated at the same table, only without his brother. The heavy brought coffee and Les got straight to the point. He explained how he'd organised the street party to get everyone out of the flats and that there would probably be quite a number of people milling around out the front. Knowing how Grigor didn't like to discuss certain matters over the phone, Les said that he thought it best he called over. Grigor liked that. He also agreed that even though there was no problem in the first place, the explosion would now look exactly as Les had hoped: a power overload caused by the band. Grigor added that he and his brother would add a little something to the mix to make sure there was a great shower of sparks before the fireball. In the meantime, don't worry and don't bother to get in touch. The next time they would meet would be when he and Vaclav returned from Tasmania. Norton finished his coffee and wished Grigor good fishing.

Well, thought Norton, as he drove back to the Eastern Suburbs, that was only a minor detail I suppose, but now at least Grigor knows exactly what's going on. And it's always better to be sure than sorry. Now, there's only one other little thing I can think of. Norton glanced at his watch. It's not even lunchtime. With a bit of luck maybe I can knock this one on the head at the same time. As he pulled up just down from Blue Seas Apartments, he was pleased to see, as he walked up from his car, Sandra's old white utility out the front. He was even more pleased to see, as he peeked over the fence, the red-headed artist was hanging out some washing on the line in the back yard. Norton hurried to the storeroom, got the yard-broom and slowly and casually pushed it around the corner to 'accidentally' bump into Sandra.

'G'day, Sandra,' he said easily, moving the broom around some leaves and other bits of rubbish. 'How's things?'

163

Sandra turned around in her skin tight, stone-washed jeans and equally tight red tank top and gave Les one of those smiles that despite his feelings towards her now, nearly made him want to break the broom over his head.

'Oh, hello...' she appeared to think for a moment. 'Les. How are you?'

'Not too bad,' replied Norton. 'Just doing what a good little caretaker should be doing.' Sandra smiled as she continued hanging out her washing. Norton kept sweeping, pushing the rubbish into a small pile near the fence. 'That party should be a ripper on Saturday night,' he said.

'Party?' said Sandra, pausing momentarily from what she was doing. 'What party?'

Norton stared dumbly at the artist for a second then screwed up his face in mock remorse. 'Ohh, Christ!' he said, making a futile gesture at the air. 'Me and my big bloody mouth. I'm not supposed to have said anything. Bugger it.'

Sandra stopped what she was doing and stared directly at Les. 'Just what are you talking about, Les?'

Norton affected a sheepish grin. 'Ahh, shit! I wasn't supposed to have said anything.' Sandra's eyes narrowed. 'I was talking to the girls on the roof the other day.'

'Franulka and the girls in the band?'

'Yeah. I just happened to mention that this Saturday was your birthday. And right out of the blue they decided to throw a surprise street party out the front.'

'A street party?'

'Yeah. They're going to call it the Prince Charles birthday bash, 'cause it's his birthday too. But really, it's a surprise birthday party for you. And I've gone and given the bloody thing away.' Norton shook his head in disgust. 'Jesus, I'm a nice bloody goose!'

Sandra continued to stare at Les. 'A surprise birthday party, just for me. I don't know what to say.'

'I know what bloody Franulka will say when she finds out you know. Stuff it.' Norton kicked at the pile of rubbish in mock annoyance then turned to Sandra,

164

anguish and remorse etched deep in his craggy face. 'Look Sandra, do us a favour, will you?'

'Sure, Les.'

'Don't let on to the girls that you know anything.'

Sandra smiled and gave a dainty shrug of her smooth, brown shoulders. 'Yeah, that's okay. Though I have to admit, I do feel rather flattered.'

'Yeah. It certainly is nice of them. So just make sure you're there on Saturday night, and act like you don't know anything. Okay?'

'No worries.'

'And if you should see me, or anyone else, stacking up stuff out the front, just sort of, you know... edge your way around it.'

'I understand, Les. I won't say a word.'

'Ohh, good.' Norton looked relieved and began sweeping the rubbish again. 'I know one thing for sure. The way the girls were talking, it's going to be one hell of a party.'

'Yes. Knowing them, I'm sure it will be.'

'Anyway, I'll get this finished and get out of your road. Before I put my bloody big foot in it again. I'll see you later, Sandra. And remember, not a word.'

'You needn't worry, Les. No one will know a thing. Bye bye.'

'Good on you, Sandra. See you later.' Norton gave her another sheepish grin and pushed the pile of rubbish around the side passage.

As soon as he was out of sight, Norton tossed the broom back in the storeroom and hurried back to his car. Christ, he thought, as he got behind the wheel, if ever they make lying an event at the Olympic Games, I'd take out a gold medal every time. He gave a quick smile towards the sky. I'm not really a liar, you know — I've just got a bad grip on the truth, that's all. But at least she'll be there for sure now, thinking she's the belle of the ball — instead of in her flat bonking some bloke when the place goes up. As Norton drove past the old block of flats an evil grin broke out across his face. Well, goodbye, Blue Seas Apartments, my million-dollar investment. The next time I see you, you cockroach-infested pile of shit, you'll look like Hiroshima in 1945. And fuckin' good riddance too. Norton drove home and made a bit of lunch.

He pottered around the house for the rest of the afternoon mulling things over in his head; but there was nothing he could think of now to get unduly concerned about. It was all go. He thought of giving Price and Billy a ring, but decided to leave it till tomorrow. Before he knew it, it was getting on for five o'clock and time to get ready for work.

Norton reflected on what it would be like working in a kitchen; greasy, smelly and fuckin' hot. And from what his recollection of the surroundings, the waitress and the food, the last and only time he was at the Devlin Dining Room, it wouldn't be any different. He got into his daggiest pair of jeans, most worn out running shoes and an old blue T-shirt with 'Kings Cross' on the front that he never wore. He tossed a sweat band made from a red T-shirt, that was so old and faded from sweat it was closer to pink, and a couple of pieces of fruit into a small overnight bag and headed for Coogee.

Devlin Place was little more than a dead end running off Coogee Bay Road between the Coogee Motel and a music shop called Guitar City about half a kilometre up from the beach. There was a Chinese restaurant next to the motel. On the opposite side of the road there were a beautician, a video shop and several other small businesses, as well as a few old semis and an equally old Spanish style block of flats. The Devlin Dining Room was part of the motel, with the main window fronting on to the street. The motel driveway ran between the restaurant and the office with the entrance to the restaurant in the driveway. Norton found a parking spot not far from the music shop, locked his car and walked down.

He paused momentarily out the front of the restaurant

and looked in the window. It was much the same as the last and only time he'd been there. Tan brickwork out the front, same as the motel, and inside was a mishmash of red and brown over well-worn brown carpet.

There were about a dozen or so tables with red table-cloths, a goldfish tank near the entrance and a few prints and cheap paintings on the walls. The menu was written up on a large blackboard next to a swing door that led into the kitchen and that was about it. Maxims de Paris it wasn't. Norton had a squint through the window at the menu which appeared to be a mixture of French provincial and home style cooking. He decided to go in the back rather than walk through the restaurant.

The back entrance to the restaurant was to the right of the motel, in a small courtyard bricked off from the motel car park, the entrance itself being a rickety fly-screen door full of holes situated next to the toilets. The door faced a brick building that was probably a storeroom of some sort and the rest of the small res-taurant courtyard was full of old cartons, a couple of garbage bins, a mop and bucket and what looked like about two hundred thousand filthy, empty bottles. Some dust-caked windows in the kitchen faced this uninspiring scene and that was about it. Norton shook his head, rapped on the flyscreen door and stepped inside.

Still wearing the same jeans and T-shirt he'd had on at the hotel, Quigley was standing at a large, old wooden table in the middle of the kitchen, trimming a fillet of beef. He glanced up at Les and gave him a brief smile that was again as much a smirk as anything else.

'Hello, Les,' he said quietly.

'G'day Bob. How's things?'

Quigley glanced at his watch. 'Right on time.'

'Yeah,' nodded Les. 'It's only about ten minutes from my place.'

The kitchen wasn't all that big, barely four metres by six. As he stood there watching Quigley, Les had a quick, clockwise look around. Next to the back door

167

and beneath the windows was a double sink that Norton tipped hadn't seen a sprinkle of Ajax since the 2nd AIF came back from Gallipoli. Next to it was a small dishwasher that looked like a cut-down iron lung and in pretty much the same condition as the sink. A shelf ran from it into the corner, above which was a cupboard full of plates and soup dishes. Next was an ancient, eight burner stove and oven behind where Quigley was standing, with a pot full of something boiling away on top. Next to it at about eye level, was a sort of oven or pie warmer and beneath this were three, small deep freezes which ran from the corner to the wall of the kitchen fridge. The door to this was next to the swing door that lead to the dining room. There was a pantry in the other corner, then more cupboards and shelves full of plates and cups, tablecloths, napkins and other restaurant junk that ran down to a hot water urn near the back door.

In the middle of the kitchen was the huge, old table where Quigley was standing, on which were chopping boards, bowls of herbs, stacks of butter, tins, vegetables, jars of spices, carving knives, whisks, ladles and other restaurant odds and ends. Between the table and the freezer wall sat a small chest of drawers that held the cutlery. The floor was grey lino and everything else was either yellow, brown or black and all grimy, greasy and badly in need of a bucket of hot water, a scrubbing brush and some Flash. God, what a bloody pit, thought Norton. Did I really eat here once? I thought they closed places like this down after they sprung Oliver Twist.

It was warm outside but the kitchen was hotter. Norton found a place amongst the tablecloths for his overnight bag, took out his sweat band and looked at Quigley.

'Well, Bob. What do you want me to do?'

The way Quigley looked at him, Les was convinced he must have '24 Carat Mug' written across his forehead in luminous green paint. Oh well. Let him think what he likes, thought Les, wrapping an old sweatband around his head.

'You know how to cut up vegetables, Les?'

'Sure.'

'Okay. Start on those carrots and broccoli.'

Norton picked up a small carving knife and gave it a couple of hits on a steel while Quigley showed him how he wanted the vegetables cut up then put into two containers of water which were nothing more than grimy, battered, plastic ice cream cartons. While Les was doing this Quigley pointed out where everything was and what it was and showed him how to work the dishwasher and where the dishracks for it were kept. He told Les not to throw out anything that came back on the plates — all foodscraps went into two plastic buckets under the table one for meat scraps the other for vegetables. Any vegetables that looked like they hadn't been touched went into another ice cream container on the table.

While Norton chopped away, Quigley drank bottles of Powers and constantly smoked cigarettes while he told Norton how good the food was in his restaurant, how good it was going, how good a chef he was, how good his car was going, and how many sheilas he was throwing up in the air. He also added that he was doing a job on one of the waitresses who was nineteen.

Norton felt like pulling a few squelches on Quigley and asking him who was he trying to kid — the place was a brothel, the food was ordinary at the best of times, and didn't he think Les had ever had a root? But he changed his mind, deciding to act the dummy and kept nodding his head as Quigley went on with his bullshit, almost as if he was awe struck. Norton cut up the vegetables plus some par-boiled potatoes in their jackets and some herbs and was beginning to think that, apart from putting up with Quigley's ego-tripping the work was pretty easy and the next three nights could even be a bit of fun.

'That'll be plenty of vegetables, Les.'

'Righto, Bob.'

Quigley wiped his hands on a greasy teatowel and lit another cigarette. 'I'm going inside to change the menu around. I'll get you to clean out the fridge.'

169

Quigley told Les where the mop and bucket were and to get the Ajax and a scrubbing brush. Any ideas Norton had of the job being 'a bit of fun' quickly disappeared as soon as he saw inside the fridge. It was about two metres by four with racks and benches round the walls and it was even filthier than the kitchen. There were chewed up cartons of butter and other food on the floor amongst plastic containers of cream and milk. Tubs of vegetables and fruit and trays of half-cooked meat and chicken sat on the racks — everything from floor to ceiling was covered in slime, grease and other gunk, and several broken eggs sat amongst congealed blood on the dirty, wooden floor. Two thoughts struck Norton as he took it all in: the bastard who had been there before him must have had a nice holiday, and how come a health inspector hadn't put his head in before now? It was botulism city. Norton shook his head for a moment, then began stacking the contents of the fridge onto the floor outside so that he could mop the fridge out. Besides the cartons of food, there were half-empty bottles of wine and soft drink and cartons of Powers and other beers, which Norton tipped were leftovers from the restaurant and Quigley's private stash.

With a bit of elbow grease, Norton got into it, and got the fridge cleaned up about three hundred per cent better than what it was. At one stage he went out into the kitchen to get some more hot water, when what must have been one of the waitresses arrived. She was skinny, with straight, black hair, and was wearing a pair of black ski pants and a white top. She was definitely no oil painting, with black circles under her eyes and lines around her mouth, and if this was the nineteen-year-old Quigley was knocking off she must have been fighting six rounders since she was fifteen — she looked closer to thirty. She totally ignored Les as she threw a purse, a packet of cigarettes and her car keys onto the bench near the pantry. She got a bottle of Bundaberg Rum from the pantry, poured enough in a glass to start up a two-stroke motor, and hit it with a smidgen of ice and Coca Cola. She glugged half of it down, then lit a cigarette and walked out into the dining room. Fuckin' hell, thought Les, as he waved away the fumes and the cloud of cigarette smoke she left behind. It's lucky she didn't blow us both up.

Norton cleaned out the fridge and restacked it about the same time as Quigley finished whatever he was doing in the dining room.

Quigley had a glance round the fridge and gave it a look of grudging approval. 'That's good, Les,' he said.

Good? thought Norton. You're fuckin' kidding, aren't you? I'll bet it's the first time it's seen any hot water in a year. 'Yeah,' he nodded, washing his hands in the sink. 'It was a bit of a mess. How long has the other bloke been working here?'

'Layton? Oh, about six months or so. You know him do you? Layton Mitner?'

Norton shook his head. 'Can't say I do.'

'He'll be in later. He's an old mate of mine.'

If he's half as grubby and half as big a smartarse as you, Quigley, thought Norton, I can't wait. 'So what do you want me to do now?'

'There's a kilo of prawns in the fridge. Peel them, then I'll get you to make some garlic bread.'

Norton got the prawns from the freezer and began peeling them, putting the peeled ones into another battered ice cream container. Quigley pottered around in front of him, trimming beef and chickens and preparing other things for the restaurant. Norton was going to start up a bit of a conversation, then he thought no, bugger it. The three lousy nights I'm here I'll just act the complete wally and switch right off — what's there to talk about anyway? He was relieved when Quigley turned on a radio that was sitting on top of the pie-warmer; even though it was barely audible. But, Norton's relief turned to further frustration when he found it was tuned to one of those Western Suburbs stations that churned out nothing but golden oldies, greatest memories and takeaway food ads one after the other. With

Bobby Goldsboro moaning his way through 'Honey' followed by Roy Orbison and 'Blue Bayou' Norton knew that Saturday night couldn't come quickly enough.

After a while the skinny waitress came back in, poured another rum and coke and lit another cigarette. 'That's all the tables done, Robert,' she coughed. 'I might go through the bookings.'

'Okay, Carol,' answered Quigley.

Even though they hadn't been introduced, the waitress still ignored Les, who didn't actually go out of his way to smile and catch her eye either. She gulped down her rum and Coke then without bothering to say 'excuse me', grabbed a handful of the prawns Norton had peeled, shoved them on a buttered bread roll and began gnawing at it while she smoked her cigarette at the same time. Norton was trying to remember the last time he'd come across a pig like her — probably lying in a gutter somewhere a few streets up from the Kelly Club. She moved to the opposite side of the table and got into a muted conversation with Quigley, as pieces of bread and prawns fell from her mouth onto the floor. Under closer scrutiny she was even skinnier than he'd thought; she reminded Les of Popeye's girlfriend Olive Oyle, and if it hadn't been for her Adam's apple, she would have had no shape at all. The way they talked, it was now obvious that she was the one Quigley was skiting about rooting. Lucky guy, thought Les. Wish I could find myself a young spunk like her. He peeled on and after a while Quigley actually showed a modicum of manners.

'Oh, Les,' he said. 'This is Carol.'

'Hello, Carol,' replied Norton.

'Harrumphgh, Les,' answered Olive Oyle, through another mouthful of prawn roll, causing more of it to fall on the floor.

When Norton finished peeling the prawns, Quigley got him to squeeze lemon on them plus a splash of vinegar and put them back in the fridge. Then Les started on the garlic bread, which simply meant cutting into some bread rolls three or four times and painting them with melted butter and crushed garlic, using a filthy old paint brush Quigley produced from somewhere then wrapping them in aluminium foil before putting them back in the fridge.

When Les was halfway through the garlic bread, waitress number two arrived. She was a bit on the dumpy side with straggly blonde hair, wearing a black minidress and a white shirt. She said hello to Quigley then, like Carol, she tossed her cigarettes, car keys and purse into the pantry corner and got out a cheap bottle of Scotch. And like Carol, she also poured herself a stiff drink and lit a cigarette. Again Les may as well not have been there as she got into conversation with Quigley and Carol. Eventually Quigley introduced her as Mendle. Hello, mused Les, what a quinella: Olive Oyle and Mendle As Anything.

By now a few customers had begun to drift in; although this brief interruption in no way hindered Quigley or the waitresses drinking or smoking one cigarette after another. The blower above the stove was on but the cigarette smoke in the kitchen was now burning Norton's eyes. It was also starting to piss him off as well. He was about to make a sarcastic remark about passive smoking and health regulations when he felt something rubbing up against his leg. It was an old, red alley cat, who had let itself in through a hole in the flyscreen door. Les was about to automatically kick its arse back out the door when Quigley spoke.

'Here you are, Rusty,' he said, and cut up a few scraps of beef which he dropped straight onto the floor near the sink.

The cat got stuck straight into it, its tail up in the air moving slowly from side to side. Jesus, thought Les, what next? Normally by now, especially working in a restaurant surrounded by food, Les would be getting a bit on the peckish side. Also with the heat he would have had a pronounced thirst and be absolutely tonguing for a beer. But between the cat eating off the floor, the filthy state of the freezer, and the way Carol ate,

173

somehow made him completely lose his appetite. And the way they all slopped booze down their throats like mule skinners in the Last Chance Saloon was enough to turn Norton off drinking for the rest of his life.

The moggy left the way it came in, accompanied by a flurry of barking, growling, hissing and spitting. Norton glanced over between washing pots and dishes and saw an old grey mongrel dog with its nose through the hole in the flyscreen door.

'Hello, Bootsie,' said Quigley.

Quigley opened the door and dumped some more food scraps on the floor. It was the dog's turn to get on the feedbag, which it did, accompanied by much grunting and slobbering all over the floor. That's it, thought Norton, shaking his head, if a rat comes out of one of the cupboards and Quigley says 'hello Tiddles' and starts feeding it, I'm knocking off.

Unbelievably, there were customers, and Norton was kept busy washing dishes, scrubbing filthy, blackened pots and getting things for Quigley from the pantry and the freezer, while the owner and his two waitresses smoked at least a hundred cigarettes each and drank themselves into oblivion.

The night progressed with Norton switched off as best he could. He managed to save his eyesight and lessen the damage to his lungs by going out amongst the empty bottles in the backyard every now and again for a bit of fresh air. In the meantime, he'd found a new job; emptying the girls' ashtrays for them. He also found out that the stuff he'd seen boiling away on the stove earlier was called demi-glace and all the scraps and leftover wine went into it to be reduced down to stock. He also found out where all the vegetables that didn't go into the bucket under the table went: back out into the restaurant. Norton just blinked when he saw what he swore were the same vegetables go round about four times. Christ, is it Saturday night yet? he thought, as 'Tie a Yellow Ribbon Round The Old Oak Tree' gurgled out of the radio sitting on top of the pie-warmer. But

174

it was tolerable — until Saturday night anyway. Then who should arrive, acting like he owned the place, but Quigley's mate Layton Mitner with a cigarette hanging out of his mouth.

He was about two inches taller than Les and about two stone lighter; but acted like he was six inches taller and four stone heavier. He had a long, sallow face like Quigley and was about the same age with lidded brown eyes, and weak, brown hair combed up to give it a bit of body. He was wearing grey trousers and brown shoes and a green and black shirt, and acted like Joe Cool in front of the two waitresses, but looked about as sharp as a wet fishfinger. For some reason Norton disliked him the minute he laid eyes on him.

'G'day, Bob,' he said, bursting through the flyscreen door like Elliott Ness.

'Hello, Layton,' replied Quigley.

'You been busy?'

'Yeah,' nodded Quigley. 'Not too bad.'

Layton let the girls know he'd arrived then got into a muted conversation with Quigley. Except for Layton checking out his every move, Norton was once again ignored. Eventually Quigley made a half-hearted effort at some manners.

'Oh, Les. This is Layton.'

'Hello, Layton,' replied Les, about to offer his hand.

Quigley's mate gave him a brief once up and down and a muttered 'Les', not bothering to offer his hand, and went back to his muted conversation with Quigley.

Oh well, fuck you then, thought Les. Suits me, and continued with his chores.

Out of the blue Quigley gave him an odd order. 'Les? Those bottles out the back. Go and push them into the corner a bit, will you?'

'Okay,' shrugged Norton, happy to get away from the cigarette fumes for a while.

Push them into the corner? Buggered if I can see what difference it'll make, thought Les, as he surveyed what was literally hundreds of empty wine and beer bottles.

175

Oh well, who gives a stuff? Norton began moving the bottles away from the restaurant into a corner, mainly with his feet and legs. He glanced back at the kitchen window and saw Layton and Quigley in a huddle beneath the cupboard in the corner between the sink and the stove. The cupboard door was open and obscured his view somewhat, but there appeared to be an exchange of something between Quigley and Layton, then Quigley placed something in the cupboard and closed the door. After he did he put his head through the door and called out to Norton.

'Don't worry about that, Les. You can leave it till tomorrow night.'

'Okay,' shrugged Norton.

Les went back into the smoky heat and began washing more dishes. Mitner had a plate of food and although Les had his back to him he could feel the ex-kitchen hand's eyes boring into his back.

'Bob tells me you've been working up the Cross,' said Layton.

'Yeah,' replied Les.

'Up with all the poofters, eh?' Mitner had a high-pitched, girlish laugh which he let go at the end of just about every sentence. 'I thought you might have. All the poofters wear pink headbands and blue T-shirts.' This was accompanied by more giggly laughter. 'I suppose you go to the Gay Mardi Gras too. With all your poofter mates from round the Cross.'

The two pisshead waitresses gave a bit of a titter and even Quigley seemed a little amused. Mitner was starting to play to the crowd, now thinking Les was just too plain dumb to have any comeback. Norton stared down into the sink as his blood started to, if not boil, begin to simmer a bit. Will I break this cunt's jaw now or won't I? He ground his teeth and said nothing. No, not tonight. I still need that alibi. But I guarantee if he's around when I knock off next Saturday night, I'll stick his head straight through that fuckin' freezer door. In fact if he's not here, I might work an extra night just

176

to do it. And I might shove his mate's head through the fuckin' thing as well.

'Listen, Les,' continued Layton. 'If you've got AIDS from some of your poofter mates, you can't work here, you know.' This was accompanied by another burst of giggling laughter.

'Go on, eh?' said Les.

'Yeah. You can't handle food if you've been copping it up the arse,' giggled Mitner.

'How about skinny big mugs with big mouths,' muttered Norton. 'Are you allowed to handle them?'

'What?'

Norton somehow managed to keep switched off, even though, if Layton mentioned the word poofter once, he mentioned it two hundred times. He also managed to get in Norton's way as much as possible, making Les weave around him as he worked. Before he went, he left his plate on the bench for Norton to scrape off and clean. He didn't bother to say goodbye to Les but told Quigley that he'd see him tomorrow night. Norton couldn't wait.

The night limped along. Quigley, a constant beer at his side, managed to keep cooking and the two waitresses, in between their steady drinking and smoking, managed to get the food out to the customers and bring the plates back in.

Before long, some other customers started coming round the back. They were mainly surfie looking types in their early twenties and younger, mostly men, but a number of young women too. They'd come to the back door, look at Les for a moment, then step inside and go over to Quigley. A few words would take place, Quigley would go to the cupboard next to the stove, there would be an exchange of money and something else, and then they'd leave. The two waitresses carried on as normal and Les, knowing he was expected to be too dumb to realise what was going on, carried on as if nothing unusual was happening either. Jesus, just what sort of a shit fight have I got myself into here? he thought.

Somehow the customers at both the front and back dwindled off and it was time to clean up and go home.

The girls swept and vacuumed the restaurant; Les cleaned up all the kitchen, taking out the bottles and putting the rubbish in a dump-bin at the back of the motel. One of the last jobs he had to do before mopping the floor was to take the blackened rings off the stove and scrub them in the sink with a copper scourer. Les was glad now he'd thrown an old pair of rubber gloves in his bag, as the burners were close enough to red hot. As he got the last burner off the stove, Norton blinked in disbelief at what was beneath. It looked like the scene of the Exxon Valdez disaster. There was oil, grease, fat, pieces of meat and vegetables and other shit almost a foot deep which must have been around twelve months old. It wasn't only filthy: it was downright dangerous. If a match or a flame of some description had gone down there, it would have literally gone off like a petrol bomb. God almighty, thought Les. What a bloody pigsty.

It was almost twelve when Norton knocked off. The other three seemed to stay back and continue drinking; Les wasn't offered a beer and it appeared Quigley wanted him out of the place and the sooner the better. Norton was given eight dollars an hour, which came to $52, which Quigley magnanimously made up to $55, as well as grudgingly telling Les that he hadn't gone too bad. Norton was tempted to go down on his hands and knees in gratitude.

'Can you come in at five tomorrow?' said Quigley. 'We might be a bit busy Friday night.'

Norton shuddered. An extra half-hour in this pit. 'Yeah, righto, Bob,' he answered, tossing his sweatband in his overnight bag.

'Okay. See you tomorrow night.'

The two waitresses muttered a disinterested goodbye and that was it. Norton walked to his car, leaving them to their booze and cigarettes and whatever else there might be with him not around.

Sitting behind the wheel Norton couldn't believe how

178

much he stank. It was a mixture of sweat, garlic, and cooking smells, but mainly cigarette smoke. Also, his throat was sore, his eyes were still stinging and he was getting a headache. He felt like taking the $55 Quigley had given him and throwing it out the window. Instead he drove straight home to have a shower and two Panadols.

Warren wasn't in when he got home. Oh well, at least someone's having a good time thought Les. In fact, no matter what Warren does tonight, apart from getting run over by a bus, he'd have to have a better time than I did. Shit! What am I gonna tell him in the morning?

Norton's clothes were absolutely putrid and he couldn't ever remember feeling so dirty and smelly; the shower was pure bliss. He intended watching a bit of TV after it but couldn't believe how tired and dried out he felt. He made a mug of Ovaltine and after dropping the two headache tablets found himself yawning like a lion before he was halfway through it. Stuff this for a joke, I'm going to bed. As he lay on the pillow, Norton's last thoughts before drifting off were that he was a complete and utter mug for taking on that kitchen hand job, even if it was a perfect alibi. It was plain punishing. Plus he now had to put up with Quigley's smartarse mate Layton. And I've got another two fuckin' nights to go. Christ! Norton shook his head. I must be crooked on myself. You wouldn't wish that joint on your worst enemy. Not the Burma Railway? Hah! It makes the Burma Railway seem like a month on Lindeman Island. Oh well. I suppose it's all for the best.

Norton blinked his way into consciousness around eight. Like the previous day it was cloudy, but still warm.

Warren was in the kitchen sipping coffee and reading the paper when Les walked in, still wiping water and tiredness from his eyes.

'Well, cut my legs off and call me Shorty,' grinned Warren. 'If it isn't Bogdan the kitchen hand. How was it last night, Boggers? Have a good time, did you?'

'Yeah,' nodded Norton, feeling the kettle before switching it on. 'It was tops. I had a ball.'

'Yeah, I'll bet you did,' answered Warren, smiling at the look on Norton's face. 'The place is a brothel. The food there's killed more people than road accidents.'

Les stood and blinked at Warren. 'How did you know?' he said, before he realised it.

'How do I know? I used to go to Randwick High School with Quigley. He was a grub then. The only reason he stays in business is because his uncle's a health inspector at Randwick Council. Even then, I still don't know how he keeps going.'

Norton was about to say something but changed his mind. 'You didn't tell me this yesterday, you cunt,' he muttered, shovelling coffee and honey into a mug.

'I didn't want to spoil your enthusiasm.' Warren threw back his head and roared laughing. 'You fuckin' Dubbo.'

Norton shook his head and somehow couldn't help but agree. As he sipped his coffee he told Warren a bit about the restaurant. He didn't mention Layton and he didn't mention the hustle between him and Quigley in the corner. Warren seemed to laugh even louder at the low night Les had gone through; then he settled down.

'So how long are you going to maintain your new career as catering hygiene supervisory officer at the Devlin slop pit?'

'Till Saturday night.'

'Saturday night! You're kidding.'

'I told Quigley I would. And I'm a man who keeps his word, Warren.'

'Tight-arsed wally'd be more like it.'

'You're entitled to your opinions, prick features.' Norton took another sip of coffee and sat down. 'So, what happened to you last night? You weren't in when I got home.'

'I went out. To the opening of a nice, shiny new bar in Darlinghurst.'

'Darlinghurst, eh? What did you wear? Your dressing gown, or the sequin top with the matching handbag?'

180

'It wasn't that type of bar, gorilla head. In fact, I had a good time. Took it easy on the piss, met not a bad sort there and finished back at her place for a cup of coffee.'

Norton looked astounded. 'Don't tell me you finally got a root.'

'No. But we'll put this one down as a probable. I'm taking her out Saturday night.'

'Lucky girl. Why don't you bring her over the Devlin for a feed?'

'Les. I want to get into her pants, not get her into hospital. The pumping I intend doing on Saturday night isn't with a stomach pump.' Warren sipped the last of his coffee and folded the newspaper. 'No, I don't know where I'll take her. Could you suggest anything? Would the kitchen hand know of any good parties or anything this Saturday night?'

Les stared at Warren and tried to keep a straight face. 'How the fuck would I know of any parties on Saturday night? I'll be up to my arsehole in cockroaches and dirty dishes.'

'And deservedly so too.' Warren put his cup in the sink and walked round and gave Les a fatherly pat on the shoulder. 'In the meantime, Bogdan, don't work too hard. And do us a favour: don't bother bringing any food home from the restaurant with you. I'd rather commit harikari than eat any of that shit. It'd be better for your stomach. See you, Boggers.'

'Have a nice day, Warren.'

Norton was forced to let it go at that. It hadn't been a bad serve Warren had given him and he was forced to cop it sweet. At least he now knew how Quigley could have his restaurant like a pigsty and still stay in business. Les did have one chuckle though. Did he know where there was a party on Saturday night? Did he what! A ripper — not far away and with a band thrown in. Bad luck about that, Woz, old mate. Maybe next time. So what to do now?

Norton drained his coffee and grabbed a couple of

oranges. A run in Centennial Park wouldn't go astray. He changed into a pair of shorts and did just that.

While he was jogging through the grass and around the ponds Les mulled Saturday night over and over in his head. There was only one loose cannon that needed tying down now, not an overly important one, but a detail that could be fixed up with a phone call and that would definitely be it. There was another thing on his mind that he wasn't quite one hundred per cent sure about, but it had nothing to do with the party. Just the flats.

After his run and a half hour or so of exercises Les returned home, got cleaned up and into a clean pair of jeans and T-shirt. After a decent breakfast, Les got on the phone and attended to the loose cannon. Warren's indexed address book was next to the phone; he opened it, thumbed to D for Dapto and dialled the number.

'Hello. Could I speak to Larry Dapto, please.'

Dapto was an easy going if somewhat overweight rock promoter, who sometimes wore a beard and sometimes didn't. He was a good friend of Warren and had worked with him in a couple of advertising agencies. He'd got out of the game to promote a couple of those mini Woodstock-type rock festivals. Les had got to know him through Warren and had bumped into him at parties, and up at the Kelly Club and round about. Larry loved his food and drink and a one-liner and was now in the film game. He'd co-produced a couple of Australian movies but was now concentrating on making rock videos from his home somewhere in Paddington. Les always found Dapto easy going enough and evidently the only time he ever got the shits was when he blossomed out to sixteen stone and some friends in an advertising agency where he was working entered him in a Meatloaf look-alike contest. To this day Dapto never found out who it was; but he'd never lost his sense of humour.

'This is Larry speaking.'

'Hello, Larry. It's Les Norton.'

'Les. Hello, saaannn. How's things?'

'Pretty good, mate. How's yourself?'

'As a bean man. As a bean.'

'That's good.'

'So Les, me old China. What can I do you for?'

'Larry. Are you still into making rock videos?'

'Certainly am, saaannn.'

'Well, I might have something for you. These sheilas with a band are having a street party this Saturday night. It's for a friend, but I know they're really gonna turn it on. It might be an idea for you to go out and film it.'

'What's the band?'

'The Heathen Harlots.'

'The Heathen Harlots! Hey man, they're a fucking hot outfit — stuck with a wombat manager who should be cleaning brascoes.'

'Yeah. Like I said, it's for a friend's birthday or something, but they're doing a whole lot of new songs and all. It might be worth your time to get a bit of a crew together and go out and film it.'

'Hey, not good enough, saann. This sounds un-fucking-real.'

'It will be, Larry. But if you do go, don't tell the sheilas I told you about it. I think they're trying to keep it a bit on the quiet side.'

'As a bean, saaann. No worries.'

Norton gave Dapto the address and told him roughly what time it would be starting. He himself wouldn't be there till late as he had a job he had to go to but he'd see him there some time or other. Dapto thanked Les again and said there was a definite drink in it for him. Les said thanks. They exchanged one or two more pleasantries then Les hung up.

Well, that's about it, smiled Les. I can't think of another thing. If those sheilas see Dapto out there with his camera they'll probably think he's something to do with the bloke from America. Though as long as those foul-mouthed molls are getting paid, I don't think they'd give a stuff if Larry was from one of the moons around Jupiter. Now, is there anyone else left to con? No, I reckon that's about it. But I also reckon it's about time I gave my ever lovin' boss a ring. It's been almost two weeks.

The casino owner's answering machine was off and Les got straight onto him.

'Hello, Price. It's Les.'

'Les, me old son.' Price sounded ecstatic. 'How are you mate?'

'Pretty good, Price. How's yourself?'

'Good as gold. Wouldn't be dead for quids.'

'That's the style. I rang a couple of times, but all I got was your answering service.'

'Yeah. I rang back, but you must have been out. What have you been up to, old fellah?'

'Ohh, not much. Just taking it easy. Getting a few early nights for a change. Going to the beach and that.'

'Billy said he rang you. You know what's going on up the club?'

'Yeah. Sounds like you're copping it sweet yourself. Playing five hundred and that with your mates. What else have you been up to?'

'That's about it, Les. Finish there and go straight home. Getting plenty of early nights myself for a change.'

'It doesn't hurt.'

'Ohh, you can say that again. You seen Billy lately?'

'No,' lied Les.

'Wait till you do. He looks like a million dollars. Training like mad, lost over half a stone. He's got me thinking I might even start having a run myself. Hey, you know if you want to come up and do a night, it's sweet.'

'No, that's okay, Price. Leave it to Billy. He's got a family to support.'

'Fair enough. But if you're short of a quid . . .'

'No, that's all right, Price. I'm plugging along okay.'

'From what they tell me, I think you've got more money squirrelled away than any of us.'

'I wish you were right,' chuckled Les.

'So when are you going to call up one night? Just have a drink or a coffee. Or call over home for a feed one day. Jesus! Don't make a complete stranger of yourself, Les.'

'No, I'll be up soon. In fact, I reckon there's a good chance I might even see you over the weekend.'

'Okay. Do that for sure.'

'All right, Price. Well, I'll get cracking. And I'll see you shortly.'

'Righto, Les. Good to hear from you, mate.'

Norton smiled at the phone for a while after he hung up. Well, while I'm here, I may as well give young William a ring.'

There was no mistaking Billy Dunne's voice over the phone.

'How's Billy the kid?'

'Is that you, Les?'

'Yeah. How are you, mate?'

'Good, mate. What's doing? I thought you might have been around to do a bit of training with me.'

'I was, Billy, but you look that fit I don't know whether I'm game.'

Billy laughed. 'I'm fit. But I ain't that fit.'

'Yeah, I dunno. Listen, I rang Price. Thanks for saying you haven't seen me.'

'That's okay, mate. No worries.'

'So, how's it going up the club? Everything sweet?'

'Yeah, couldn't be creamier. We're starting to get out by around twelve now.'

'Half your luck. And while we're talking about luck, I might even have a little something for you, Billy, old pal.'

'Yeah?'

'Yeah. A reward for your fabulous powers of deduction, Holmes. A nice, lazy five grand.'

'Five grand! Fuckin' hell!' Billy paused on the phone for a moment. 'Hey, wait a minute. You didn't do what I think ...'

'Exactly, Holmes.'

'You...' Billy couldn't help but laugh. 'You're a no-good cunt, Les. You know that, don't you?'

'Indeed I do, William,' laughed Les. 'And you can give me a lecture on the evils of drugs and a jolly good thrashing too. Next week, when I drop the five gorillas in your skyrocket.'

They talked and laughed for a while with Billy realising Les didn't want to say too much over the phone. But when Les hung up, Billy was looking forward to seeing his old mate early next week; five grand or no five grand.

Well, that's about it thought Les. Nothing to do now but wait until Saturday night, then on Sunday go and inspect the charred remains of my sumptuous villa with tears in my eyes. I suppose I could take a run over to Whittle's and get him to snooker away the rest of that bikie money. No, fuck it, I'll leave it till next week. It's safe where it is. A bit of a craggy grin crept across Norton's face. In the meantime, I guess I'm just stuck between the Devlin and the Deep Blue Seas. What a way to go.

It wasn't much of a day outside. Norton spent the rest of it pottering around the house and yard and doing a bit of work on his car, then he cooked a feed. One half of him was trying to put the old block of flats out of his mind; the other half was still hoping to Christ nothing would go wrong. Before he knew it, it was time to go and bundy on at the restaurant. He put on an old, white Billabong T-shirt and threw a white sweatband in his overnight-bag. At least this time, as he reluctantly drove over to Coogee, he knew what to expect.

Quigley was in the same place at the table when Les walked in that night, trimming beef or whatever, with a beer and a cigarette in one hand and still wearing the same T-shirt he was wearing on Wednesday. Christ, thought Les, I'll bet he whistles and the fuckin' thing jumps up off the floor onto his back.

186

'G'day, Bob,' he said, stowing his overnight bag in the same place as before. 'How's things?'

'All right, Les,' replied Quigley slowly, giving Norton a look that said he was now totally convinced that Les had 'prime Australian galah' stencilled across his forehead in capital letters.

Norton stood at the table and wrapped his sweatband on. 'So, what do you want me to do? Chop up some more vegetables?'

'No,' answered Quigley. 'There's not that many bookings tonight. I might get you to do something else first.'

Bookings? mused Les. Do people actually book to eat in this rat's nest?

'I might get you to do the stove.'

Norton's heart sank and his anger rose at the same time; he knew exactly what to expect. You greasy, stinken, fuckin' piece of shit, Quigley. You're sure getting your pound of flesh out of me, aren't you, you prick?

'There's a stack of newspapers in the pantry. Get them and I'll show you what to do.'

Norton got the bundle of newspapers and spread them out on the floor around the stove. Quigley switched it off and moved the demi-glace. Les put on his rubber gloves, removed the rings and burners and got into it. It had to be one of the filthiest jobs Norton had ever done — it was everything he could do to stop himself from telling Quigley to get fucked and walking out. There were literally gallons of putrid, rancid fat and blackened grease on the bottom of the stove, full of food scraps, cigarette butts, matches, dead cockroaches and flies, scraps of cloth, paper and other gunk that not even the CSIRO laboratories could identify. It had been that long since the stove had been cleaned parts of it were solidified, and Les had to smash them apart with a hammer and a big screwdriver. Fat and grease went everywhere; on his face, in his hair, all over his clothes. The more Les scrubbed the more shit there seemed to be; and all the time Les could feel Quigley sniggering at him. Well, this might be hard, fumed Norton, but

187

I know what's going to be harder. Stopping myself from tearing both Quigley and his mug mate Layton apart if he comes in here gobbing off later on tonight.

He got the stove cleaned and put back together with not so much as a compliment or a thanks from Quigley. Olive Oyle arrived with a crash of car keys, a giant slurp of rum and Coke followed by a cloud of cigarette smoke. She didn't bother to say hello to Les. But she had a big smile and a hello for 'Robert' before disappearing in another cloud of cigarette smoke into the dining room to do whatever it was she did with the tables. After that it was the same routine as the night before; chop vegetables and herbs, wash pots and pans and get this and that for Quigley. The only variation: Quigley had about a dozen half-rotten bream in a bucket which he got Les to gut and scale. It was all Norton could do to stop from throwing up.

Although he'd managed to clean himself up a bit, Les still stank of rotten fish and rancid grease when waitress number two arrived with more crashing of car keys, a huge slurp of cheap Scotch and another cloud of cigarette smoke thick enough to lose a bus in. Like Olive Oyle, Mendle As Anything didn't bother to say hello to Les; she said hello to 'Robert', though, then joined the other waitress in the dining room.

Norton switched off and soldiered on. The radio groaned out Tom Jones' 'Green Green Grass Of Home' and as the night ground on, Les was wishing that was where he was. A few meals went out and at one stage, as Les got something from the fridge, he had a quick glance through the small window in the swing door that led to the dining room. There were barely eight customers in the restaurant but at least twice that many had come to the back door; mostly the same young surfie types like the night before. Once again, they'd look at Les, go over to Quigley who'd go to the cupboard in the corner, money would again change hands, the surfies would leave and Les Norton, the prize dummy, would chop or wash away as if nothing was happening.

Quigley lit another cigarette and went to the toilet at the same time both waitresses were in the dining room. Les had a quick look around then opened the cupboard in the corner. There was a small, rectangular, plastic container sitting on a pile of plates. At one end of it were several small, al-foil squares which Norton tipped were grams of hash. At the other end were a number of small plastic bags about a third full of white powder. Les tipped this to be speed — the customers coming to the back door weren't on the nod or scratching at themselves like strung-out smackies and the way they were dressed he sure as hell doubted if they could afford cocaine. Not a bad little business you've got here, Quigley, mused Norton, closing the cupboard door. The food goes out the front door; the dope goes out the back door.

Then it dawned on Norton what else was going on. Layton was Quigley's supplier who also worked in the restaurant doing as little as possible while they washed the money. No wonder Quigley didn't worry too much if he didn't get run off his feet with customers. And by Layton's attitude and the way he gobbed off at Les as if he was eight feet tall, Layton was an obvious cokehead. He was probably taking a few nights off — then after Les had cleaned the place up he'd be back and Les would get the arse. Quigley came back in and Norton watched the owner's reflection in the kitchen window as he bent over the sink. You shifty pair of smartarse cunts.

As he was watching Quigley, a young kid who couldn't have been a day over fifteen came to the back door carrying a skateboard. He looked at Les, went over to Quigley and the same ritual went on behind Norton's back. Norton was disgusted. This wasn't just someone moving a bit of green around between a few friends or whatever. These were two slimy dealers who would sell dope to anyone just to get their money so they could shove half of it up their nose. Les spat in the sink. He'd never given anyone up in his life, but as soon as was

189

finished in this shithouse he'd be dropping thirty cents on these two arseholes.

The word arsehole had barely flashed through Norton's mind when who should come charging in the back door, his eyes reddened and spinning around from an obvious snout full of blow, but Layton. Here it comes, thought Norton, gritting his teeth as he shoved a rack of dishes in the dishwasher. Layton was wearing his Friday night kill 'em gear; black jeans, brown shoes and a black shirt he must have ironed by rolling up in a Holland blind. He stank of Brut aftershave and if Les wasn't mistaken he'd had his hair permed. Layton totally ignored Les, he said a quick hello to Quigley then let the two girls know Joe Cool was in town and swanned around in front of them for a while. Eventually he went across to Quigley. Norton knew what Quigley was going to say five minutes before he opened his mouth.

'I'll get you to take that garbage out, Les,' said the owner. 'Those ahh... fish heads are starting to go through the kitchen.'

'Yeah, righto, Bob,' replied Les, happy anyway to be able to get out of the cigarette smoke for a few minutes.

Norton pulled the garbage bag out, tied the top and headed for the dump-bin at the rear of the motel. As he rounded the corner from the toilets, Les stopped and looked back. Quigley and Layton were once again in the corner doing their hustle. Les shook his head, spat on the ground and continued on down the drive.

Back in the kitchen he put his head down as he scrubbed some pots in the sink and told himself to be cool while he waited for Layton to start mouthing off. Only one more night to go, Les. One more, that's all. After a few minutes talking with Quigley, Layton went over to the urn and made a cup of coffee. He looked at Quigley, then at Norton and smiled.

'I see you're wearing your white headband tonight, Les,' he said, adding his giggly laugh. 'Is that the go with all the poofters up the Cross, is it? Pink ones

190

Thursday. White ones Friday. It matches your T-shirt this time though.'

Norton stared ahead and gritted his teeth. Only one more night, Les. Just one. That's all.

'I suppose you're missing your mates up the Cross tonight, Les.' Layton turned to the others. 'Friday night's the big night for all the poofters. Especially if you've got a white headband and a matching T-shirt.' This was accompanied by another burst of giggling laughter. The two half-pissed waitresses must have thought this amusing; they gave a bit of a titter as they took some more meals out to the dining room. Then Layton started sniffing the air. He turned from Quigley to Les. 'Hey, Les, I thought you took all those fish heads out? Something still stinks in here.' He moved over and began sniffing Norton. 'Oh, it's only you, Les. Is that your last boyfriend's aftershave?' Les was seething.

Then Layton picked a piece of stove grease from Norton's hair. 'Hey what's this? Did he blow in your hair, Les?' He gave a great giggle of laughter. 'I reckon you'd give a good head job, Les. You'd have the experience.'

That was it for Norton. Fuck waiting till next week. He picked up a pan from the sink and was just about to backhand Layton with it right in the mouth when the phone near the pantry rang. The two girls were in the dining room, Quigley had his hands full and Norton of course, wasn't expected to have brains enough to be able to talk over the phone.

'Hey, will you grab that, Layton?' said Quigley.

'Yeah, righto, Bob.' Layton took his coffee, walked over and picked up the receiver. 'Hello. Devlin.' Then he smiled over at Quigley. 'It's for me, Bob.'

Quigley nodded his head, Les put the pan back in the sink and let out a massive lungful of pent-up rage.

Layton talked and giggled on the phone for a while then hung up and got a plate of food. He slung off at Norton a couple more times but kept his hands off him, seeming more content to swan around in front of

191

the two waitresses. Eventually he left, saying goodbye to everyone but Norton and once again leaving his plate for Les to scrape off and clean.

Norton was now filthier on himself than ever for taking on this job. He had over sixty grand sitting in his wardrobe and could have been out somewhere, anywhere in Australia, having a ball. Instead, he was in a smoke-filled dump putting up with idiots and taking shit from two penny-ante dope dealers. The only semblance of a pat on the back he could give himself was the amount of restraint he'd shown. But he swore to himself that, even if Quigley laid him off tomorrow night, he was coming back next Thursday and kicking Layton from one end of the restaurant to the other. And Quigley too, if he put his head in. Then he was ringing a bloke he knew in the drug squad.

The night dragged on. Quigley and his two waitresses smoked about two hundred cigarettes while they all got drunk and the radio churned out all the worst possible pop music from the sixties and seventies. Norton couldn't ever remember being so down in the dumps and dirty on himself. In fact, he was starting to get dirty on the world. But the night had to end sooner or later, and it did; just after twelve. Quigley paid Les from a little black cash-box near the pantry, slinging him an extra five dollars and making a big man of himself for doing it, then he pissed Les off without once again the offer of a beer or a thank you but a 'be here at five thirty tomorrow'. Norton left the three of them to carry on with what ever they did, more than glad to be out of the stinken joint.

Oh well, thought Les, sitting behind the wheel of his car. Only one more night to go. Then it'll be my turn to have a laugh. And a big one. And as for restraint, I'd better not kid myself. If that phone hadn't rung I'd have wrapped that dirty black frying pan right around that dope-dealing arsehole's head. Again Les felt tired, drawn and dirtier than ever and was looking forward to a shower and a good night's sleep. Then it dawned

192

on him that Blue Seas was just up the road and this was about its last night on earth. He looked at his watch, twenty past twelve, and smiled to himself. I might go up and just have one last look at the old block of flats and see who's around.

He pulled up in Soudan Street, down from and opposite to the garage on the corner, switched off the engine, and sat in the car listening to the radio while he stared ahead in a bemused sort of way at Blue Seas Apartments. There was scarcely any moon and in the streetlight the old block of flats seemed to look even more decrepit than ever. Sandra's utility was out the front and so was the hippies' kombi-van. It was almost sad in a way. The old block of flats probably had its share of memories in its day and it was hard to believe it was once a clean, modern block of flats and that the suburb running down to Coogee, with its trams and aquarium, was almost a holiday resort area. Christ, I wonder what will be here tomorrow night? thought Les. Fire engines, police, people running around everywhere. And a dirty great pile of glowing ashes where the old flats used to be. I just hope no one gets hurt. That's all.

He glanced at his watch again just as the grey BMW swung into Aquila Street and pulled up not far from Sandra's old white utility. Well, what do you know, mused Norton, the hint of a smile flickering round the corners of his eyes. Right on time. The familiar spritely figure in the trench coat and hat got out, had a quick, furtive look around, then walked briskly into the foyer. Well, I'll say one thing. Whoever you are mate, you sure don't mind a bit of a late night root. Then Les chuckled out loud. But I'd make this one a good one, if I were you. I reckon it might be your last for a while. In my block of flats, anyway. Still chuckling to himself, Norton started the car and headed home, looking forward more than ever to having a shower and going straight to bed.

Norton was up the following morning around eight-thirty, not sure whether he was pleased to find it almost a perfect, sunny day or not. One thing he did know. After seven-odd hours in that smelly kitchen he had no trouble getting to sleep. The heat from the oven left him dried out and drained and the fumes from the others' non-stop cigarette smoking made the air outside the Kelly Club in Kings Cross seem like a walk through a pine forest in the Snowy Mountains. He made a cup of coffee and sipped it on the back verandah as he gazed out into the back yard. Oh well, one thing's for sure. It'll be a good night for a party. The papers were out the front; he brought them in and was flicking through them at the kitchen table when Warren surfaced around nine. He was sort of smiling at Norton in his blue velour shave-coat and for a Saturday morning, after his customary Friday night on the piss, he hadn't brushed up too bad.

'Do you have to make so much fuckin' noise out here, Les? You know I like to have a sleep in on Saturday morning.'

'Sorry, Warren,' replied Norton. 'I didn't realise my reading was disturbing you. Next time I'll put the fuckin' TV on.'

'Inconsiderate bastard.'

Norton kept reading but found his eyes following Warren around the kitchen as he fossicked around, making himself a cup of coffee.

'So, how was it last night, Bogdan? Have a nice time in the Devlin incurable diseases ward?'

'Yeah,' replied Norton. 'It was great. Just like the night before. Seven hours in a Bombay toilet block surrounded by cunts. I can't wait to get back.'

'I don't know why you just don't tell him to stick it in his arse. You're mad.'

'Because that's not how I operate Warren. I said I'd help him three nights and I'm going to. Quigley ain't that bad a bloke.'

'Quigley not a bad bloke!! You're kidding. He's a cunt. He thinks he's God's gift to women and he's killed more people than road accidents with his cooking.' Warren poured a cup of coffee and peered suspiciously at Norton over the rim. 'Something doesn't quite gel here. I know you too well, Les. I reckon you're up to something.'

'Up to something?' Norton glared at Warren. 'What in the fuck could I be up to working in a shitpot restaurant? All I'm doing is trying to earn a quid to keep this roof over our heads. And you treat me like a criminal. Jesus, you're good.'

'Yeah, I dunno. You couldn't possibly need the money that bad. Something's definitely going on.'

'Ohh, go and get fucked. Anyway, leave me alone, Woz. I'm trying to read the papers.'

Warren slipped the *Sydney Morning Herald* across the table as Les pulled the Positions Vacant section out and began going through it. He decided it might be an idea to change the subject before he gave himself away.

'So what did you do last night, Tom Cruise? You don't look too bad for a Saturday morning. Generally you look like you've been shot out of a cannon.'

'Not much. Had a few drinks back at the office after work. Went for a bit of dinner at a German place near Taylor Square. Then cruised round a couple of bars. I took it easy on the piss. I'm saving myself for a big one tonight.'

'You still taking that bag out, are you?'

'Melissa? Yes. And she's not a bag. She's quite a good sort.'

'The run you've been having lately ratboy, anything'd be a good sort to you now.'

'Hardy-ha-ha-fuckin'-ha!'

Les and his flatmate exchanged a few more pleasantries as they breakfasted and read the papers. After a while Warren made a fresh cup of coffee and walked out into the backyard.

'Hey, it's not a bad day outside,' he said, when he came back in. 'I'm going to go up to the Paddington Bazaar. Why don't you come up?'

Yeah, that would be all I need, thought Les. Go

walking round the Paddington Bazaar and bump into Sandra. Hello, Les. Looking forward to the party tonight? Haven't seen you cleaning up round the flats lately.

'No, I promised Billy I'd have a run with him later,' he lied. 'Why don't you come and have a run with us? Then we'll do a few rounds down the surf club.'

'Yeah,' nodded Warren. 'That doesn't sound like a bad idea. I'd have no trouble keeping up with you and your punch-drunk mate.' He sipped his coffee and gazed back out into the yard. 'No, it's too nice a day. I'll go to the bazaar. But I'll make it next week for sure.'

'I'll tell Billy when I see him. He'll be estatic. Warren Edwards, the human dynamo. Couldn't pull a wet tampon out of a sloppy drop kick.'

Around eleven Warren got changed and headed off to Paddington, leaving Les alone in the house wondering what to do with himself. Sitting around on his own, Norton soon found that, despite the banter and wisecracking with Warren earlier, he was now starting to get a bit edgy. He told himself nothing could go wrong; he'd covered every conceivable angle and he had two professionals on the job. But somehow he just couldn't control the feeling in the pit of his stomach. Christ, I'm blowing up a block of flats in front of God knows how many people dancing and having a party. Shit, if you took something like that for granted, there'd have to be something wrong with you. He made some more coffee and found himself pacing around the house. At midday his curiosity got the better of him. He strolled down to the TAB at Sixways and put some bets on, then drove over to Blue Seas Apartments.

Aquila Street wasn't quite what what you would call a hive of activity, but there were a number of people roaming about getting things together. Les parked just down from the garage opposite and sat in the car for a while sussing things out while he figured out whether he should show his face or not. The thing that did surprise Norton was a small fork-lift truck stacking pallets up in the middle of the street from a stack almost in front of the old block of flats. So, that's going to be your stage, is it? mused Les. Clever little devils, aren't you? Wonder how you managed to organise that? But then knowing you loveable, little lot, you'd just flash your ample pussies around and I imagine you'd be able to score just about anything. Sandra's utility wasn't there; she was obviously at the Paddington Bazaar. But the hippies' old kombi was there, and so was the purple wagon with Heathen Harlots on the side. Norton had just spotted it when who should come from inside, helping two of the hippies with a speaker, but Syd, the group's roadie and minder. He still had his neck in a brace and he was moving a little gingerly, but he was certainly up and about.

Franulka appeared from somewhere in an old pair of jeans and a sloppy grey sweatshirt. There was no missing her; even in that daggy gear she still looked disgustingly horny. She said something to Syd then went over to the bloke driving the fork-lift, pointed and said something to him also. It wasn't hard to see who was organising the show. The other girls in the band appeared with more people coming and going from the flats opposite — everybody seemed to be pitching in and doing their bit. Gwen was at the rear painting something on a big sheet of canvas or tarpaulin. Well, girls, smiled Norton, I've got to give it to you. You've sure got your shit together for this one. He sat there watching them for a few minutes more still wondering whether to put his head in or not. No, I don't think I'll bother. What's that old saying? Out of sight, out of mind. Besides, if I do go over, they'll only find me something to do. And I don't particularly feel like lumping speakers and other junk around — it's too nice a day. And I don't feel like talking to Syd all that much either. No, I think they can get on quite admirably without me. He watched the proceedings for a minute or two more then drove home.

Back in his house Les didn't know what he wanted

197

to do. It was too nice a day to be inside, but he didn't feel like going to the beach and being around people. Yet he didn't feel like his own company either. He didn't want silence, but he didn't want the TV or the radio on either. He put the kettle on to make a cup of coffee. While it was heating, another old saying went through his mind. You make your bed, you have to lay in it. Yes. Let's just hope I don't have to wear the bloody thing as well. Before the kettle boiled he abruptly switched it off.

'Ahh fuck this!' he cursed out loud.

He walked back down to Six-Ways and put some more bets on, then came home, got into a pair of shorts and his Nikes and went for a run in Centennial Park.

While Les was doing his best to enjoy his run the work at Aquila Street continued. The stage made of pallets began to take shape, ending up about six by three metres, and about two metres off the ground. They'd managed to scrounge up a roll of grey Axminister which, when it was laid over the top, almost looked as if it was tailor-made for the job. The night was certainly shaping up to be a success.

While all this movement was going on, nobody seemed to notice two beefy, dark-haired men carrying small overnight bags and wearing blue overalls with Otto Bins stencilled across the back. One was carrying a small aluminium stepladder he'd taken from the boot of a blue Mercedes which they had parked several hundred metres away. The two men had a quick but thorough look around, then moved inside the old block of flats; once inside the foyer, both men appeared to know exactly what they were doing. Moving straight up to the roof, they took what could almost pass for large tubes of toothpaste from their overnight bags and began squirting lines of what could also pass for Stripe toothpaste all over the place except that instead of being red and white, these lines, around four inches long, were black and grey. They squeezed plenty of the resinous smelling

198

'toothpaste' on to the tarred roof, methodically working their way down the stairs and around the fuse box to the laundry. Using the small stepladder they squeezed more lines of 'toothpaste' up onto the ceiling. As one tube would run out, they would put the empty into an overnight bag and get out another one.

Once inside the laundry, the swarthier of the two men produced two small packages about the same size as an oblong shaped tub of margarine. He removed the greaseproof paper and kneaded the light, green putty-like substance until it was a little flatter, then jammed it behind one of the meter boxes above the coppers in the laundry. Satisfied that it was secure, he worked two small devices consisting of a hearing aid battery and what looked like a transistor into the mixture. Happy with the first one, he jammed the other into a niche in the wall at the other end of the laundry and worked another device into that also. While he was doing this, the other man took two small squares of blue, putty-like substance from his overnight-bag. He jammed one above the laundry window where it faced the street and worked one of the electrical devices into it, then did exactly the same behind the fuse box at the foot of the stairs.

Satisfied everything was in order the two men picked up the stepladder and their overnight bags and walked slowly, even casually back to their car, leaving the people working outside the old block of flats to carry on absolutely none the wiser.

Back in Cox Avenue Bondi Norton had showered after his run and grilled himself a steak plus salad and vegetables. No matter what his innermost feelings were, nerves, anxiety, whatever, he still hadn't lost his appetite and he knew there was no way he'd eat anything in that restaurant. He knocked that over pretty smartly, had a mug of coffee then settled down to watch the Wide World of Sport and listen to the races. It was a beautiful day outside and, around four-thirty, Norton besides his nervousness, was almost cursing his good

199

luck. His straight out bets and his doubles had done no good, but an All Up Parlay in Brisbane had won him just over six hundred dollars. Work that out, he thought, shaking his head. I'm another six hundred in front, there's nearly seventy grand in my wardrobe and I'm going to work for seven hours in a stinken hot, cockroach-infested kitchen where I have to put up with two of the greatest drop kicks I've ever met in my life. Norton shook his head again. I think George Brennan was right when he said my brains were in my arse. Before Les knew it, it was getting on for five. He changed into his daggiest jeans and an old blue T-shirt, tossed a white sweatband into his overnight bag and headed for the restaurant.

Quigley wasn't in the kitchen when Norton arrived at work. The back door was open, there was an open bottle of beer on the table and the demi-glace was bubbling away on the stove, but no Quigley. The back door was open, Les let himself in, stowed his bag, had a quick look in the dining room and waited. Oh well. A few minutes later Quigley appeared from the direction of the toilets, blowing his nose, his eyes red and runny and spinning around in his head like two Ferris wheels. He saw Norton, blinked and tried to act cool.

'Hello, Les,' he said, then fumbled around lighting a cigarette and taking a mouthful of beer.

'G'day, Bob,' answered Les, putting on his sweatband. One look at Quigley's sallow face and watery red eyes told him he'd been throwing more up his nose in the toilets than Vicks Sinex. At least he'd changed his T-shirt. 'So, what do you want me to do? Chop up some vegetables?'

'Yeah. And a few herbs. But don't do a real lot. There's not that many bookings.'

That's understandable, mused Norton. But I imagine there'll be a few bookings at the back door. Well then, I wonder what filthy, low job you've got lined up for me tonight?

It took Norton twenty minutes to find out what it was because that's how long it took him to finish the vegetables. Quigley got him to clean out the three deep-freezers. He switched them off then told Les what to do. First he had to get rid of what was in them. As usual it was more accumulated filth and garbage. There were plastic bags of different fish, mainly niggers and what had to be shark, plus the half-rotten bream Les had cleaned the night before. There were about twenty blue swimmer crabs that had now turned into brown swimmer crabs tinged with green. Pieces of meat, chickens, ducks, things that were entirely unidentifiable. A solitary lobster, cartons of ice cream, pieces of crab shell, prawn heads, matches and just rubbish in general. It was filthy and neglected just like the stove had been, but instead of being covered in rotten grease it was frozen solid.

Knowing he was just getting used up, and on top of his already edginess, Norton's temper began to rise. He pulled out a frozen beef fillet and was seriously thinking of letting Quigley have it right between the eyes, but he somehow managed to cool down. Just a few hours more Les, that's all now and it will all be over. Once he had all the food out Les then had to smash the accumulated ice away with a meat cleaver before he could start on the freezers with a bucket of hot, soapy water. How long since they'd been cleaned was anybody's guess — the ice, now turned a dirty grey, was over a foot thick in parts. Norton wouldn't have been surprised if there was a mastodon or a Neanderthal man still clutching a spear frozen in there. Cursing inwardly, Norton hacked away at the ice. His hands, even with rubber gloves on, were stinging and numb from the cold. While Norton was working, Quigley turned the radio on and pottered around at the table drinking piss and smoking cigarettes as Gene Pitney's 'Only Love Can Break A Heart' seeped out of the speakers like a weeping cut.

Norton was still working on the freezers when waitress

number one arrived in her usual jangling of car keys, booze and an encompassing cloud of cigarette smoke. Tonight she was wearing a black mini and her legs looked like two white tomato stakes that could have done with a shave. As usual Norton could have been invisible bent over the freezers. It was. 'Hello Robert.' A few more words then she disappeared into the dining room.

After much scrubbing, smashing and silent cursing Les got the third freezer finished as waitress number two arrived, also wearing a black mini. She too ignored Les, said 'Hello Robert', lit a cigarette, threw a triple Scotch down her throat and joined Olive Oyle in the dining room. Apart from saying hello when he got to work, Norton had scarcely uttered a dozen words all night. His mind was working overtime however, and what was going through it didn't give Les a great deal to smile about. His next few words didn't bring him any joy either.

'Okay, Bob,' he said through gritted teeth, as he wiped his hands on a tea towel. 'What do you want me to do now?'

'You see all those plates in the corner cupboard?'

Quigley got Les to get every plate out of the 'dope' cupboard near the sink and scrub the bottoms of them from where they were blackened from Quigley putting them straight on the stove to heat up. Norton spent another pleasant hour or so bent over the sink with a pot scourer and a can of Ajax, scrubbing charred soot from the bottoms of about a hundred plates and soup bowls. The only thing that kept him sane was the pleasant thought of coming back the following week and breaking both Quigley's and his mate Layton's jaws. By the time he finished scouring the plates, a few customers began to trickle in and it was back to the normal grind of washing dishes and scrubbing pots. The only difference tonight was watching the clock tick round and wondering how things were going up at Blue Seas Apartments. But he need not have worried. While Les was having a complete bummer

202

at the Devlin, things were going swimmingly up in Aquila Street.

It was almost nine and there was a crowd of about a hundred, which was increasing steadily. All the speakers and instruments were up on stage and the sign Gwen had painted in green and gold saying The Prince Charles Birthday Bash was hung up as a backdrop. All the neighbours were cool and they'd been in touch with the cops who weren't all that interested. There were three heavy metal bands playing at Selina's at Coogee, so they knew they'd have plenty on their plate there, rather than worry about a street party in what was little more than an overwide alley about a hundred metres long.

Everybody from the flats across the road was there with their eskys and friends; friends of the band were there, so was Burt, Rosie, and Sandra and all the hippies were helping the girls in the band. It was carnival atmosphere on an absolutely delightful night with the mob from the pub across the road now starting to show a little curiosity.

As the girls got up on stage all the men's 'curiosity' turned to pure lust. The girls were wearing much the same gear they had on when Les saw them out the front the morning they got back from Canberra. Alastrina's tits were just about hanging out of her string top. Isla looked better than ever in her crutch-tight jeans full of razor slashes that had been doubled up, round the backside. Riona's behind looked sensational and her crumpet was just about bulging right out of her black leggings and through her cut off jeans. Even Gwendoline, fussing around at the mixer as she got a cassette together to record the night's performance, looked extra horny in her school uniform complete with a straw hat. But it was Franulka who stole the show. She looked almost unbelievable in her Elvira gown with the cut-away top and the huge split up the front, where if you were down the front of the crowd you could get a glimpse of a sensational pair of purple knickers trimmed with pink.

203

Larry Dapto was onto it like he had Clark Kent's X-ray vision and told his two-man camera crew that at one stage of the night they were to zero in on Franulka, even to the extent of sticking the camera lens right up her dress.

Gwen had a bit of Top Forty music playing softly through the speakers as the girls began moving around on stage and getting behind their instruments. At a nod from Franulka she turned it off, then the sexy lead singer adjusted the mike and gave it a couple of taps 'toc toc' with her finger.

'Hello, there,' she breathed huskily into the microphone, throwing in a lascivious grin for all the men including poor Syd in his neck brace. 'We're The Heathen Harlots and we'd like to welcome you to the Prince Charles Birthday Bash. We hope you have a good time. This first song's a bit laid back. But we just want to tune our instruments.'

Franulka tapped her foot a couple of times, and smoother than Yellow Box honey, the girls slipped easily into the Rolling Stones' 'Terrifying'.

They were spot on. Evocative and crystal clear at the same time with just the right acoustics echoing off the surrounding flats. A hush went through the crowd as the girls moved lazily around on stage, each taking a turn at the lyrics while they checked their instruments, got their 'sea legs' and the nod from Gwen on the mixer. This one song drifting across the street was enough for the drinkers in the hotel; it emptied out in about two minutes. By the time the girls finished the first song the crowd had almost doubled and was increasing steadily.

'Thank you,' said Franulka, as the last chord echoed off the surrounding buildings and blended in with the muted applause from the crowd. She ran her eyes over the crowd and saw Dapto and his camera crew filming steadily. The other girls saw him too and Franulka gave them a wink and a nod. 'Like I said,' she continued, 'we're The Heathen Harlots, doing our bit for Charlie

204

boy on his birthday. And we think we've now got our instruments tuned.' Franulka caught the eye of a male punter ogling her. 'Is your instrument tuned, big boy?' The punter, grinned, yelled and waved his can of beer. 'Good. Okay, that last song was nice. But let's... let's have a bit of rock 'n' roll.'

There was silence for a moment, then Franulka nodded to the other girls and literally screamed into the mike. *'My man is red hot.'*

The girls yelled back. *'Your man ain't diddly squat.'*

'Well, I got a guy, he's six feet four. Sleeps in the kitchen with his head in the hall. My man is red hot.'

'Your man ain't diddly squat.'

'He ain't got money, but boy he's really got a lot.'

The Heathen Harlots belted into a scorching version of Robert Gordon's 'Red Hot'. And when Franulka ran her tongue around the mike and sang, *'He ain't got money, but boy he's really got a lot'*, nobody in the audience needed to be told twice what she was referring to.

They attacked that song, literally tearing it to shreds as they bounced all over the stage. The crowd went wild. In seconds there wasn't a foot not tapping, a head not shaking or a backside not wiggling. Cars pulled up and windows opened, as Aquila Street turned into a mass of singing, dancing people.

His eyes bulging out like two oranges, Dapto turned to his camera crew. 'Not fucking good enough,' was all he managed to say.

After that the girls slipped straight into Steve Hoy's 'Flick Through The Pages' before the applause and cheering had a chance to die down, with Isla somehow belting out an even bigger backbeat than the original. They moved, they swished across the stage shaking their pert backsides and wiggling their tits at the audience. Franulka stepped to the front, threw her guitar to one side and did a ripping high kick. There was an audible gasp from the men in the crowd as those purple and pink knickers flashed in the light and they got a glimpse of the most perfectly sensational ted imaginable. There was only one word for it and the way Franulka threw it up: magnificent. It was that good, several men went down on their knees in homage and if there had been any Druids in the crowd they would have slaughtered a goat to it. From then on it was just gut-wrenching, get down, sock-it-to-me-baby-and-roll-me-over-and-give-it-to-me-one-more-time-big-daddy rock 'n' roll. Not only were there four glamours on stage — the Heathen Harlots knew how to play music. And seeing Dapto filming they were convinced he was some film producer from the States, so they were giving it heaps and making every post a winner.

They did Romeo Void's 'In The Dark' and 'Never Say Never', Hunters And Collectors' 'Looking For Love', Eddie Cochran's 'Skinny Jim', John Hiatt's 'Tennessee Plates', James Reyne's 'Harvest Moon', and Skyhooks' 'You Just Like Me 'Cause I'm Good in Bed'. They did a couple of their own but mainly covers. And every one raunchy enough to make a boy scout push an old lady in front of a train and steal her purse.

The crowd had seen nothing like it and neither had Dapto. 'Just keep rolling,' he yelled at his camera crew. 'I'm going back to the car to get more film!' He forced his way through the crowd that had now filled Aquila Street and were dancing like dervishes. Like the song said, it was the party to end all parties. Turn of the century.

While the crowd in Aquila Street was singing, dancing and having the time of their lives, the man responsible and paying for it wasn't having a great deal of fun at all. His cup of happiness far from running over was more like a very shallow saucer full of misery. He was almost choking from the heat and cigarette fumes, his hands were still stinging from cleaning out the freezers and he was sick of pretending to not notice the fifteen or so punters that had come to the back door for their deals of whatever. The uneasiness in the pit of Norton's stomach was increasing by the half-hour. He knew the party would be in full swing by now, and he knew that soon it would be ending very abruptly, and he was beginning to think it might be better if he was up there to keep an eye on things. But instead, he was stuck in this pit of a restaurant. The only slight variation to the night so far was that the cat and the dog had come back — they hadn't been around the previous night and Les was sure they must have died from food poisoning.

Quigley fed them on the floor as usual. The dog had left earlier but the cat kept hanging around, getting under Norton's feet as he tried to work and rubbing itself against his leg in an effort to cadge more food. Norton, his temper a little on the short side tonight, finally kicked its red arse out the door. The cat then sat at the door peering at Les through the hole in the flyscreen like he was a rapist and a mass murderer. The cat finally psyched Norton out and, full of remorse, he got some meat scraps and a few chicken bones and put them just outside the door. Les toiled on, managing to keep switched off and conceal the turmoil inside him. He was so worried about the old block of flats that he almost forgot about Layton until he bowled in about twenty past ten.

Tonight Quigley's mate was decked out in his Saturday night, all black, kill 'em gear; black shirt, black trousers, black belt, red socks and scuffed, unpolished brown shoes. It wasn't hard to tell where the profits from their dealing was going because, like his mate Quigley, Layton's eyes were red and spinning around in his head like two bubbles in a piss pot. As usual he ignored Les, said hello to Quigley then did a Joe Cool in front of the two pissed waitresses for a while before settling down next to the owner. About five minutes later Les got told to take the garbage down the back; when he got back he assumed the resupplying had taken place so he continued working around the sink. The two waitresses were in the corner throwing more booze down

207

their throats. Quigley was involved in something he was cooking and couldn't talk so Layton must have thought this was as good a time as any to start on Norton the boofhead, Queensland kitchen hand.

'You're still here, eh Les,' he cackled, adding his annoying laugh.

Norton clenched his teeth and stared down into the sink, muttering a barely audible 'mmhh'. He was telling himself to be cool, but somehow Les could feel Layton's opening remark had caused the dam holding back his emotions to start to crumble.

'I thought for sure you'd be up the Cross with all your poofter mates tonight,' said Layton.

Norton took in a couple of deep breaths and slowly began to count back. 10... 9... 8... 7... The good karma goes in. The bad karma goes out.

'But I suppose you'll go straight up after work... then they'll all be straight up you.' Layton almost went into a high-pitched giggling fit as if this last remark was hilarious.

Norton shook his hands over the sink then walked across to the back shelf and dried them on a tea towel. As he did, one of the waitresses knocked an eggbeater onto the floor. She had her hands full and Les automatically bent down to pick it up. He'd just bent over when he felt something being jammed in his backside. Almost in disbelief Les stood up and slowly turned around. Layton was standing there, holding a carrot and laughing.

'How did that feel, Les?' he roared. 'Like a big cock going right up your arse?'

That was enough for Norton; something in the pit of his stomach went off like a grenade. He threw the eggbeater onto the table and snatched the carrot out of Layton's hand.

'No,' he hissed venomously. 'More like a big one going right down your fuckin' throat.'

Les grabbed Layton by the collar of his shirt with his left hand and jammed the carrot into his wide open mouth, and kept jamming till it was almost halfway down Layton's throat. Layton's eyes bulged as he spluttered and choked. Quigley stopped what he was doing; the two waitresses gave a little gasp.

'You greasy, fuckin' piece of shit,' snarled the enraged Norton. He ground the carrot further into Layton's mouth then spun him around and kicked him straight up the arse in the direction of the back door. It wasn't a karate kick, it wasn't a kung fu kick, nor was it a tae-kwon-do kick either. It was just a good old-fashioned kick right up the arse like your father used to do, but with a lot more weight behind it. Layton zoomed across the floor, and straight out the door, wrenching the flyscreen completely off its hinges, before he crashed into the wall behind in a mess of buckled and broken wire mesh and a screeching, startled red cat.

The girls screamed and Quigley dropped what he was doing as Norton, his fists clenched with rage, strode to the back door ready to decapitate Layton. He tore the flyscreen off Layton, flung it to one side, grabbed him by the shirt and pulled back a massive right fist.

The big-mouthed, tough-guy dope dealer threw his hands over his head and screamed out to Quigley, 'Bob! Quick, ring the cops.'

Norton blinked at Layton and hesitated for a moment. Then he heard a voice behind him.

'Leave him alone, Les, or I'll call the police.'

Norton blinked again and turned around. Quigley was standing in the doorway, the two startled waitresses behind him.

'You'll *what*?' said Les, almost unable to believe what he was hearing.

'You heard. I'll ring the cops and have you up for assault. The girls saw what happened.' Quigley's voice was shaking.

Despite his anger Norton suddenly let go of Layton and laughed. He stood up and looked at Quigley. 'Are you fair dinkum?'

'My oath I am,' answered Quigley.

209

Norton walked across to Quigley and shoved him back inside the restaurant straight through the two waitresses. 'You're gonna call the cops are you? All right, shithead. Do that. The phone's over in the corner. And while they're here we'll show them this.'

Norton strode past Quigley over to the dope cupboard. He didn't just open it — he ripped one of the doors off its hinges and flung it across the kitchen. The replenished dope deals were sitting in their plastic container. Norton tore the lid off and there had to be around thirty there, bags and foils, at roughly $100 each. He strode back over to the ashen-faced Quigley and shoved the container in his face.

'And what do you call this... Robert? Your thirty different herbs and spices?' Norton laughed contemptuously. 'You'll call the police? You fuckin' dope-dealing cunt. I ought to break your fuckin' neck.' Quigley seemed to pale even more at the look on Norton's face. Then Norton suddenly smiled diabolically. 'But seeing they're only spices, why don't we spice things up around here? What have we got there? About thirty?' Norton walked over to the stove and tipped the lot into the demi-glace bubbling away on its burner then grabbed a wooden spoon and gave it a good stir.

Quigley gasped in horror as around $3000 worth of deals disappeared amongst the slop and whatever else that was boiling away in the pot.

'Now,' said Norton, turning to the two shocked waitresses, the horrible smile still on his face. 'Tell them out in the dining room that the chef's special is coming up.'

The two girls didn't move and stood there with their mouths open.

'Don't worry about it. I'll do it myself.'

Using a table cloth, Norton picked up the boiling pot of demi-glace by the handles, walked over to the swing door, kicked it open and flung the pot, the demi-glace the lot out into the dining room. There wouldn't have been half a dozen people at either end of the restaurant.

They could hardly believe their eyes as this great pot of steaming swill came sailing across the room and splattered up against the wall.

Norton then walked over to the now terrified Quigley and grabbed him by the T-shirt. 'Now, arsehole. You're gonna put an assault charge on me are you? Well we might as well make it a good one, mightn't we?'

Norton strode back out to Layton still laying with his back against the wall. Quigley's partner in crime threw his arms in front of his face just as Norton's fist caught him above the eye, splitting it to the bone. Layton gasped with pain as the blood bubbled out and Les could hear the two waitresses scream. He brought back his fist and drove a short right straight into Mitner's face, almost disintegrating his nose in a shower of blood and splintered bone. Norton gave him another one in the mouth and Layton let out an awful scream as all his front teeth caved in and his lips burst all over his face like an overripe plum. Layton had lost interest now, but Les kicked him in the solar plexus, then dragged his blood-spattered, unconscious body to its feet and flung him out amongst the bottles and boxes in the yard. There was a crashing and tinkling of broken glass and that was the end of Layton. He just lay there and bled onto the concrete and broken glass.

Smiling fiendishly, Norton walked over to Quigley who was propped horrified in the doorway and shoved him back into the kitchen through the two waitresses behind him who had suddenly sobered up somewhat. 'Now, prick features. How would you like to be next?'

Quigley didn't know what to do. He just stood there staring at Norton then he began to shake. Layton was laying out in the backyard looking like dogmeat, the two waitresses were ready to leg it, leaving Quigley alone in the kitchen with fourteen stone of enraged Queenslander whom he'd been treating like a piece of shit for three nights. If the dope-dealing owner had never prayed before, he certainly was now.

Les gave Quigley a bitter once up and down and felt

like spitting on him. 'You know when I think about it, you're not even worth belting. You weak cunt. When dope dealers can go running to the cops, the place is fucked. But I'll tell you something.' Norton jabbed his finger in Quigley's chest. 'Even if you don't, there's a fuckin' big chance I will. I know a couple of detectives that'd love to get their hands on a pair of cunts like you and your mate out the back. And don't worry about your uncle in Randwick Council. I might ring the board of health. They'll close this shit fight of a joint down in five minutes.' Quigley was still shaking. He flinched as Norton suddenly raised his hand. 'Now, smartarse. You owe me five hours pay. Give it to me.'

Quigley swallowed hard, then fumbled into the black metal money box, grabbed fifty dollars and thrust it at Les. 'That's near enough,' he spluttered.

Norton snatched the money and shoved it into his jeans. 'Thanks.' He brought his fist up to give Quigley a backhander, then changed his mind. He peeled off his sweatband, tossed it in his overnight bag and headed for the door. As he reached it a young surfie appeared who Norton vaguely remembered from Thursday night because of his spiky blond hair. 'G'day, mate,' said Norton pleasantly. 'What do you want? Some hash or speed?'

Norton's face was also familiar to the surfie so he thought everything was cool. 'Ohh, just a bag of goey, man.'

'Come right in, mate.' Les then turned round to Quigley. 'Well, don't just stand there, Robert. You've got a customer. Why don't you take him and show him the drug smorgasbord out in the dining room?' Norton glared once more at Quigley then left; if the fly screen had been there he would have slammed it.

Back in his car, Norton's anger subsided as did the pent-up rage he had for Layton and he couldn't help but laugh. He'd certainly settled the score with both him and Quigley; the spatters of blood along with blobs of

212

demi-glace on his T-shirt were proof enough of that. He stared out of the windscreen and wondered what to do. It looked like he'd blown his alibi by about an hour, but maybe not. He could still prove where he was that night. He had another look at his T-shirt. I suppose I should go home and have a shower. I can't really go anywhere looking like this. There was an old blue sweatshirt with the sleeves cut out laying on the back seat. It was an old training sweatshirt Les had forgotten was in the car, but at least it was cleaner than what he had on. He drummed his fingers on the steering wheel for a moment, then another strange smile crept over his face. He reached in the back for the sweatshirt. No, fuck going home. Why don't I go to a party? He looked at his watch: ten forty-five. And I'd better hurry too. There's a big chance it'll be all over in three-quarters of an hour.

The band's first bracket went till ten, then they took a thirty-minute break. The crowd had gone wild — the Heathen Harlots had rocked their tits off. During the break Dapto noticed Gwen fiddling around with the cassettes and was more than happy to find she was getting it all down on tape. He didn't say anything then, but already Dapto's rock 'n' roll, man-with-the-big-cigar mind had the cassettes synched with the video he was shooting and sold and distributed worldwide. The Heathen Harlots Live At The Prince Charles Royal Gala Performance. Produced by Larry Dapto, distributed by Larry Dapto, T-shirts and posters by Larry Dapto and most of the profits going to Larry Dapto. The shot of Franulka flashing that sensational looking ted would sell 100,000 copies in outback Queensland alone.

After a few well-earned beers and a couple of joints to settle their nerves, the girls climbed back on stage to a rousing cheer from the audience which was close to 500 now. Brassy as they come and the ultimate show-girl Franulka flounced over to the mike and did a bit of a parody on something Mick Jagger had made famous.

'Are we havin' a good time?' she asked, putting on a cockney accent. A great scream of approval went up from the crowd. 'Well, I think I've just split my knickers,' More howls and screams of approval. 'You don't want my knickers to fall down now, do you?' The crowd — mainly the men — screamed their approval that loud you could have heard them in Wollongong. Franulka wiggled her tongue at the crowd, then turned to the band. 'A one, a two, a one, two, three, four . . .'

They slipped straight into a thumping version of Ian Hunter's 'Big Time'. In five seconds the place was jumping again. They blitzed that, then did James Reyne's 'Rip It Up', Aerosmith's 'Big Ten Inch', Little Richard's 'The Girls Can't Help It'. The crowd went insane. If they weren't dancing themselves silly and having such a good time there would have been a riot.

There wasn't a parking spot within cooee of Blue Seas Apartments and Les could hear the band as he topped Coogee Bay Road. Christ, he thought, as he detoured past the crowd around the empty Royal Hotel, what have I done? He found a parking spot on a bus stop down from the hospital in Avoca Street and walked. He got to the garage and stood up on the wall just as the girls tore into The Flamin' Groovies' 'Jumpin' In The Night'. Bloody hell, thought Les, watching the mass of dancing, shouting people — these sheilas are bloody good.

Over the heads of the crowd, Les could see that the band was set up far enough away from the flats for anyone to get hurt and they were facing towards Perouse Road, so nearly all the crowd was away from the flats too. The band's power leads were gaffer-taped across the road and went straight into the laundry, just as Les had anticipated. Down the front he could see the hippies and there was no mistaking Sandra in her stone-washed jeans and black tank top. Yep, everyone was there and it was all going according to plan. Then an odd feeling struck Les as the music got to him and he noticed just what a great party it was turning out to be. If I'd have known it was going to be this good and those tarts could play like that, I'd have got Grigor to blow the joint at two-thirty.

The band finished that song and the crowd barely had time to get their breath back when the girls thumped into Lonnie Brooks' 'I Got Lucky Last Night'. Franulka did a couple more high kicks and the mob roared. Norton grinned to himself as he got a glimpse of purple knickers. Been there, done that. He rubbed at the bruises round his neck that were still healing up. And believe me, fellas, it ain't quite worth it. A fair-haired bloke of about twenty was boogieing around with his girlfriend next to him. He caught Norton's eye; Les winked and smiled back and the bloke offered him a bottle of beer from a carton of Tooheys Red sitting on the garage wall. Norton accepted one gratefully and thanked him.

'Ripper party, mate,' said the half-drunk bloke.

'Reckon,' agreed Norton. 'How long have you been here?'

'About an hour. Me and me girl was over the pub and heard the music. So we grabbed some piss and come over.'

'I just finished work myself,' said Les.

'Yeah? Well, don't worry about it, mate. 'Cause I reckon this party's gonna go all night.'

Norton sipped his beer and gave the bloke an odd look. 'Don't bet on it.'

Les left the bloke and his girl to their dancing and moved in amongst the crowd a little closer to the stage. He could see Larry Dapto and his crew filming away but decided to give him a bit of a wide berth just in case. Yes, thought Les, sipping his beer as he looked around him, everything is going exactly to plan. When Les Norton throws a party, Les Norton throws a party. He glanced at his watch. Bad luck it's gonna end in half an hour.

Norton blended in with the crowd and finished his beer. There was a carton of VB unattended on the ground; he managed to snooker a can and sucked on

215

that as he moved among the crush of happy, dancing people. It was a sensational party, probably one of the best Les had ever been to. There were heaps of girls, everybody was out to have a good time and the Heathen Harlots must have pulled something special out for the occasion because their performance was nothing short of thaumaturgic. Franulka and the girls were dynamite as they pranced and boogied around the makeshift stage, while behind them Isla was laying down a backbeat on the skins that was as solid as a rock. They pounded out a few more songs, then after a scorching version of Cold Chisel's 'Rising Sun', Franulka hung onto the microphone while she waited for the yelling, cheering mob to settle down,

'Thank you, music lovers,' she crooned over the mike. 'And now we'd like to do something a little different. Will you please welcome up on stage the Nimbin Didgeridoo Quartet.'

Norton had to blink as the four hippie men got up on stage, carrying their didgeridoos. Hello, he mused, what sort of a scam is this? But like the crowd, Norton was in for the shock of his life. The hippies set up a microphone at about waist level and aimed their didgeridoos at it. Then on a signal from Franulka, they and the band began an awesome version of Gondwanaland's 'Log Dance'. Everybody stopped what they were doing and gaped. The girls crashed and flayed at their instruments like they were performing a Chopin concerto and the hippies had their didgeridoos barking like a pack of African wild dogs. It was a spellbinding performance and a perfect touch in amongst all the pounding rock 'n' roll. When they finished the whole street stopped and cheered. Norton whistled and clapped till his hands were sore. Jesus what bloody next? he thought. Taken away by the music he never noticed the time till he looked at his watch. It was almost eleven-thirty. Shit! There ain't gonna be a next. Unexpectedly he felt a tap on his shoulder. He turned around and there was Syd, wearing a neck brace, expressionless.

216

'Hello, Les,' he said.

'G'day Syd,' replied Norton evenly.

'How're you feeling?'

'Not bad Syd. What about yourself?'

A thin but ironic smile slowly crept across the big roadie's face. 'I suppose I could be a lot worse.'

Norton returned Syd's smile; though it was just as thin. 'I suppose we both could be a lot worse.'

'I reckon you could be right.' Syd looked evenly at Les for a moment, then offered his massive paw. 'It was my fault the other night. I'm sorry. No hard feelings?'

Les accepted Syd's hand. 'No, no hard feelings. I was a bit pissed and I just didn't realise what was going on, that's all.'

'Yeah, fair enough. Anyway, don't stand there on your own. Come over and have a drink with us.'

Without thinking, Les replied, 'Yeah, righto, Syd. Thanks.'

They went across to the side of the stage closest to the entrance to Blue Seas Apartments. Sandra was there drinking a can of UDL and the hippies were getting into a couple of cellar packs of Coolabah.

'Hello, Len,' said Sandra. 'Great party.'

'Yeah. It's a ripper,' replied Norton apprehensively. He glanced at his watch. Eleven twenty-eight.

Then Franulka and the girls on stage noticed Les. Franulka had hold of the microphone as the hippie men got off stage to more thunderous applause.

'Well, we're glad you like our — and the Nimbin Didgeridoo Quartet's — version of 'Log Dance'. But right now we'd like to welcome someone else up on stage: the man who organised this party. Our man of the year and if it wasn't for him none of us would be here.'

Norton saw Franulka and the other girls smiling down at him. Oh oh, he thought. That's all I need. Now half the fuckin' world's going to know. There goes my smother. Les was about to give the girls a sickly, sheepish grin and try to get out of going up on stage when suddenly he noticed something that filled him with dread. He grabbed Sandra by the arm.

'Hey, Sandra,' said Norton urgently. 'Where's Burt and Rosie?'

'Oh, they went inside a while ago.'

'Inside!!?'

'Yes. Burt couldn't handle the crowd. And all the noise was making Rosie a bit scared, so they decided to go inside.'

Norton felt his blood turn to ice. Here was the glitch he had been dreading. The one thing he never thought of and the angle he never covered. An old blind man confused and frightened in the crowd of people. The dog would be scared and confused too. Either that or Burt was half full of ink and wanted to go in and do a bit of porking. He snatched a look at his watch. Right on eleven-thirty.

'So, ladies and gentlemen,' continued Franulka. 'Would you please put your hands together and welcome up on stage, an entrepreneurial rock 'n' roll genius. He not only cleans our flats, but he's going to be our new agent. Ladies and gentlemen... Les —'

Franulka was just about to say Norton when there was a small sharp explosion in the laundry, and another in the foyer. A great shower of white sparks sprayed out of the laundry window. The microphone suddenly went dead, the lights went out and a hush fell over the crowd.

That's the bloody start of it thought Les, as a cold sweat formed on his brow; in three minutes all that would be left of Burt and Rosie would be a pile of black pork crackling in what was left of Burt's bedroom. The band and the crowd stared at the shower of sparks trying to figure out what was going on.

'Fuck!' said Syd. 'Looks like we've overloaded the system.'

Norton stood and sweated. Could he let Burt and Rosie die? Well, in a way yes. The dirty old bastard. But imagine the horror he'd be going through: blind and terrified, trying to find his way out through the smoke and flames, as he slowly burnt to death. And the old dog Rosie. Screaming in agony as she too slowly roasted in the inferno. Burt maybe. But how could anyone let a guide dog burn to death?

'Christ all-fuckin'-mighty,' wailed Norton. He shoved his way through the crowd, jumped the fence and dashed into the foyer.

All the lights were blown in the flats but the first thing Les noticed was the great shower of white sparks cascading from the fuse box casting some light across the stairs. In the eerie white light Les raced across to Burt's door. He was about to start kicking it down when there was a huge explosion in the laundry; the laundry door was blown off its hinges right across the foyer, followed by one of the coppers. If Norton had have left his rescue attempt another couple of seconds, there was a good chance it would have cut him in half. He cleared his ears and shook his head as another explosion in the laundry shook the whole building and he was knocked off his feet.

Outside there was mild panic as the party of the decade came to an abrupt halt and everybody started running for their lives. Within seconds of the explosion, the laundry was a mass of flames and a huge, orange fireball was spreading up the flats, billowing, rolling and turning in on itself as it crept up the building. Syd and the girls grabbed their instruments and whatever else they could and got off the stage. The hippies seemed to be standing there transfixed, till Sandra grabbed them and started dragging them away.

'Don't stand there,' she screamed. 'That's the bloody gas mains exploding. The whole bloody place'll go up any second.'

Norton picked himself up as the building crackled and burnt around him. It was the weirdest sound, almost like being in the middle of some violent, electrical

219

thunderstorm. Already the heat and smoke was intense and there was this odd smell in the air, something like ether. Up the staircase and all along the ceiling dozens of little fiery explosions were going off like tiny napalm bombs. Les didn't know what Grigor and his brother had done but he remembered them saying there would be an explosion followed by a fireball and about three minutes later the building would implode. So he had to get his finger out or he'd be imploded with it.

It took him three attempts to kick the door in — the first one loosened it, the second one splintered it around the lock and the third smashed it in. Les found his way to Burt's bedroom in the light from the flames. Instead of finding a terrified blind man and his howling dog, Norton could only see two inert figures. Burt was blind all right — he was sprawled out across the bed, blind drunk, and so was Rosie. Christ, he cursed. I could have left them in here and they wouldn't have known a thing. Shit! Burt was in his trousers and singlet snoring his head off; Rosie's paws were tied to the front of the bed with leather thongs and she was out like a light, snoring her head off and slobbering into the pillows. Even through the smoke, the smell of cheap brandy was almost overpowering. Filthy, drunken old pig, fumed Norton. Typical, he's fallen asleep on the nest. As the inferno raged through the flats and the heat intensified, Les found he couldn't get Rosie untied or even wake her up; she'd just roll her fat stomach to one side and her tongue would loll out. In desperation, Les ran into the kitchen and ripped all the drawers out till he found a sharp knife. The crackling noise now sounded like a tropical monsoon lashing a tin roof. Frantically Les hacked at the leather thongs as the smoke choked him and stung his eyes. Finally he cut through, then hoisted old Burt up on his shoulder in a fireman's carry and began dragging Rosie along the floor by her collar.

The foyer was a mass of flames and thick acrid smoke with visibility less than two metres; Les choked and gagged as the fumes burnt his eyes and the heat seared

220

his lungs. He gritted his teeth, got a grip on Burt and Rosie and made a charge for the door just as part of the ceiling above him gave way in a shower of sparks and burning debris. Somehow he managed to make it through the door and out into the front of the flats. Safely in the street Les stopped to catch his breath and looked behind him in time to see a huge fireball envelop the old block of flats. It spun and boiled around the outside, rose about ten metres above the roof then, as the roof collapsed from the intense heat, the flames seemed to suck back down into the hole like a small, nuclear explosion in reverse, and the entire block of flats collapsed in on itself in a blinding cauldron of flames that rapidly began to burn itself out.

It was precise, almost surgical, and, in a terrifying way, quite beautiful to watch. The two swarthy men standing not far from the hotel carrying what looked like a couple of children's toy walkie-talkies certainly thought so. They pushed the aerials in on their 'walkie-talkies', pocketed them and complimented themselves on a good job, as they looked forward to their trout fishing holiday in Tasmania. It was definitely one of, if not the best, they had ever done.

'That has to be one of the bravest things I've ever seen, Len,' said Sandra, as she, Syd and the girls in the band came running over to give Norton a hand with Burt and Rosie.

'Man, you've got some balls, all right,' agreed Syd, 'I wouldn't have gone into that building for all the money in the world.'

'Ahh, I dunno,' shrugged Norton modestly. 'I just couldn't stand here and let the old bloke and his dog burn.'

Dapto had it on film, the whole crowd saw it and Norton was everybody's hero; he could do no wrong. There was even talk about handing the hat round. With old Burt and Rosie safely on the ground, somebody managed to find a couple of blankets. Norton was singed and the back of his sweatshirt was smouldering, but he was okay. However, not that okay that he couldn't play on his injuries if he had to.

'Do you think we'd better get Burt over to the hospital?' said Gwen. 'He looks like he's suffering from smoke inhalation.'

Franulka sniffed the air. 'If you ask me, they both smell like a couple of Christmas puddings.'

Part of the crowd returned and gathered round, including the hippies. In the background, what was left of Blue Seas Apartments burned steadily on and everybody seemed more interested in watching the old block of flats in its death throes. Nobody had ever seen a gas main blow up before and all agreed it was a truly wondrous thing.

'Good thing we managed to save our instruments,' said Isla, the glow from the flames reflecting on her face. ''Cause every-fuckin'-thing else is gone.'

'Yeah. Absolute Gowings, man,' nodded one of the hippies.

'Don't worry too much,' said Norton. 'Every flat's got a fire insurance policy on it for twelve and a half thousand.'

'What was that, Les?' said Franulka.

'It was part of a special clause the owner put in all the leases. You all get over twelve grand. So the agents told me when I got the job.'

'Are you fair dinkum, Les?' asked Alastrina.

'Yep. Plus you've still got the rest of that money coming for the gig. I'll get that to you tomorrow.'

Alastrina and the others brightened up immediately. 'Well, that's okay,' she said. 'I wouldn't have had more than twelve and a half bucks worth of stuff in the flat.'

'Yeah. Me either,' said Riona.

'I kept all my good stuff across the road,' said Sandra. 'After all those break-ins.'

The hippies looked like they'd just won the lottery. Their loss on the night would have been a wok, a bong, some brown rice and a couple of bags of bean sprouts.

'You should have that money in about two or three weeks,' said Les. 'There'll be no hassle with the insurance company. We all saw the gas mains go up, right?' There was a profound general chorus of agreement. 'So, have you all got somewhere to stay?'

'My friends across the road can put us all up,' said Sandra.

'Okay. Well, just leave it all to me.'

In the background, Norton could hear the approaching wail of two fire engines. After that would probably come the cops and even if he was the hero of the day, he wasn't quite in the mood for playing questions and answers with the wallopers.

'Look,' he said. 'Can you people look after Burt and Rosie?' He threw in a bit of a grimace. 'I'm going over to the hospital and get something for these burns.'

'Yeah, good idea, Les', said Syd. 'You want a hand?'

'No, I'll be right, thanks, mate. I should be back later and I'll find you in those block of flats opposite. If not, I'll catch up with you tomorrow.' Acting as if he was in a fair bit of pain, Norton stood up and the girls all crowded around him.

'You're a brave man, Les,' said Franulka.

Norton was about to say something along the lines about if he'd known more about her and Syd she was definitely right but changed his mind. 'Anybody would have done it,' he shrugged. 'I'll see you when I get back.'

Norton lost himself in the crowd as he walked in the general direction of the hospital, then doubled back to his car.

Christ all-bloody-mighty, panted Les, as he sat inside his old Ford and wound the window down for a bit of air. How bloody close was that. He reached over and also wound down the passenger side window. The ramifications of what had just happened and how close he'd once again come to death dawned on him. Fuckin' Burt and his rotten bloody dog. I'd clean forgotten all about them. About another half a minute and I'd be

223

in there with them. Phew! Les let out a burst of air, looked up at the night sky and made a mental sign of the cross.

But he'd done it. Blue Seas was gone and not a soul got so much as a scratch. It was bad luck that a few people had to lose their possessions. But... that's the way things go. And there would be no hassle with the insurance company or the police. If they sent round an investigator or someone from the arson squad, they wouldn't even find a spent match. Those two bloody Romanian gypsies would be ten lengths in front of anyone in this country. Plus there were at least five hundred people who would swear they saw the gas mains explode as the result of a power overload from a rock 'n' roll band running their leads into the laundry. Norton had done it. He'd pulled off the perfect crime. He sat in the car shaking his head, not knowing whether to laugh or what. It was hard to imagine. Barely a fortnight ago he'd found himself out of work with his big investment in real estate not worth a zac, and even costing him money. Now it was gone — just a big glowing pile of smoking ashes.

But what a weird old two weeks it had been. Brawls with bikies, a horrible, vicious fight with a giant, maddened roadie. A drug rip-off that could have gone either way. A couple of good roots. Then those two creeps in that grottsville restaurant. And lies. Christ, who hadn't he lied to? He made Tom Pepper look like George Washington. But now it was all over. So how much was he in front? Forget about mental arithmetic; Les was flat out writing down the date. The place was insured for about $120,000; the land was valued at $75,000; he had about $70,000 at home, less what he'd promised Billy and those sheilas in the band. How much was that? The best part of $250,000. Norton couldn't help but grin at himself in the rear-vision mirror. A quarter of a million, eh? Not a bad earn, Les, old son, not a bad sort of an earn at all.

Les was just about to start chuckling when the grin

disappeared to be replaced by a look of horror, as something else, something catastrophic also dawned on him. He'd told everybody in Blue Seas that each flat was insured for twelve and a half grand. Ohh no, he groaned, how could I be such a dill? Christ it's a good thing Jimmy the bikie's dead or he'd be in the whack up too. Shit! What was I thinking at the time? It was just a spur of the moment thing, too — just to get everyone's attention away from their own predicament and in absolute agreement about the gas mains exploding. And now he had to pay for it, when he needn't have given the cunts a cracker. It was all sweet anyway. And he'd have to pay up because you can bet your life if he didn't they'd be up at Hymie and Fymie's real estate agency asking for it. And when the two kosher kids told them to piss off, the stench of a rather large rat would pervade the air. Norton shook his head and cursed himself. Fifty bloody grand. Christ! That's taken the edge off my earn. Fuck it! Why me all the time.

Then a very strange look crept across Norton's face. It was thoughtful and edged with a very sly smile; and related to something that had been nagging at him for almost all of the last two weeks. Yes, he thought, as he drummed his fingers slowly on the steering wheel, why should I fork out the extra fifty thousand dollars? Norton glanced at his watch then up towards Perouse Road. It was getting on for twelve-thirty. Yeah, why indeed. I think I know someone else who can put his hand in his kick for the fifty grand. He fuckin' deserves it, too. He locked the car and walked back up to the Royal Hotel.

There were still plenty of people milling about, watching what was left of Blue Seas Apartments slowly disappearing into the night sky in a cloud of grey smoke, steam and glowing ashes. The police had arrived and were keeping the crowd away and the traffic moving. Two fire engines had hoses going everywhere, but only two were pouring water on to the shell of what had once been home for six different lots of people, about

225

twenty million cockroaches and an unknown number of rats and other wee beasties. The police didn't seem all that concerned and the firemen were going methodically, but unhurriedly about their business. It was all over bar the shouting.

Standing outside the hotel, watching the lights flashing on the police car and the two fire engines, for some reason Les still couldn't help but feel a slight twinge of sadness for the old block of flats. Like he had surmised earlier, the old building probably contained memories from a bygone era in Randwick, and it was the first thing he'd ever invested in in his life — even if he was never all that interested in it and despite the fact that it turned out to be a giant lemon. However, Norton wasn't standing outside the hotel just to be nostalgic or in an attempt to embellish the moonlit scene around him with some sort of gentle ambience. His eyes may have been drifting over the crowd, the flashing lights and what was left of the flats, but Norton was concentrating more on the road coming from Randwick Junction; and according to his watch, what he was looking for should be coming from that direction any minute now.

The grey BMW cruised slowly across Coogee Bay Road into Perouse Road, then slowed down even more as it got to opposite the Royal Hotel. Norton followed its progress and smiled as the driver did a U-turn and nosed into the hotel driveway before the cop on duty had a chance to wave him on. Barely a metre away Norton stayed in the shadows and amongst the other people, and with a smile that was trying hard not to turn into a grin, watched as the familiar spritely figure in the trench coat and hat, got out and locked the car. Les could sense his confusion as he stepped gingerly between the people watching and stood on the edge of the footpath, gazing across at what had once been Blue Seas Apartments. Oh well, thought Norton, guess I'd better go over and say hello. See if I can be of any assistance. The poor chap does look awfully confused.

Les stepped between the people and tapped the figure in the trench coat lightly on the shoulder.

'Hello, Price,' he said quietly. 'How's things?'

Slightly startled, the silvery-haired casino owner turned quickly around. He blinked at Norton for a moment or two before he spoke. 'Les? I... what? What are you doing here?'

'What am I doing here?' answered Norton. He jerked a thumb towards where the fire brigade were playing a hose on what had once been Blue Seas Apartments and was now not much more than a cloud of steam and ashes spiralling into the night sky. 'That's my block of flats, remember? I'm the owner.'

'I... ohh, yeah. Right,' blinked Price Galese.

'I heard about it on the radio, so I came straight over.'

'Yeah, right. Yeah.' Price continued to blink at Les then turned back to what was left of the old block of flats. The impromptu stage was still there with the Prince Charles Birthday Bash banner still flapping behind it. 'Christ! What happened?'

Les gave a bit of a shrug. 'According to one of the fire brigade blokes, some sheilas living in the flats have got a band. They threw a street party and overloaded the power in the laundry, and the gas mains blew up.'

'Jesus Christ! Was anyone hurt?'

Norton shook his head. 'No. Evidently everybody was out in the street when the place went up.'

'Bloody hell! It looks like a bomb hit it.'

'Yes, it does, doesn't it?' Norton tried hard not to smile at the look of anguish on his boss's face. 'So what brings you over here, anyway, Price? You're a bit out of your way, aren't you? And you look like Philip Marlowe in that outfit.'

'Huh? Oh... I... ah, I had to give one of the boys a lift home. I was driving past. And I... ah... I saw the fire trucks, so I thought I'd stop and have a look.'

'Ohh, right. Yeah,' nodded Les.

Price turned away from Norton and moved a little further along the footpath towards the old block of flats;

his apprehension and nervousness was now bubbling to the surface. Les let him go and studied him from behind for a few moments. And as the remaining pieces of the jigsaw puzzle fell into place, he felt like going over and kicking his boss right up the arse. Norton may have pulled off the perfect crime; but for the last few years, Price had pulled off the perfect mistress.

You rotten, shifty old bastard, thought Norton. No wonder you talked me into buying that stinken block of flats. That way you didn't have to take the risk of putting her up somewhere and with slackarse me owning the place you knew I'd never come over, and there'd be no chance of anybody else buying the dump and tossing her and the rest of them out. Buy this block of flats, Les. A great investment, Les. You'd be a mug if you didn't, Les. You arsehole. A lousy 100 bucks a week, plus a few bucks here and there for a painting or whatever, and not a soul knew she existed — except maybe George. Good one, Price. And you wouldn't have told her some bloke working for you owned the joint. In fact I don't know what you've told her. She's not all that bright, and you've got to be one of the best con men that ever existed. You taught my everything I know. Norton continued to study his boss, staring over at the flames. And the last couple of weeks the moll wouldn't have mentioned Les the new caretaker, because half the time the bitch didn't even know I existed. She sure didn't want nothing to do with me, the moll. Yes, Price, old fella. I was conned into buying that lemon just so you could have somewhere to do your late-night bonking. You bastard. I ought to break your neck. And haven't you made a nice pig of yourself the last few nights you've been getting away early? Bad heart and all. Norton gave a bit of a sour chuckle. But you weren't the only one seeking Miss Garrett's favours. Hope the others were wearing condoms.

Norton stared after Price and then somehow found he still couldn't help but admire him. I've got to give you one thing, though, when it comes to getting a mistress

228

or whatever; you've still got taste. She's got to be one of the best sorts I've ever seen. And not a soul knew about it. Despite himself Norton had to laugh. I hope when I'm sixty I'm still bonking good sorts like that forty years younger than me. But all that moralising over the years about being a good Catholic. Oh well, who gives a fuck? Norton shook his head, then walked over and once again tapped his boss on the shoulder and this time tried to look concerned.

'I'd get back over here, if I were you Price. All these drunken mugs around. Anyway, what do you want to be hanging around like a gig for? You've seen one fire, you've seen the lot.'

Price was still more than a little vague. 'Yeah, I suppose you're right, Les,' he replied slowly. He walked back towards the BMW with Norton, but his eyes were still on the fire. 'Are you sure no one was hurt?' he asked again.

'Positive,' answered Norton. 'In fact the only casualty up here tonight's been me.'

'You?' Price screwed his face up slightly and gave Les a quick once up and down. 'What's up with you? You look all right to me. There's not a mark on you.'

'Oh, I'm not talking about physically, Price,' said Les. 'I'm talking... monetarily.'

'What!!?'

'Well, I've done my arse, haven't I? The fuckin' joint wasn't insured. The land's not worth two bob. Plus I've done the money I put up in the first place. I'm right up shit creek in a leaky boat.' Les moved his face a little closer to Price's. 'I only wish I'd never let you talk me into buying the cunt of a joint in the first place.'

'Hey, hold on a sec, Les. Nobody put a gun to your head and made you buy it. You were pretty keen, if I remember.'

'In fact,' said Les, ignoring Price. 'Seeing as you talked me into buying that shit fight, I was thinking of snipping you for a lazy $50,000, just to show what a good bloke you are.'

229

'What!!?' Price Galese looked shocked. 'Get out! Listen, like I said, nobody made you buy the place. You're a big boy now — you can stand on your own two feet.' Price shook his head. 'Besides, it's not like the old days. The casino's finished, I've had to sell a couple of horses — I couldn't find fifty grand even if I wanted to.'

'Ohh, I dunno,' drawled Les. 'You could always sell one of your paintings.'

'Paintings? What fuckin' paintings? I haven't got any paintings. There's a couple back at the house and they're worth fuck all. I'm not into art.'

'Yeah? That's funny. I heard you had a really valuable collection.'

'Well, you heard wrong.' Something in the tone of Norton's voice made Price give Les a bit of a suspicious, once up and down. 'Where did you get this shit anyway?' he asked.

Norton gave a bit of a shrug. 'Off an art dealer in Double Bay. He said paintings by some sheila called Sandra Jean Garrett are worth a fortune these days.' Norton moved his face almost right up to Price's. 'And he reckons you've got the lot.'

Price stiffened. His jaw dropped fractionally, his eyes widened then narrowed. 'Why, you dirty low cunt, Les Norton. You miserable, despicable bastard.'

Norton looked evenly at his boss. He gave him another friendly pat on the shoulder then tugged gently at the lapel of his trench coat. 'That's right, Philip Marlowe. And if you behave yourself and weigh in that fifty grand, I won't tell a soul just how many you've got.'

230

Robert G. Barrett
The Godson

'I wonder who that red-headed bloke is? He's come into town out of nowhere, flattened six of the best fighters in Yurriki plus the biggest man in the valley. Then he arrives at my dance in an army uniform drinking French champagne and imported beer like it's going out of style. And ups and leaves with the best young sort in the joint... Don't know who he is. But he's not bloody bad.'

Les Norton is at it again!

Les thought they were going to be the easiest two weeks of his life.

Playing minder for a young member of the Royal Family called Peregrine Normanhurst III sounded like a deadset snack. So what if he was a champagne-guzzling millionaire Hooray Henry and his godfather was the Attorney General of Australia? Les would keep Peregrine out of trouble... So what if he was on the run from the IRA? They'd never follow him to Australia...

Robert G. Barrett's latest Les Norton adventure moves at breakneck speed from the corridors of power in Canberra to the grimy tenements of Belfast, scorching the social pages of Sydney society and romping through the North Coast's plushest resorts to climax in a nerve-shattering, blood-spattered shootout on a survivalist fortress in the Tweed Valley. *The Godson* features Les Norton at his hilarious best, whatever he's up against — giant inbreds, earth mothers, Scandinavian au pair girls, jealous husbands, violent thugs and vengeful terrorists.

If you thought Australia's favourite son could get up to some outrageous capers in *You Wouldn't Be Dead For Quids*, *The Real Thing* and *The Boys from Binjiwunyawunya*, until you've read *The Godson*, you ain't read nothin' yet!

Robert G. Barrett
You Wouldn't Be Dead For Quids

You Wouldn't Be Dead For Quids is the book that
launched Les Norton as Australia's latest cult hero.

Follow Les, the hillbilly from Queensland, as he takes
on the bouncers, heavies, hookers and gamblers of
Sydney's Kings Cross, films a TV ad for Bowen Lager
in Queensland and gets caught up with a
nymphomaniac on the Central Coast of New South
Wales.

In one of the funniest books of the past decade you
will laugh yourself silly and be ducking for cover as
Les unleashes himself on Sydney's unsuspecting
underworld.